BLIND
TO SIN

BLIND
TO SIN

A JACKSON DONNE NOVEL

DAVE WHITE

Copyright © 2017 by Dave White
Cover and jacket design by Adrijus Guscia
Interior designed and formatted by E.M. Tippetts Book Designs

ISBN 978-1-943818-29-7
eISBN 978-1-943818-67-9
Library of Congress Control Number: 2017930076

First trade paperback publication February 2017

Polis Books, LLC
1201 Hudson Street, #211S
Hoboken, NJ 07030
www.PolisBooks.com

POLIS BOOKS

ALSO BY DAVE WHITE
Available from Polis Books

Jackson Donne series
When One Man Dies
The Evil That Men Do
Not Even Past
An Empty Hell

Witness to Death

To
Duane Swierczynski
Great writer, friend and mentor

"One great power of sin is that it blinds men so that they do not recognize its true character."
Andrew Murray

PROLOGUE

2006

T HE ALARM SOUNDED *at a volume somewhere north of ear shattering. What ever happened to a good old silent alarm? There was only one other time she could remember an alarm this loud.*

The tellers had never been involved in a bank heist before. They scattered and filled the bag with cash, all while crying and screaming.

Tammy clearly hadn't yelled shut up enough. She tried again, but the two tellers kept weeping.

To her left, three patrons were on the ground, fingers laced together and resting on the back of their heads. She'd taken all their cell phones and put them on top of the table where people could fill out deposit slips. No one touched them. But that didn't surprise Tammy.

Few people needed their phones when an AR-15 was pointed in their faces. Today was no different.

The alarm continued to ring.

"What is taking them so long?" Kenneth screamed.

Tammy looked in his direction. His ski mask was tight on his face, and a line of spittle soaked into the fabric near his lip. He aimed his own automatic weapon at the skull of the bank manager.

Tammy winked at him. The man she married was panicking.

"We've got three minutes," she said. "I can finish a cigarette before they get here."

Kenneth nodded.

Walking over to the tellers, she tapped the barrel of the gun on the bulletproof glass.

"If you don't hurry the hell up, we'll find out if this works."

One of them – her nametag said Arlene – nodded through her tears. She zipped the duffel bag and nodded toward the emergency door. Tammy met her there. The door opened, and Tammy took the duffel bag and aimed the gun. Arlene screamed and fell to the floor.

Tammy shot out the two security cameras. The room screamed. Kenneth took care of the other ones.

"Okay," he said. "Let's do this."

Tammy handed him her gun, slung the bag over her shoulder and pulled her ski mask off. Kenneth pulled her close and kissed her deep on the lips.

"I've missed this," he whispered when he broke the kiss.

"We're getting too old for this," she said. "We have a son."

"Don't tell Elliot that."

"See you on the other side."

Kenneth emptied the clip of one of the AR-15s into the ceiling, making sure everyone kept their heads down. The tellers ducked behind the counter. He dropped the gun, wrapped his free arm around Tammy and guided her forward toward the door.

"I think we're going to be clear," she said.

"That took longer than three minutes," he said. "We have to be sure. You stay safe."

They exited into the winter day; the snow flurries of ten minutes earlier had turned into a full-on storm. The getaway car was across the street, Elliot revving the engine. The alarm gave way to police sirens.

Someone on the corner was snapping pictures with one of those flip phones. Tammy's stomach went sour. In the old days, no one ever had a camera.

"Back off," Kenneth shouted. "Or I'll shoot her."

The phone man took two steps back. Two squad cars, CLIFTON emblazoned on their side doors, rounded the corner. One of them had a speaker on the car and screamed for Kenneth to stop where he was.

He did. Tammy took a breath. Elliot was supposed to pull a U-turn, get them in the car and get the hell out of there.

But that wasn't what happened. As the police cars screamed to a stop in front of them, Elliot burst from the driver's seat and barreled across the street.

"What the hell?" Kenneth whispered.

Rushing up to them, Elliot pulled Tammy free from Kenneth's grip, duffel bag and all. He dragged her across the street and she screamed. The cops poured out of their cars, guns trained on Kenneth.

Tammy took one last look at him. He shrugged, dropped the gun and raised his hands.

Elliot forced her into the backseat. He got in the driver's seat and peeled out.

"No!" she screamed. "What about Kenneth?"

"This was always part of the plan. That guy with the phone. He's got your face. We've got to hide you."

Tammy looked out the back window. The cops already had her husband down on the ground in cuffs.

"We're going away for a while, Tammy. We have to."

Tammy turned back toward the front of the car and watched Elliot navigate the road. The world came back into focus. Elliot pulled onto Route 21 and headed toward Newark. Toward the airport.

"Where are you going?"

"We are taking a vacation. It's okay. Kenneth will understand. This is an emergency situation."

"They got him," she said.

"They did."

"And we are going to hide." She didn't need time to figure out what was happening, but she did feel the need to vocalize it.

"Your face is going to be in a bunch of papers tomorrow. You're going to be portrayed as a hostage."

"And you a hero." Tammy shook her head.

"They're going to be looking for us. We're going to disappear for a while."

The road wasn't slick yet, and Elliot was pushing seventy. There were traffic lights coming up and she prayed he didn't run them.

"Disappear? We can't do that."

"We have to."

"You're panicking."

"No. I'm not. This has always been a contingency."

Tammy blinked. "But what about Matt?"

Elliot's eye flicked up to the rearview mirror. "Matt?"

"Matt. My son?" Tammy gritted her teeth. "Matt Herrick. What is wrong with you?"

"Me? Stop worrying. He'll be fine. He's eighteen." Elliot slowed for *a red light. "He'll figure things out."*

Tammy pulled the duffel bag close and bit back tears. Forty-eight hours later, they were in Kansas. A quiet town with one restaurant. She hadn't heard from Matt and didn't try to contact him.

On the news, they talked about the hostage who got away. Her picture was plastered everywhere, a blurry cellphone image. Her mouth was wide open in a scream. They thought she was calling for help. But Tammy knew she was telling Elliot to wait. Elliot's arm was wrapped around her, pulling her from Kenneth. His face was obscured from the camera. Only his dark hair was visible, black against the pale shade of her skin.

Perfect for an iconic image.

And an escape.

The news anchors wondered about the man whose face was out of the photo. The one who, the reporters said, saved the unknown woman in a daring rescue.

Elliot had saved her. And now, in that podunk Kansas town, he felt like she owed him.

"We'll go back to New Jersey soon," Elliot would say. "When it's safe."

"And find Matt?"

PART I

THE HUNTER

CHAPTER 1

LUCA CARMINE COULDN'T believe his luck.

Of course, in prison, luck was relative, but today he felt really fortunate. He'd only been transferred into North Jersey State Penitentiary yesterday, and already he was seeing the benefits. The man who'd walked by him in the gym was the one who'd caused all of Luca's problems years ago.

Jackson Donne didn't look like he used to. Not the way Luca remembered him. He was leaner, and much more cut. There were lines on his face, and he'd started to go gray. Must be a tough life in this prison for him to turn that way. Donne was talking to some other man, an older white guy, probably in his sixties. There were sitting on the bench press Luca wanted to use.

Sniffling, then straightening his pants, Luca strolled up to them. If Donne recognized Luca, it didn't show on his face when Luca cleared his throat.

"Yo, I want to use that."

Donne didn't say anything, but his pal said, "Sorry. Taken."

Luca wiped his nose.

"My turn."

The man shook his head. "Taken."

Luca pressed his lips together, trying to think of the right words to say. Nothing came. He turned on his heel and headed toward a different machine. Donne didn't recognize him?

A fire started to burn in his stomach.

SHARPENING A TOOTHBRUSH was easy, if you had patience. It wasn't that it took a long time, really only five minutes, but with constant guard surveillance, you had to make sure someone was covering for you. Luca's cellmate was willing to do just that. Not that the cellmate knew what he was doing for Luca. But screaming, yelling and slamming your hands on the prison door made the guards have to deal with the psychopath instead of Luca.

He used the edge of his cot to sharpen the brush. The plastic peeled away from the brush and landed on the floor in a dusty pile. Luca kept spinning the brush, giving the tip of the handle a sharp point. When he was finished, he tested it with his finger and drew blood.

The next morning, he tucked the toothbrush into his pants just before gym time.

REVENGE.

When the moment came for Luca, his heart didn't pump harder. He skin was cool and his muscles were loose. This was fate.

Donne was by himself in the corner. He wasn't working out or talking to anyone. He leaned on the wall, eyes flicking back and forth from bench to barbells to whatever the fuck. Luca walked toward him at top speed, making sure as he did, the guards were watching other things. Donne and Luca made eye contact.

Luca was five feet away when Donne stopped leaning and stood up straight. Luca reached into his own waistband and gripped the shank. He pulled it free. If Donne saw it, he didn't react.

"Hello, Luca," Donne said.

The bastard did recognize him. Oh well. It'd be the last thing Donne would say.

Donne's eyes flicked away again as Luca pulled back his arm. What was Donne looking at? Something over his shoulder.

Then he felt a forearm around his throat and a hand on his

chin. Tight. The shank slipped from his hand and clattered against the ground. Someone screamed.

The hand on his chin pulled, and Luca heard a snap.

His own neck.

Then, as the lights dimmed, he heard Donne's voice.

"Thank you."

CHAPTER 2

IGH SCHOOL BASKETBALL never ended.

It was April, the season had been over for more than a month, but the court still smelled of sweat. The odor intensified due to the humidity and heat trapped in the walls of the brick oven-like building.

Matt Herrick sat in the St. Paul's High School gym, watching Kyrie James take jumper after jumper. Herrick would interrupt his rhythm occasionally, telling him to square his shoulders, or get his feet set. Once, he walked over to James and modeled perfect form: shoulders and feet facing the basket, releasing the ball at the apex of his jump.

The ball hit the back rim. James chuckled.

The missed shot was rebounded by a guy in a black suit. A badge was pinned to his lapel. Herrick couldn't make out what it said. The man had a shaved head. He had to be six-five, but James towered over him.

"Two more, Kyrie." Herrick nodded toward the suit. "Give him the ball."

The suit delivered a bounce pass to James, who squared up and swished the ball from twenty feet. He retrieved it, went back to the foul line and nailed another jumper.

Herrick said, "Ten a.m. Saturday. Don't be late. Lots of coaches are going to be there."

James thanked him and jogged back to the locker room. Herrick turned to the suit, who had unbuttoned his jacket.

"You can put the air on now," the suit said. He held up an ID. It read *John Mack, Corrections*.

"We don't have air conditioning. Been a while since you've been in a school?"

Mack shook his head. "Damn, I thought you were just trying to sweat the kid out. What my coach used to do to me."

"What can I do for you?"

"Matt Herrick? I've seen you on the news."

"That's me. What can I do for you?"

Corrections didn't just saunter in any old day. The knot in Herrick's gut told him it was about something he wasn't in the mood to discuss. Mack strolled over to the bleachers and had a seat. Herrick took a breath and then followed him.

"Your dad is Kenneth Herrick, right?"

Herrick nodded, the knot in his stomach tightening and confirming his suspicions.

Mack pursed his lips and scrunched his nose. Herrick waited.

"Your dad killed somebody last week."

Herrick blinked. "My father's in prison."

Mack adjusted in his seat. Beads of sweat formed on his shaved head. He wiped at his nose.

"He snapped a guy's neck. Luca Carmine. Ever heard of him?"

Herrick shook his head.

"Used to be a bodyguard for Henry Stern, the senator who got shot. They put Carmine away after he killed a woman—"

"Kate Ellison," Herrick said. The story was familiar to him. Jackson Donne's girl. "Wait, my dad killed the guy you arrested for shooting Kate Ellison?"

Mack said, "Well, I didn't ar—"

"You know what I mean. Was Jackson Donne involved?"

Mack pinched the bridge of his nose. "How did you know that?"

James popped out of the locker room in new shorts and a different T-shirt. He walked across the gym floor, Beats headphones covering his ears. He gave Herrick a nod. Herrick waved. When James was gone Herrick turned back to Mack.

"What happened in there?"

"Your dad came up behind Carmine in the gym. Snapped Carmine's neck in one move. Our guards surrounded him and dragged him away. He's in solitary."

"You know I don't really talk to my dad or visit him, right? He and I, we're not on the greatest terms, being that he's a master criminal and all."

Mack adjusted his position on the bleachers. The wood was warm, and the suit couldn't be all that comfortable in this weather. Herrick didn't want to gloat about his shorts and T-shirt. After all, how much could you gloat when you were wearing a whistle?

"That's the thing, we're hoping you could help us out."

"With what?"

"What do you know about Elliot Cole?"

The knot in Herrick's stomach loosened. Unfortunately, it was replaced by thousands of needles pricking the lining.

"My dad's old partner. The one he—" Herrick shut up.

Mack waited. Herrick didn't continue.

"Your dad's old partner is trying to buy your dad's way out of jail."

The gym went cold.

"Can he do it?" Herrick pictured Cole, someone he hadn't seen in nearly twenty years. Back when he lived in Newark. Back when he thought life was normal. "You just said my dad killed a guy."

Mack shrugged. "Money can do wonders if you put it in the hands of the right people."

"Why are you telling me this?"

"I figured you'd want to know about your dad. And, maybe you want to talk to Cole. Figure out what his deal is."

"Me?" Herrick sniffled. The smell of old gym sweat was brutal. "Isn't that your job?"

Mack leaned in and whispered, "When you're playing with that kind of money, I don't trust a lot of people I work with. Sometimes going the quiet route helps. If I have something to go on, even off the record, maybe I can play this right."

Herrick scratched the back of his neck. "I'm still not sure what's going on."

"Your dad killed someone. I don't think he deserves to be out on the streets after that. Do you?"

Herrick shook his head.

"But when a lot—and I mean a lot—of money is in play,

especially through back channels, things can go wonky."

"If it's through back channels, how do you know about it?"

Mack touched his ear. "Hear things."

Herrick stood up, went over to the padded wall and picked up a free basketball. He dribbled it out to the foul line. Balance, eyes, elbow, follow through. He swished a free throw.

"Come on," Mack said. "Help me out."

Herrick didn't respond. Instead, he swished another free throw.

Mack said, "There's one more thing."

Herrick rebounded the ball and dribbled back to the free throw line.

"Cole is trying to buy Jackson Donne's way out of jail too."

Herrick bricked the shot.

CHAPTER 3

||||||||||||||||||||||||||||||||||||||||||||||||||||||||||||||||||||||||||||||||||||||||||||||||||||||||||||||||||||||||||||||||||||||||||||||||||||||||||||||||||

AFTER CALLING SARAH and telling her he'd be out late, Herrick drove to Alpine. It was an upper crust town in Northern Bergen County, full of celebrity houses, great schools and enormous mansions. What it didn't have, however, was highways. One of the few towns in New Jersey not near a major artery, drivers had to navigate a series of side roads to get into the town.

Herrick completed his journey over an hour later, stopping in front of the kind of house seen only in movies. A huge lawn, a fountain and two Bentleys in the driveway.

Do as the rich do, he guessed.

This was not Elliot Cole's house. This was someone Herrick was sure Mack didn't know about. Not for the reason Herrick was there, anyway.

Herrick rang the doorbell, and then scuffed his shoes on the welcome mat. A man in a smoking jacket and turtleneck answered, and looked Herrick up and down. Good thing he'd changed out of his basketball shorts.

"Mr. Vavilov?" Herrick extended his hand.

Adrik Vavilov did not accept.

"And you are?" The thick Russian accent Herrick remembered as a kid had faded to almost nothing.

"Matt Herrick. Kenneth's kid."

Vavilov's eyes lit up and he pulled Herrick into a massive hug. "Matt! You look just like your father. And none of this Mister, stuff. It's Uncle Adrik! Let's have a drink! Come in!"

Herrick went in. The foyer was a large, tiled room with a winding staircase to his right and a giant glass chandelier hanging from the ceiling. He followed Vavilov — Uncle Adrik — through it into a pristine kitchen.

On the long island was a glass, half full of clear liquid, ice and a lemon.

"Can I get you something? Your father preferred bourbon, but I only have rye. Pig Whistle."

Herrick was a fan of both bourbon and rye. One of the tastes passed down through genes. But not while he was working. Rule number one.

"I'm okay."

Uncle Adrik took a sip of his drink. Then he grinned. "You've grown."

Herrick shrugged. "Time passes. You used to have a big Russian accent."

"To what do I owe the honor?"

Herrick passed his license across the counter top. Uncle Adrik took it and looked it over.

The faint smell of a roast wafted in the air.

Uncle Adrik passed the license back, took a drink and smacked his lips.

"Well, Mr. Private Investigator Herrick, I am still confused as to why you are here."

"First off, if I'm calling you Uncle, you're calling me Matt."

"Not Nephew Matt?"

Herrick shook his head. "My father."

Uncle Adrik finished the drink. Waited. Herrick said nothing. There were lines along Vavilov's chin, but Herrick wasn't sure if it was wrinkled skin or scars.

"Mr. Herrick, I am not a mind reader. Perhaps you want to talk to me instead of dropping two word phrases and then leaving me to parse the meaning."

Herrick took a deep breath. His uncle went over to the freezer, grabbed a handful of ice cubes and dropped them into his glass. He then pulled a bottle of tonic from the fridge and a bottle of gin from a cabinet. He came back to the counter and mixed his drink.

"You used to bankroll my father's schemes. Now Elliot Cole is trying to buy my dad out of prison. Doesn't take much to put two and two together and talk to you."

Uncle Adrik pursed his lips. His cheeks flushed. "That has nothing to do with me."

A woman — in her twenties, blonde and wafer thin — walked into the kitchen and stopped at the oven. She pulled it open and the smell of roast grew. She glanced at them, opened her mouth, then shut it, turned and left.

"My wife," Uncle Adrik said. "Knows her place."

Herrick wasn't sure if he wanted to call him uncle anymore.

He took a breath, then said, "Great. You don't know anything about my father being bought out of prison? I find that hard to believe."

"If your father can find freedom, that is wonderful for him. No matter the way it has to happen. But I haven't dealt in the world of Mr. Herrick or Mr. Cole in a very long time."

The old man took another sip.

"Explain," Herrick said.

"When your father went away to prison, he did a very brave thing. He didn't mention me. He didn't mention Mr. Cole. He kept his mouth shut. He didn't even mention..." He trailed off and stared at the ceiling. It didn't feel like a family reunion anymore.

Herrick waited, but the atmosphere in the room had shifted. He felt a small pain somewhere deep in his gut.

"When that happened, I took it as a sign. No more crime for me. The Italian mob, those Verdereses, was starting to make their move in New York, and it was too much to compete with anyway. This was, as I said, years ago. Before the Intrepid. Before the craziness, but I could see it all coming. So I stopped. I invested my money. Wisely."

Herrick's uncle finished off the second drink. His cheeks were red.

"So, no. I haven't spoken to or about your father in nearly ten years. The same goes for Mr. Cole. You were smart to come and talk to me, Mr. Herrick. But not smart enough. I'm not involved in this."

Herrick shifted his weight. "You haven't heard a thing?"

"Not a peep." Then the old man tilted his head and yelled, "Elena! Is it time for dinner?"

A thick Russian accent came back, "Ten more minutes."

"You can show yourself out?"

Herrick got off the chair. He spoke through gritted teeth. "I like the smoking jacket look. It still fits you, Uncle Adrik."

A smile. "You remembered."

"Other than time passing, you don't look different. Same — tall, thin, priestly."

Vavilov laughed now. "Priestly? I like that. You mean still?"

"Calm."

He brushed his hair with his hand. "When did you last speak with your mother?"

The pain in Herrick's gut started to spread. His ribs ached, and felt cold.

"Been a while."

Uncle Adrik nodded. "Maybe it's time. Good night, Matt."

Herrick walked out of the house. By the time he got to his car, it felt like his entire torso was covered in ice. But maybe Uncle Adrik was right.

It was time to track Mom down.

CHAPTER 4

ELLIOT COLE LOOKED at himself in the rearview mirror and brushed his hair to the side. He licked his thumb and used it to fix his eyebrows. He got out of the car and walked into the prison.

A chill ran down his spine as he walked through the door, and it wasn't from the initial blast of an air conditioner, because there wasn't one. He passed his ID through, and took a glance up at the security cameras. The appointment had been made weeks ago, the warden expected him, but he didn't want to be seen here.

Flying too close to the sun. This must be what "edging", as the kids said, is.

Cole patted his thigh while he waited to be called. The guard behind the desk stared at the computer, the soft blue glow reflecting on his face. Cole sniffled. This was taking too long. Didn't they know who he was?

No. Not exactly.

The guard finally nodded at him and called his name. Cole stood up, tugged at the lapels of his jacket and walked to the door. The guard buzzed him in and then stepped around the counter.

He escorted Cole down a long, sterile hallway with plain doors on either side. Cole assumed they led to offices, but didn't know for sure. Didn't care, actually.

The guard stopped at one of the doors, pushed it open and

pointed for Cole to enter. He did.

Fred Aguilera sat behind the desk, and wiped his brow. He nodded at Cole.

"Hot in here, right?"

Cole grinned, and felt the warmth under jacket. He didn't dare take it off. There might be pit stains.

"Too hot," Cole said.

"That's why you're here, right? I mean, it's April, and I'm already breaking a sweat. I got this stupid box fan, and a couple of wall units in my office and meeting room and that's it. The guys are suffering out there." Aguilera ran his sentences together. "I'm not even ready to turn mine on yet. I mean, it was forty friggin' degrees last week."

Cole nodded. "Too soon."

He wanted to get this moving, but he had to slow play it. Aguilera was the warden of this joint, and Cole had to let him play it out.

Aguilera sniffled and put the handkerchief he'd used to wipe his face on the desk. He leaned back in his chair and it creaked underneath him. His bald head glistened.

"The governor called me this morning."

"Did he?" Slow. Play.

"Yeah. And I asked him what it would take to get central air put in this building. And he said, with infrastructure and the pension costs — all that? It would be a while."

"Did you remind him it was the twenty-first century?"

Aguilera smiled. "We go through this every summer. They send more box fans. A few more wall units. But they refuse to go central. He said I'd have to find a way to raise the money myself."

Cole licked his lips and waited.

"Remember that dinner we were at a few years ago? The fundraiser?"

Cole blew air out his nose. "We met there. I don't forget meeting power brokers."

"You and your lovely wife. How is she?"

Cole looked to the ground. The tiles were grimy. The place needed a mop, a bucket and a hell of a lot of soapy water. It was worse than the first row house he'd looked at in Paterson.

"Not something you want to talk about, I get it."

"The governor," Cole prodded.

"Oh, right. Right." Aguilera wiped his nose. "Well, I told him I could probably raise the money if he did me a favor."

Cole nodded. *Here we go.*

"Now, you know him. Money from a private source? That's his sweet spot. So he asked how, and I told him about Kenneth Herrick and Jackson Donne."

"How much will the renovations cost?"

Aguilera told him.

Cole nodded. "I can do that."

"The governor said he would pardon them. On the down low. No news story. No press conference. He'd sign off real quick and his guys would bury it. Make sure no one even sends an email."

"Emails often get him in trouble."

Aguilera laughed. "He's got to vet better."

Cole agreed. He was putting together an army back home. And Kenneth Herrick was a key piece. And Kenneth wanted Donne. Vetting, though, was the key to putting this army together. Having the right men. The ones who wouldn't turn on him or screw things up. He'd done enough background checks in his years, during all of the plotting and the planning. He'd never made a mistake.

Maybe that was why he still felt a chill, despite the heat.

"You'll have the money no problem. Just like every other donation I've made. To clean up your 'gambling' history from the internet." He made air quotes.

Aguilera swallowed. "It-it will come from a third party, of course. Having the cash trace back to you would be bad form."

Cole nodded. "Like always."

"Good. There's one other thing you should know, Elliot."

Now Cole felt the sweat at the back of his hairline. He reached back and wiped the beads away before they could ruin his sport coat. A little electricity ran through his body. The kind of zip he enjoyed. Made everything worthwhile.

"Kenneth Herrick is currently in solitary."

Cole leaned forward.

"He killed a guy."

"Can I see him?"

"Didn't you hear me? He's in solitary."

"The gambling can be brought out into the open at any time. Leaked to NJ dot com, perhaps?"

Aguilera sniffled again. "When this is over, we'll both have something on each other."

"Cost of doing business," Cole said. "But, as long as you stay in line, we'll be fine."

"Let's go," Aguilera said.

"**A**RE YOU INSANE?" Cole asked.

Kenneth Herrick sat on the cot in the solitary cell. They were both dripping with sweat. None of the wall units were used in this wing of the prison. The hallway smelled like old shit, and puke.

"It had to be done."

Cole jammed his hands in his pockets. "Why?"

"We need Donne alive."

"I don't trust him. I've looked him up."

"I do. He's my guy. He'll do what I say."

Cole took a deep breath through his mouth. He could taste the odors, they were so viscous and horrid.

"He'd better."

"How long?"

"A day or two. Keep your mouth shut."

"It'll be good to be out."

Cole grinned. "We're old now. The world is different."

Kenneth shook his head. "Get us out of here."

Cole called for the guard.

CHAPTER 5

Jackson Donne's stomach was in a knot. It was only twenty minutes until breakfast, and Kenneth Herrick was somewhere off in solitary, which, ironically, left Donne very much alone.

Sure, the man who'd killed Kate and had made an attempt on Donne's life was now dead, but that didn't mean he was any safer. Too many people knew his name now. Too many people had heard what he'd done, and how he'd kept himself out of prison while putting away a ton of other people.

Donne sat up on the small cot. He'd made it through the night, and that was a bonus. But Herrick had been the law of the land around here, and that was why Donne had been untouched.

Now, though, Donne was an exposed nerve, just waiting to be touched.

The first days of his sentence were horrible, a blur of verbal and physical assault. He'd had his arm broken, and been concussed twice. But then Matt Herrick gave him Kenneth's name, and things changed. Donne had a friend. Someone who'd been behind bars long enough to hold respect amongst the rest of the crooks.

Sometimes Herrick would have to send a message. But never like he did with Luca. He'd never killed someone. He'd busted a few heads. Sent a threatening message or two. But killing seemed over the line. And Kenneth Herrick, for the year that Donne had known him, never seemed to be the one who would step over the line.

Inmates were just starting to wake up, and the noise level was increasing. Shouts, yells and cursing all echoed off the walls. Donne's chest and back tightened, like someone had reached inside him and put a tight fist around his muscles. The white noise of prison voices always caused him to tighten up. He took a deep breath.

Breakfast was announced, and the inmates started to line up to head into the cafeteria. It reminded Donne very much of high school. He got in line between two Muslims who'd been at his side since Herrick got carted off. Zuti put his hand on Donne's shoulder.

"Today, two men have been asking about you," he whispered.

Donne said, "The day is barely an hour old."

"They are impatient, it seems."

Donne felt the fist in his chest grip tighter.

"What are they asking?"

The other man, Yousef, grinned. "Are you the man from Narcotics in New Brunswick?"

Donne nodded. "Long memory. What did you tell them?"

Zuti shook his head. "We don't know you. Let's eat."

They moved into the kitchen area of the cafeteria. Donne could smell eggs and bacon. The workers behind the counter scooped the food onto a tray, didn't ask what you wanted and didn't care.

Yousef passed his tray across. "Don't give me the bacon."

The worker put two strips on his tray anyway.

"Mother fucker," Yousef said.

Donne picked the two pieces off the tray and placed them on his own. "More for me."

"There are a lot of people talking about you, Jackson."

"I'm sure it's all good."

Zuti shook his head. "Mostly, people can't understand how you're still alive."

"That seems to be the essential question of my life."

They sat at a table in the corner. One where Donne could survey the room, and few people could sneak up on him. Zuti and Yousef weren't protecting him, so much as giving him a head's up that shit might go down. That was exactly how Zuti explained it fifteen minutes after Herrick went to solitary. *I am not stepping in front of a shiv for you.*

Across the room, two black guys stared at his table. Donne tried to search his memory for recognition, but found nothing. Could be a coincidence. He took a bite of the soft, watery eggs. Forced it down.

And then a spoonful of scrambled eggs splattered against his shoulder. Scanning the room, Donne couldn't tell who it came from. The room erupted in laughs.

A guard walked over to Donne and said, "Choke that food down and come with me."

"I never question a man in uniform," Donne said. He finished eating as fast as he could.

The guard took him from the cafeteria to the warden's office. That was different. Donne hadn't seen Fred Aguilera since the day he'd been brought in. Kenneth told Donne the more someone was out of that office, the better. Fred, whose full name was Fedele, was nicknamed Fe-Deadly by the guards. He never failed to fire or punish someone as harshly as he could. Donne was half surprised Herrick wasn't put to the chair after killing Luca Carmine.

Aguilera offered Donne a seat. There was sweat sparkling off his bald head. The office had to be eighty degrees. The last thing Aguilera wanted was to cost the state a dollar more because he had to put the air conditioning on in April.

"You are an interesting man, Mr. Donne," Aguilera said.

Donne didn't respond. Aguilera was toying with him, but Donne could wait it out.

"And I'll be honest, you made the right friend."

Silence is your friend, Donne thought.

Aguilera spread his hands. "You're not going to say anything?"

Donne took a breath. "Not until I can figure out what you mean."

Aguilera touched the side of his nose. "You're smarter than I give you credit for. I thought you were just living off your friendship with Mr. Herrick."

Donne shrugged.

"Well, maybe you are. It seems Mr. Herrick has powerful and wealthy friends." Aguilera got up and walked over to the air conditioner. He turned it on. A gust of cold air washed over Donne. "And they are willing to make a large donation to the prison. Help us make things a lot better."

Donne rubbed his face.

"This is all off the record, of course, Mr. Donne."

"What are you talking about?" Donne finally asked.

Aguilera sat back behind his desk and grinned.

"How would you like to be a free man?"

CHAPTER 6

ERRICK DROVE BACK to his Hoboken apartment and lucked into a parking spot on the street. He parallel parked, and then climbed the stairs to his abode. He tried the doorknob and found it unlocked. His chest filled with warmth.

Sarah Cullen had Crosby, Stills and Nash going on the computer. He could see her behind the kitchen bar working at the stove. Her back was to him, and she was swaying gently to the music. Something Herrick couldn't recall the title to, despite the familiar harmony. The smell of onions and spices filled the air.

"Hey," he said.

She didn't jump, instead turned toward him and grinned.

"Tacos," she said. "You want a margarita?"

"No, thanks." He flared his nose. "How many have you had so far?"

She flipped him the bird. "Can you count?"

Herrick tossed his keys on the table and sat on the couch. "You know, there's probably something to be said about you fixing my dinner and a drink when I get home from work. Something about gender stereotypes."

"Or, I got home first and I like to cook."

Herrick leaned forward and rubbed his face with both hands. "Weird day."

"Kyrie's workout was a bust?" Something sizzled on the stove and Sarah turned the knob down.

Herrick shook his head. "That went great."

Crossing her arms, Sarah said, "Don't make me wait."

So he told her. When he was done, she said, "Jesus Christ."

"You're telling me."

The microwave timer went off, and the music streaming service shifted into an advertisement at the same time. Sarah went to the stove and started fixing plates. Herrick went over and closed the laptop.

"When was the last time you saw your mom, Matt?"

Herrick shrugged. "Before I went to Afghanistan. My parents are the reason I enlisted. I was orphaned and couldn't afford college."

Sarah put the taco in front of him. The refried beans steamed on the plate.

"You're not an orphan. We're talking right now about your mom and dad. They're alive."

Herrick said, "I guess I'm being metaphorical."

Sarah kissed him on the cheek. "Wise man."

"When I was seventeen, my dad got arrested and my mom ran off with Elliot Cole. My dad's old partner."

"What's the next step?"

Herrick sat back and ran his hand through his hair. The taco sat heavy in his stomach. Sarah was eating hers in a salad, and she nibbled on some lettuce.

"Adrik is not funding my father's release. He doesn't even seem to be in the game anymore."

Sarah kept nibbling. "Why don't you go talk to your father?"

"He's in solitary. He killed a guy, and they won't let him see anyone."

"So why would they let him out?"

Herrick rubbed his index finger and thumb together. "Cash money."

An hour later, the plates had been cleared. Herrick had the Mets on, but wasn't really listening to them. Baseball wasn't his thing, it was just background noise. The NBA playoffs weren't starting until later, and Herrick's mind was racing. He wouldn't be able to focus on the roundball anyway.

Sarah sat next to him with a glass of wine, a cabernet. She

sipped it.

"Gave up on the margaritas?"

"Pain in the ass to make."

Herrick said, "I'm going to have to talk to Elliot."

Sarah took another sip of wine. "Knew you'd get there eventually."

"I'm full of good ideas. Sometimes the one I need takes a while to get to the top."

Sarah didn't respond.

"I haven't seen my mother in so long. I wonder if she and Elliot are still together."

Sarah leaned in and kissed him. "I'm sure you'll find out."

Herrick's heart beat a little faster, but it wasn't from the kiss. He couldn't find the words to continue the banter. Instead, he returned her kiss.

They went to bed.

CHAPTER 7

TURNED OUT ELLIOT Cole wasn't all that difficult to track down. It wasn't because he had a Facebook or LinkedIn account. Nor was he listed in the phone book. In fact, Herrick didn't even have to start asking around about him. Nope. All Matt Herrick had to do was just show up at his office the next morning, brew some coffee and take a minute to peruse the sports section.

Because fifteen minutes after he did that, a man walked in with a gun.

Herrick sat back in his chair and crossed his arms in front of him. "Can I help you?"

"You're coming with me."

The guy held a revolver in his left hand. He was a big Latino guy in a tracksuit. His features didn't register with Herrick, mostly because the gun took up most of his attention.

"Where are we going?" Herrick asked.

"Elliot Cole wants to see you."

Herrick grinned. "He could have called."

"Let's go." The guy waved the gun toward the door. The traffic on Washington ground by outside the window.

Herrick stood up. "Listen, you don't need that thing. I want to talk to Elliot too, and I'm not armed anyway. I hate guns."

"I'm doing my job."

ick walked around the desk and kept his hands where the gun could see them. "Where are you parked?"

"I'll show you when we get outside."

Taking a breath, Herrick said, "Do you know where we are?"

The gunman took a step forward. The gun was inches from Herrick's chest. "Hoboken. You think I'm an idiot?"

"I think you're about a quarter mile from the PATH train. There are cops and jittery people going to work in Manhattan streaming through these streets. You walk outside with a gun out in the open, they will swarm around you. You'll be in prison before either of us can blink."

The gunman's nose squinched up and he gritted his teeth. His gun arm extended. Herrick grabbed him at the wrist and snapped it left. The gun clattered to the floor. Herrick kicked it away.

"Okay. Now let's go see Elliot Cole," he said.

Before the full name could come out of his mouth, the gunman reared back and punched Herrick in the face. Herrick fell backward and crashed into the desk. He felt a warm liquid spill from his nose. Using the back of his hand, he slowed the blood.

"Don't fuck with me," the gunman said. "*Now* let's go see Elliot Cole."

"Okay," Herrick said. His nostril throbbed.

After retrieving the gun, they both left the office and found the gunman's car a block away on Willow. No one called the cops.

HERRICK'S NOSE STOPPED bleeding by the time they parked in Paterson. They were in the middle of a rundown neighborhood — broken glass on the ground, cars on blocks and a couple arguing. The road was otherwise empty, no pedestrians or traffic. The gunman told him to get out, and Herrick complied. No need to restart the blood.

The gunman led him to a two-story walk-up and opened the door. Not the kind of neighborhood Herrick expected Cole to live in. He stepped through the door anyway.

The inside was completely different. Shiny wood floors, art on the walls. The smell of Pinesol. The gunman pointed down the hallway. Herrick followed it. The gunman remained behind. Herrick snuck a peek at him. Leaning against the door, arms crossed, he appeared to be snarling.

Herrick made it to the corner of the hallway and Cole, complete with stark white hair, goatee and rail Elliot standing in the doorway. He wore khakis and a black po build, rt.

"You didn't have to threaten me, Elliot," Herrick said.

"You've been snooping around. Adrik told me. Manuel was doing his job."

"Why are you buying my father out of jail?" Herrick put his hands in his pockets.

"Cut right to the chase, huh?"

Herrick shrugged. "I need an answer. My dad took the fall for you and now you want him out? And Jackson Donne too?"

"You get a lot of information quickly."

Cole stepped out of the way and let Herrick into the room. There was a bed, and next to it medical machines beeped and whirred. Herrick moved in closer and his heart rate tripled. His mother lay on the bed, sleeping.

"She's very sick, Matt. And I need your dad's help to save her."

CHAPTER 8

ERRICK APPROACHED THE bed. The air smelled like old roses and rubber. It was the kind of odor that would imprint itself in Herrick's brain. He could tell already—a whiff of rubber would likely send this day, this moment, crashing back to him.

His mother was asleep. An IV trailed from her arm up to a bag hanging from a metal pole. Next to her was a heart rate monitor. It beeped in slow rhythm. Herrick tried to match his breathing to it.

The body in the bed was certainly his mother, but it'd aged ten years. The familiar blonde in her hair was now fading, and she was showing gray at her roots. There were lines on her face where there hadn't been before. She was straw thin. Herrick reached out to touch her.

"Don't wake her," Cole said. "She just had surgery and she's going through chemo. She needs her rest."

Herrick pulled his hand away and turned back.

"She didn't sleep last night. I told her about your father."

"What's wrong with her?"

"Cancer. Stage four in her lung. But we're waiting on results of the segmentectomy tests. We don't know if it's spread yet. This is her second round of treatment."

Herrick put his hands in his pockets. "Why don't you take her to a hospital? Sloan Kettering?"

Cole tilted his head toward the hallway. "Let's talk in the kitchen."

They walked down the hall. Manuel's hulking figure shaded some of the sunlight that seeped in. Herrick nodded in his direction. The nod wasn't returned.

Inside the kitchen, Herrick took a seat at a bare wooden table. The rubber and rose smell faded, replaced by coffee and dish soap. Cole poured himself a cup and then offered one to Herrick.

"Have orange juice?" He didn't want to get jittery.

"This isn't a hotel," Cole said, but then found a carton and poured a glass full.

"It's been a long time, Elliot."

"Not long enough. I wish we didn't have to talk."

Herrick took a breath and stared at the glass Cole had placed in front of him. He tried to remember the last time — maybe the only time — he and Cole had spent alone together. A time without Adrik or his parents around. Cole wasn't even his babysitter. There was only one moment that came to him.

"I don't think I've seen you since Lattieri Park," Herrick said.

"That fucking day." Cole chuckled. But the grin quickly faded. "Your parents were on the outs with me then. Can't remember why I pissed them off. I think our heists were getting more and more dangerous. But they left me to babysit you. That day."

"I thought you might remember. I beat your ass at HORSE." Herrick took a pull of juice.

"Who didn't you beat?" Cole tapped his fingers on the countertop.

"Why are you buying my father out of prison?"

Cole shook his head. "He's going to help."

"Help with what?"

Cole shook his head. "You're going to help too. But it is your dad's job to tell you. Not mine."

Herrick took another drink of the orange juice. Too pulpy.

"You're going to walk away from me and wait to hear from your dad. If you care about your mother, you're going to forget you even saw us. Let your father walk from prison and then help him."

"I don't even know what it is."

"It's better that way."

"Plausible deniability?" Herrick tried.

They sat for a few minutes. Herrick drank his orange juice and waited for Cole to fill in the blanks. Cole let his coffee sit and watched the steam float away from it.

Finally, Herrick said, "What about Jackson Donne?"

Cole sat back and spread his hands. His cheeks flushed.

"What about him?"

"You're buying him out too."

Cole stood up from the table and leaned against the counter. The guy liked to lean.

"You know more than I thought you did."

Herrick nodded. "Might as well tell me everything."

Cole grinned. "Go home, Matt. Go coach your team."

"It's the off-season, I'm bored."

"Work out Irving. Or go sleep with your girlfriend. Then wait for the news from your father." The words were sharp.

"I don't want to see him again. Ever again."

Herrick's chest burned, and the fire rose up his throat into his face. He counted to ten, forcing himself to stay in his seat.

"You know a lot too."

Cole took a breath. "Your father," he said. "Your father forced me to get Donne out too. I'm not happy about it."

Herrick didn't say anything.

Manuel came into the kitchen, glared at Herrick and then turned his attention to Cole.

"She's up," he said.

Herrick stood up. "I want to see her."

Cole said, "Get him out of here. Be gentle. Somewhat." Then to Herrick, "You were never here."

Before Herrick could make a move, Manuel grabbed him by the collar and tugged. Herrick's feet went out from underneath him and he felt his momentum shift and gravity take hold. Manuel silently dragged him down the hall to the doorway, Herrick swatting at the big man's paw the entire time.

His struggle was to no avail and he found himself back in the backseat of Manuel's car.

Forty-five minutes later, he was alone on Washington Street in Hoboken.

CHAPTER 9

Jackson Donne sat on his cot and stared at the wall. He wondered if Kenneth was doing the same thing in solitary.

They were getting out.

Tomorrow.

But, the funny thing was, Donne didn't want to leave. It was his fault he was here in the first place, pleading guilty to murder. It was his penance. And other than being nearly beaten to death the first six months after he'd gotten here, it'd been pleasant.

He leaned back on his cot and fell asleep. That was the one thing he was able to do here no matter what. Sleep.

The past few years on the outside, it never came easily.

They processed Donne rather easily the next morning. He didn't have many items with him—most of his stuff was still in Vermont or thrown out when everyone thought he had killed a state senator. It'd been that kind of stretch for Donne. He wasn't supposed to see daylight for ten years.

But now he stepped out into the asphalt parking lot, the spring sun shining down and nearly blinding him. He used his right hand to shade his eyes and saw Kenneth Herrick leaning against a cab. He smiled at Donne and gave a little wave. Donne walked over to

him, this is a bit unexpected, huh?" Herrick stuck out his hand.
He took it. "This isn't right, Kenneth."

Kenneth Herrick shrugged. "I told my friend I wasn't leaving
without you. Come on, the meter's been running for about twenty
minutes."

He pulled open the back door to the cab and got in. Donne
walked around to the other side and did the same.

"What's this about?" Donne asked.

Kenneth shook his head. The driver of the cab pulled out onto
Woodbridge Road. They didn't speak in the car.

An hour later, they pulled into a parking lot on the edge of
West Orange. The parking lot was for a legendary pizza place
known as the Star Tavern. Kenneth smiled like it was Christmas
morning.

"Come on," he said to Donne. "I've been waiting years for
this."

He paid the cab driver with a stack of bills he pulled from a
white postage envelope.

They went inside. The place was basically a long bar with tables
scattered throughout and a few booths up against the opposite
wall. They took a corner booth. Kenneth ordered an iced tea.
Donne ordered a Flounder Genevieve IPA. Local beer, according
to the waitress.

And the first beer he'd had in over a year.

When the waitress sat it down in front of him, Donne watched
the sweat drip from the pint glass and pool in a little circle around
the bottom rim. He counted to ten before taking a sip. When he
did, the hops and malt washed over him, and he felt something
unlock between his shoulder blades. His taste buds must have
gone soft in prison, because the hops were extremely bitter and
had lost some of their citrus notes.

Whatever. It was beer.

Kenneth was staring at him as Donne put the glass down.

"Did you enjoy that?" He laughed.

"That obvious, huh?"

Kenneth nodded. The waitress came back and he ordered two
pies. A pepperoni and an onion.

"Tell me about your dad, Jackson."

Donne took another long sip of beer. "We've been friends for over a year and you're asking me now?"

"You know my son. You know me, but you've never been very forthright with me about yourself."

Donne leaned forward. "You know more about me than most people."

Kenneth nodded. "I know about your cop stuff, putting away half the New Brunswick Narc Department. I know some of your PI stuff, and that one of your fiancées should be dead and isn't, and the other one you wish was alive but is dead."

The words cut through Donne and the early sensations of a buzz.

"Sorry," Kenneth said. "That was…inelegant."

Donne finished off the beer. "Why do you want to know about my dad?"

"Because my relationship with Matt is terrible, and I'm afraid for how he's going to handle what's about to happen."

Donne signaled the waitress for another beer. She winked at him and hobbled toward the bar. The bros at the table next to them had ordered wings, and the smell of the buffalo sauce made Donne's stomach growl. Kenneth's explanation made little sense, but being hungry didn't put Donne in the mood to dig deeper.

"My father left my family when I was very young. I don't remember much about him other than his face was scratchy. He didn't shave well. That, and the day he left, I found my mother on the couch crying. But I was too young to really understand what it meant."

Donne's next beer and the pizzas came. They ate, and it was like Thanksgiving dinner. Too much and too fast, but still perfect. They finished both of the pizzas.

Donne went to signal for another beer, but Kenneth stopped him.

"No," he said. "We have to go meet a guy. And I don't need you drunk while we're there."

"Tell me what this is about."

"Work," Kenneth said. "It's always about work. And, I think, my ex-wife."

CHAPTER 10

THEY WERE IN Paterson.

The blocks were lined with rundown row houses. Littering the streets were broken bottles reflecting the sunshine back up at the few motorists who traveled by. The cab pulled up to one of the row houses, and Kenneth went through the same process of pulling a stack of bills. It looked like the envelope was nearly empty now.

Good thing Donne hadn't ordered that other beer.

His slight buzz had faded, and his equilibrium was back. The pepperoni repeated on him as he got out of the cab. Kenneth turned to him as the cab pulled away.

"Keep your mouth shut. Let me do the talking."

Donne stopped. Down the street, two guys were sitting on a stoop throwing dice.

"I just got out of prison," he said. "I'm following you around like a toddler. You gotta tell me what this is about before I go in there."

Kenneth's cheeks flushed. "And why do you think you're out of prison? Because of me." He pointed toward the door of the row house. "And because of the people in there. I need your help."

Donne stood his ground. "I didn't even want to leave prison. I had a ten-year term to serve. I've served one and change. I'm not supposed to be out yet."

"Stop whining. You got a Golden Ticket thanks to me. Come in and keep your mouth shut."

Donne bit his lip and followed Kenneth up the stairs. Kenneth knocked once and the door swung open. The space was filled by a large man, muscle bound and track suited. He bore down on Kenneth, and something in Donne's stomach curled up and went to sleep.

The big man hugged Kenneth and said, "Been a while. Come in. Elliot's waiting."

They went into the hallway—fresh wood paneling, the smell of potpourri hanging in the air. A vent pushed cool air into the room. Donne scratched the back of his neck.

Kenneth said, "Jackson, this is Manuel. Manuel—"

The big man waved Kenneth off. "I don't need no introductions."

Donne nodded toward Manuel, who pointed down the hallway. Kenneth went first and Donne followed. The scent of rubber now mixed with the potpourri. Donne could feel Manuel's presence hanging over his shoulder.

A man, tall, thin and blonde, but closer to Kenneth's age, stood in the kitchen. Next to him was a woman in pajamas, sitting at the table and sipping tea. Her gaunt face didn't look in their direction. Kenneth paused at the door, putting his hand on the jamb. He appeared to be steadying himself.

Kenneth ran a hand over his face, and then said, "Hello, Elliot."

The white haired man stuck out his hand. Kenneth didn't take it. He then offered it to Donne, who accepted the shake.

"I'm Elliot Cole," he said. "You've heard of me?"

Donne shook his head.

"I've heard of you, Mr. Donne."

"Yeah, I had my fifteen minutes of news time, it seems."

Cole spread his hands. "But you've done your time, and now I'm sure you're a changed man."

Kenneth stepped in. The woman in the chair looked up at him. Her skin was jaundiced.

"You deal with me," Kenneth said. "He's just the muscle."

Elliot's gaze went from Donne to Manuel.

The woman spoke, "You haven't asked how I am, Kenneth."

Shaking his head, Kenneth said, "Maybe I don't care."

"If you didn't, you wouldn't be here. You don't owe us."

"Tammy, I—"

The woman pushed herself up from the table. Two slow steps later, she had taken Kenneth's hand.

"I know what happened hurts you, Kenneth. But you and me, we had something. We have a son, and I need your help."

Kenneth pulled his hand away.

"I'm sick. Lung cancer. I—"

Cole stepped in. "Don't wear yourself out, I can—"

Tammy didn't let him take over the conversation. "We need to get to Cuba. They have medicine there. They can fix me, but Elliot spent his money getting you out because he needs you. We can't get there without your help."

Kenneth opened his mouth. Then he closed it. He looked up to the ceiling. Finally, he said, "What is it?"

Now Cole said, "We want you to rob the Federal Reserve."

CHAPTER 11

〰〰

DONNE FELT HIS legs go out from under him. The room suddenly got warmer. He didn't go down, catching his balance at the last moment. Kenneth put a hand on his shoulder, steadying him.

"New York?" Kenneth asked. "That's impossible. Why bother?"

Cole shook his head. "East Rutherford."

There was a Federal Reserve on Route 17 in East Rutherford, just miles from the Meadowlands. Donne didn't know much about it, other than it existed. As far as he understood, the place didn't get headlines, and didn't house gold. It was secondary. The one in New York was the big one, the one that kept gold, and took care of some major deals. It was even the plot of a *Die Hard* movie.

"I don't want any part of this," Donne said.

Kenneth turned toward him. "We'll talk later."

Inside Donne's chest, a fist wrapped itself around his lungs and heart and squeezed. "I—"

"Later," Kenneth said.

"I need millions, Kenneth," Cole said. "I'm done. Spent the last of my dollars getting you out of prison. Adrik won't help me, not anymore. Not since—" He wiped his face. "This is a job I can't do on my own. And with Tammy sick, I need help. You're the best I know."

"I've been in prison for the last ten years."

Kenneth took the seat next to Tammy. Donne wished he had thought of that. The fist in his chest was distracting his thinking.

"And now you want me to mosey into the Federal Reserve and steal millions? Technology is different. Life is different. Ten years ago, I had a flip phone. Now? I can't imagine the security. There has to be another way."

Tammy burst into a coughing fit, and Cole went over to her. He wrapped her in his arms while she convulsed and gasped for air. Donne watched Kenneth. His face was stone, exactly the same as it had been when he snapped Luca Carmine's neck.

Donne tried to picture it, going away to prison when the Red Sox were celebrating their first World Series victory. Change, to Donne, always felt glacial. Ten years ago, Jeanne was still al—she was alive now. But Donne thought she died. Ten years ago, he was barely a cop. He was a twenty-five-year-old kid trying to figure life out.

Now, he was still trying to figure life out, but as an ex-con.

"There has to be something more here, Elliot."

Kenneth's words snapped Donne back to attention. Tammy had stopped coughing. Elliot still had his arm around her.

"Robbing the Federal Reserve? This isn't a movie. You don't just create a distraction somewhere and waltz off with the money. After 9/11, the world is a different place, security is tight. People are always watching you. Isn't that what all your letters to me said?"

Cole reached into his pocket and produced a folded up piece of printer paper. He handed it to Kenneth. Donne could see that it was a news article printed off the internet, but he couldn't read it. Kenneth eyed it, then folded the paper and put it in his pocket.

"How long?" Kenneth asked, nodding toward Tammy.

Cole opened his mouth, but Tammy reached up and shushed him.

"I'm sick, Kenneth. Not dead and not three years old. You can talk to me."

Kenneth adjusted his gaze.

"We don't know. But if the cancer spread, I want to try something different. They reopened Cuba for us. We can go there now. Elliot and I need the money. I'm not ready to die yet. We need you."

Kenneth stared at her and Donne counted in his head. He got to fifteen before Kenneth exhaled.

"Listen," he said. "My friend and I are about two hours out of prison. I need some time to get settled and think about this."

Cole said, "Think quickly. I know you don't have much — if any — money right now. This is a good opportunity for you."

Kenneth nodded, looked at Donne and said, "Come on."

In minutes, they were back on the street waiting for another cab. One Manuel had called for them.

Donne's chest loosened and he was finding his breath again. A cab came around the corner. Kenneth waved at it.

"This is bizarre," Donne said.

Kenneth glared. "Wait until we are in the cab."

The cab stopped hard, kicking up asphalt. They got in. Donne clicked his seatbelt, while Kenneth gave a familiar address in Hoboken.

"This is not bizarre — it's bullshit," Kenneth said as they pulled away. "There are a thousand other ways to steal money. Less dangerous ways. But he wants to go into the Federal Reserve?"

Paterson morphed into Route 20, then Route 21. Route 3 and the New York City skyline emerged in front of them.

Donne rubbed his eyes. "Why did you ask for me to come along?"

"Because I'm old," Kenneth said. "I don't know if I can pull off even a simple bank robbery anymore. I need help. I want you to help me."

The cab driver took a glance at them in the rearview, but didn't speak. He couldn't hear the conversation clearly through the partition, Donne guessed.

"You knew this was coming?" Donne asked.

Kenneth took a long breath. "I knew something like this was coming. No one just buys you out of prison. It's why I could do what I did with...with — "

"With Luca," Donne said.

"And there's one other thing."

Kenneth took the folded paper out of his pocket and handed it to Donne. As he unfolded it, Donne saw the word "Iraq" in the headline.

"I need you, because you know my son. And we're going to have to talk to him."

Donne stared at the headline. "Money from the Federal Reserve Disappears En Route to Iraq."

Okay, he thought, maybe this Federal Reserve did garner some important headlines.

"So you're doing this?"

Kenneth nodded.

Folding the paper up, Donne had a better idea of why they were heading to Hoboken, and maybe why they were going to talk to Matt Herrick.

CHAPTER 12

COLE WAITED FOR the door to shut. Once that hard click echoed through the household, he turned to Manuel.

"You call Neil?"

Manuel nodded and his cheeks flushed. "Texted. He'll be here in five."

Cole shook his head. "You two."

He walked back into Tammy's room. She lay on the bed, staring at the ceiling. Cole sat on the chair next to her and rubbed her arm. She looked at him without smiling. Her eyes were watery, but she wasn't crying.

"Neil is bringing your next treatment."

She nodded.

"A few more days and we'll be in sunny Cuba. We'll be past this."

Tammy flared her nostrils. "We should have been past this life years ago. We should be retired now. Sipping piña coladas somewhere. I don't want you to risk your life again."

"For you, Tammy, I'll risk my life. So will Kenneth. We'll get Matt to help too."

She shook her head. "I don't want him to. Not him."

The back door creaked open and slammed shut. Cole stood up.

"We need him. We need everyone. It's too big a plan otherwise.

We need an army." He exhaled. "Get some rest. We're moving later tonight."

Neil Haskins kissed Manuel in the kitchen. Cole knocked on the wall to let them know he was there. The two broke apart. Neil ran a hand through his military style haircut. It matched Manuel's. The bag carrying the chemo stuff rested on the table.

"She gets one more treatment tonight, then we go." Cole picked up the bag and looked it over. A wave rushed over him, and it felt like the room got a shade darker.

Haskins took the bag from him and winked. "You know, for an old guy, you're pretty understanding of us."

"I grew up in the era of free love. Get to work. We're about to get busy."

Haskins laughed. "Cute turn of phrase."

He left the room, and Cole turned back to Manuel.

"He got you there," Manuel said.

"Maybe he shouldn't bring your love life up every time I see him."

Manuel nodded. "I'll talk to him."

Cole took a seat at the table next to Manuel. "You know I trust you. Pulled you from the gangs. Got you into the National Guard. Which, coincidentally, helped you meet Neil. I need to ask you one question."

Manuel went pale. "Boss, listen, we—"

"Tell me what you think of Jackson Donne."

Manuel shifted in his seat and the color came back. "I don't trust him. I don't know him, other than what's been on the news. He's a wild card."

"Did you see the way he fell to his knees when I told them about the job?"

Manuel nodded. Down the hall, Haskins was singing to Tammy. It sounded like a lullaby.

"Looks like prison made him a wuss, boss. He fell to his knees. The air went out of him."

Cole stood up again and went over to the sink. He ran the tap and washed his hands, doing the alphabet song in his head. The things that stuck with you from grammar school. Even fifty years later. He needed to be doing something while he thought over what he was going to say next. Kenneth's reaction was going to be key.

He turned off the faucet and dried his hands w
towel. Then he turned back to Manuel. Manuel was star dish
door.   t the

"Waiting for Neil?"

Manuel turned back to Cole. "I haven't seen him in days, No,
with all the work we've been doing. The prepping."

Cole nodded. "I get it. But we don't have time to slow down
now."

"What you're doing to —" Manuel started. "I don't understand
you, boss."

"It's a means to an end, just like how we have to pack everything
up tonight. Spotless. Repaint if we have to. We're out of here."

Manuel wiped his nose. "Whatever you say."

"Then, I want you to find Donne. And take care of him. Take.
Him. Out. I think your read on him is right. He's not built for this.
And, from what I've read about him, and what Kenneth said about
him when I would visit the jail, Donne has some sort of soul. We
don't have time for that."

Manuel stood up. "I'll start packing."

"Good."

Haskins came back into the room and met Manuel with another
kiss. Cole fought back the sourness in his stomach. Haskins and
Manuel were both good people to have on the job. There was no
time for any other feelings.

"Get to work, guys. You'll have time for all this when we get to
Long Valley. And just think, in a week, we'll all be rich."

They walked into the other room, leaving Cole alone. He
stared at the wallpaper near the back door. It was peeling at the
corner. He would have to fix that, because there was no way in hell
he was staying up all night to tear off wallpaper, scrub the walls
and re-paint.

Robbing the Federal Reserve was one thing. But he was too
damn old to redecorate.

CHAPTER 13

THE DOOR OPENED. It wasn't Matt Herrick standing there, but a woman. The one Donne recognized from the school Herrick worked at. Kenneth's shoulders slumped.

"He moved?" Kenneth said.

The woman—Donne could not remember her name—said, "Can I help you?"

"Matt." Kenneth nearly shouted it. "Where does Matt Herrick live now?"

The woman took a breath and stuttered. "He's out. He lives here, but…"

Donne stepped in front of Kenneth. "Hi. You probably don't remember me, but Matt really helped me out about a year or so ago. I'm—"

Instant recognition. "Jackson! Jackson Donne. What are you…? Oh, you really got out. So this must be…"

Her eyes went wide when she looked at Kenneth. Donne nodded.

"This is Matt's dad. This is Kenneth Herrick."

Kenneth stuck out his hand, and, after a second, so did the woman. They shook.

She said, "This was not how I expected to meet his parents. I'm Sarah. I'm Matt's girlfriend."

The name quickly flashed back to Donne.

Kenneth's hand snapped away. But he recovered nicely. "Well, he has exceptional taste."

"Where's Matt?" Donne asked.

Sarah put her hands on each side of the doorway. "I don't know. Working."

Kenneth took a deep breath. Then he folded his arms. "What does my son do for a living now?"

Donne snapped his head in Kenneth's direction, surprised by the question. Kenneth knew. Herrick may not have come to visit Kenneth much, but Donne and Kenneth had talked a ton in prison. He knew. What game was he playing here?

Someone in the building started pounding on drums, a half-hearted attempt at a song that seemed very familiar to Donne. The beat wasn't perfect, so he couldn't place it.

Sarah said, "He's a high school basketball coach." Kenneth opened his mouth, but she held up a hand. "I know—it's out of season, but they're doing workouts before AAU practice starts. Matt likes to keep a good relationship with the AAU guys so he can have a say in where these kids go to college."

Donne waited.

Kenneth said, "Can we come in and wait for him?"

Sarah said, "No. I don't think so."

"Why not? He's my son."

Sarah straightened her back. "Because you are two convicted criminals who appear to be out of jail based on a technicality."

Kenneth opened his mouth and then closed it. Finally, he nodded. "We'll come back."

"Don't hurry," she said. "He doesn't want to see you."

He waved at Donne and started back down the hallway. The drums got louder, pounding away with the rhythm of a rock song.

CHAPTER 14

"**T**HEY'RE OUT."

John Mack sat across from Matt Herrick in the middle of Garden State Plaza, one of the largest malls in New Jersey. They were in the food court, surrounded by the smell of fries, pizza and Chinese food. Herrick nursed a Dr. Pepper while Mack munched on a small salad from a chain.

Herrick asked, "When?"

"Today. I tried to slow the process down, but the warden down there is kind of headstrong. He saw the cash and couldn't say no." Mack chewed lettuce. "Did you talk to Cole?"

"Why is the warden making the decision?"

Mack shrugged. "I think he nudged our fearless leader in Trenton in this direction after the donation. But who knows? What about Cole?"

A family walked by them, the dad holding the hand of a toddler whose attention was drifting with all the marketing going on around them. The mom pushed a stroller with a babbling baby inside. Both mom and dad looked like they hadn't slept in a month.

Herrick told Mack the story of visiting Elliot Cole—minus the part about Herrick being dragged out of the house by his collar. Mack listened as he finished his salad, and then shook his head.

"What are they up to?" he asked.

"Hell if I know, but it can't be good."

"Stating the obvious."

Mack put his fork down, exhaled loudly, and leaned back his chair. Herrick waited. When he was a kid, his dad used to do the same thing before grounding him. In retrospect, being grounded for pushing a kid on a playground was kind of ridiculous when your dad and mom were modern day cat burglars. Herrick didn't learn that until it was too late. His parents did a hell of a job lying to him, up until the day his dad was arrested.

Uncle Elliot and Uncle Adrik were the rich ones. Mom and Dad called them corporate. They were the ones to land the front row Yankees tickets, and gave Herrick some experiences kids got spoiled on. But that was how it went. Saw some great games back in the day, and while he was there with his uncles, Mom and Dad were out Bonnie and Clyde-ing it.

"What if you raid the house in Paterson?" Herrick asked, snapping himself back to the conversation.

Mack shook his head. "Don't have any probable cause. Elliot Cole hasn't been on our radar in a long time. And I'm also only in corrections. He hasn't jumped bail."

"Would probably put the kibosh on the whole thing anyway. We'd never find out what they were up to."

Mack squinted when Herrick said "kibosh," but didn't comment. "Of course, if we stop it before we know, that's a good thing. I'll make some calls and see if we can get someone out there to at least take a look around."

Herrick's phone buzzed on the table. He snatched it before Mack could sit back up. It was a text from Sarah. *Just met your dad. Weird.*

What felt like an electric shock ran up Herrick's arm and into his chest. Air got caught in his throat. He started to stand. Sat back down and wrote to Sarah. *Are you okay?*

Yes. They're gone. He and Donne were here.

Mack said, "What is it?"

Herrick stared at the cop across from him, and his stomach knotted. His instincts told him to not say anything. Make up an excuse to leave, and get the hell back to Hoboken. But that reaction never helped him before. Lying only led to trouble with law enforcement.

He took a breath. "My dad and Donne just came to my

ent. They're gone now, though. They ran into my girlfriend."

"Hell of a Saturday for her. You going back there?"

Herrick nodded.

"I'll meet you there. I want to hear this."

Herrick nodded again. Then bolted for the parking lot. Sarah said she was all right, but it didn't ease the rock that formed in the back of his neck. A rock that wouldn't go away until he saw her okay with his own eyes.

Route 17 to Route 3 to Interstate 495. Basically hell on asphalt any time of day, and it took Herrick nearly forty-five minutes to navigate. Mack's car was directly behind him at one point, but all the lane weaving separated them. Herrick didn't even bother to try finding street parking, and tucked his car in a lot. The car he bought after he realized public transportation was slowing his caseload down. At least in a car you felt like you had control.

He got to the front door of his apartment building, pulled his key and was about to unlock the door when he felt a hand on his arm. He whirled and reached for the ASP nightstick that was usually there. Today, though, in his rush, he left it in the car.

"Matt," Jackson Donne said. "Your dad and I need to talk to you."

Herrick said, "Sarah?"

"She's fine, but you and I need to get off the street. It's important. I'm worried."

"You're supposed to be in jail. Both of you."

Donne nodded. "Yeah, I kind of wish I was. It's bad, Matt."

"Where's my dad?"

Donne tilted his head in the direction of the PATH train. "Let's walk."

"I don't want to see him."

"You really should. Let's walk."

Herrick hesitated, looking up at his apartment window. Donne took his arm.

"Let's go."

Herrick exhaled. They walked.

CHAPTER 15

ERRICK DIDN'T SAY anything to Donne as they walked. His heart was pumping hard and his fingers were slightly numb. It was after lunch, and the bars were just starting to get busy with people checking out the final innings of the matinee Yankees and Mets games. The PATH train station wasn't bustling like it would be on a weekday morning.

Donne took the steps down two at a time, a bounce in his step Herrick had never seen. Herrick used the bannister. A man leaned against the wall near the Metrocard kiosks. His face was covered in shadow, but that didn't matter. Herrick hadn't seen him in over ten years, and that didn't matter either. He knew it was his father.

They reached the platform and Kenneth Herrick stepped forward. Matt Herrick looked at his dad, and realized the time that had past. The rakish good looks of a 1970s action star were gone, replaced by wrinkles, jowls and gray hair. His dad had shaved the full black beard and mustache, but a salt and pepper five o'clock shadow appeared. Steve McQueen in the 70s meet Clint Eastwood now.

"Hi, Matt." The voice was the same, baritone and strong.

Matt Herrick looked at Donne. "Are you glad I gave you that note way back when?"

Donne shrugged. "Probably be dead otherwise."

The squeal of train brakes and the following hiss filled the station. A few commuters at the turnstile started to run.

"Wanna ride?" Kenneth said. "I used to love the subways when I was a kid."

Herrick shook his head. "I don't want to be here. You shouldn't be out of prison."

Play it dumb, Matt.

"I just wanted to see you. You never came to visit."

Herrick worked his jaw for a moment. "Dad, I was in Afghanistan because I was essentially an orphan. Because of you."

"I'm glad you survived." Kenneth was stone faced.

Herrick flashed to the boy with the bomb in the sandbox. Seconds from detonation. Herrick's hands started to shake and he balled them into fists. He rolled and cracked his neck.

"No help from you," he said.

Donne put a hand on his shoulder. "You okay?"

"I talked to Elliot Cole," Herrick said. "I knew you were out. I know he bought you out. I know about...about Mom. That's all I want to know. Jesus, I'm going to have to hire a therapist."

"We need your help," Kenneth said.

"Cole told me." Herrick put his hands in his pockets. "Stay away from me and Sarah."

A voice warned everyone to stand clear of the closing doors, and then the train pulled out into the tunnel.

"I haven't been to New York in so long," Dad said.

Herrick turned to Donne. "Take him to New York, then. Away from here."

"He's the boss."

Like it was grammar school all over again. Go tell Mom, ask your father. Herrick's body was a muscle tightened mess, like he'd spent the entire night working out for the first time in years. He wanted to punch something.

"I just wanted to see you, Matt. I wanted to know you were okay. After seeing your mom this morning, I just...I know Elliot told you to help, I'm going to tell you the same thing."

Donne jumped in. "Does that mean we are going to do it?"

"Jesus Christ," Herrick said. "When did you become a lap dog?"

"If it wasn't for your dad, I'd be dead."

"You said that already. And who gave you his name?"

Kenneth put a hand on Herrick's forearm. Herrick snapped it away. "Everyone needs to stop touching me right now and tell me what the *fuck* is going on."

Kenneth just shook his head. "It was good to see you, son. I'm sorry if this is difficult, but I had to see you. And I need your help. I hope you consider it. Come on, Jackson."

They turned and walked toward the turnstile, and hopped it. Herrick counted to ten. He wasn't any closer to understanding this, and now the world had tipped on its edge and everything else was out of focus. He leaned against the wall and rubbed his face. He counted to twenty.

A mass of loud twenty-somethings made their way past him and through the turnstiles. They were talking about visiting some bars in the Village. They were laughing and pushing and shouting. Spring in New York. Day drinking, shenanigans and flip-flops. Stuff that he'd missed while he was in the sandbox. Life went by, people moved on. Herrick stared at his shoes, exhaled hard and climbed back up the stairs to Hoboken.

His father was the reason he joined the military. Why he missed having a life.

Ten minutes later, he opened the door to his apartment. Sarah was on the couch, knees up to her chin. The TV was blasting something on Home and Garden. She turned to him.

"Where have you been?"

"Are you okay?"

They said the words simultaneously. His poker face must not have been on the ball that afternoon, because Sarah jumped off the couch and wrapped him in her arms. He squeezed her tight.

"I just saw my dad for the first time in, God, it has to be ten years."

Sarah laughed. "I just saw him for the first time ever. Why was he here?"

"He just wanted to see me. Something bad is going down, and I don't know what it is. But he wants me to help."

Sarah ran her fingers through his hair, massaging the back of his neck. The air went out of him, in a good way, like the first sip of a drink after a long week.

"What do you want to do?"

Herrick laughed. "I want a big drink, but I don't think I should."

"Okay."

"I need to go think this through. You promise you're okay?"

Sarah leaned back from him and nodded. "I can take care of myself. Anyway, he was kind of nice to me. In a creepy old man way."

Herrick shrugged. "He's a creepy old man. I'm going to go to the gym. Want to come?"

Sarah said, "Let me get changed."

Herrick did the same, and then he grabbed his basketball. The only way to clear your mind was to practice free throws.

CHAPTER 16

KENNETH STAYED MOSTLY quiet in the city, save for a few directional tips. He wanted to walk through Central Park, so they did. They watched a group of men dance on roller skates. Nearby on the pond, some of the row boaters struggled to get their boats to turn. Donne wished he had a phone to play with.

His phone didn't work anymore. Not without Wi-Fi anyway. A lot of what he'd become accustomed to had gone by the wayside in just over a year. But being out in the open and unable to distract himself with technology was a bit of a culture shock.

Probably not a good addiction to have.

It didn't seem to bother Kenneth. Then again, when he went away, the iPhone was just an internet rumor.

Donne needed the distraction. Needed to be looking at something else, distracting himself with memes or clickbait articles. Anything but thinking about reality. Anything to keep from playing the visit to Elliot Cole's house over and over again in his head.

An hour later, they walked down Fifth Avenue as Kenneth window-shopped.

"You know," he said, "when we were kids, just dating, Tammy and I would come into the city at Christmastime. But she would never want to see the tree. She'd want to go to Macy's or some of those other stores and look in the windows. You know what I'm talking about?"

Something tickled Donne's intestines, like a centipede crawling around in his gut. He knew exactly what Kenneth was talking about, because Jeanne liked to do the same thing. Kate never did, though. She wasn't a city woman.

She wasn't anything anymore.

Donne's eyes burned. He caught himself and blinked the sting away.

"I know about that stuff," he said. "The Christmas decorations. I'm more a Thanksgiving guy."

Kenneth nodded. "You know, her face just lit up at that time of year. She loved it, and her mom would do the whole Seven Fishes meal on Christmas Eve. Those were the moments when we could just be. Not worried about the law or the next job. We were with family, and that was good. Ask Matt about it one day."

"Maybe I will, if we see him again."

"We will." Kenneth chuckled. "You know, one year, we snuck in and stole one of the decorations. A caroler holding a candle in two hands. We just couldn't resist that thrill."

Family wasn't Donne's strong suit. He and Jeanne would stay at home on Christmas Eve and order a pizza. Or Chinese food. Or he would work, busting up parties full of drugs. There were too many blurred Christmas Eves in his memory. And the blurring wasn't because it was a long time ago.

"Here's what I don't understand," Donne said. "Why was it only you who went to prison? How'd you get caught?"

Kenneth stared at Donne as they waited on a corner for the traffic light to change. It did, and Kenneth crossed.

"When I went away, I told Elliot to take care of Tammy. To keep an eye on her. I didn't want her to get caught, and no one did a better job of covering his tracks than Elliot. I didn't think they would—" His voice caught. "Never thought they'd fall in love. They were too different. But times change. And now? He bought us out for a reason, Jackson."

"You're not going to do this." Donne wiped his face. "We have a chance to get away scot-free."

I can run and start over. Find Jeanne. Figure out who I am now.

"This is my chance to save her, Jackson."

"Don't be stupid. There's more going on here. You said it

yourself."

Kenneth looked up the street. "Down there somewhere? Wall Street. All the world's money. Guy like me? I'd love a chance to raid it. World's biggest heist and get away with it. No trace. Maybe this isn't just about Tammy. But it's a chance to do something big."

"And dumb."

"You owe me, Jackson."

Donne took a deep breath.

"We can get away with this, and then you can have a life. One I missed out on the last ten years."

"Robbery. Being on the run. That's not living, Kenneth."

They stopped on a corner. A guy in a suit bumped into Kenneth. Kenneth apologized and the suit kept walking.

"You showed me that article. The one about Iraq and the Federal Reserve."

Kenneth nodded. "Shows it can be done."

"And then we went to see Matt."

Kenneth hesitated. A bus blared past them. A street vendor cooked hot dogs and pretzels.

"I just wanted to see him and say hello."

Donne shook his head. "I think it was more than that."

Kenneth held up a wallet. One Donne hadn't seen before. Donne whirled. The guy in the suit was gone, disappeared in a mass of foot traffic.

"Want a hot dog?" Kenneth asked.

"Iraq. Your son was in the Middle East," Donne said. His synapses were firing in many different directions. "I can't believe you just stole that wallet."

"I'm getting a hot dog." Kenneth turned to walk toward the street vendor. "A lot of people were there, Jackson."

"It's too big a coincidence."

Kenneth ordered two hot dogs with mustard. "We need him too."

"Matt?" The centipede in Donne's guts was nibbling away now. "Why?"

"Having a guy tied to the military will help us break into a military building." Kenneth shrugged. "Maybe we won't have to break in. Don't have it all figured out yet."

He handed Donne a hot dog. Donne took it as the centipede argued with hunger pangs.

"He will try to stop you. He won't want to help." Donne unwrapped the paper around the hot dog. "You saw him before. He didn't even want to see you. If you're going to do this, and *if* I'm going to help—"

"You'll help." Kenneth wiped mustard from his lip. "He'll help too."

"*If* I do, we have to be smart. Bringing Matt in, that's a recipe for trouble. And I don't think either of us will end up in jail this time. Maybe in the ground. That sounds about right. Getting Matt involved is dumb."

Kenneth took a big bite. Toward New Jersey, the sun sagged behind some buildings.

"Give him some time." He polished off the hot dog. "We're family."

CHAPTER 17

||||||||||||||||||||||||||||||||||||||||||||||||||||||||||||||||||||||||||||||||||||||||||||||||||||||||||||||||||||||||||||||||||||||||||||||||||||||||||

TAMMY COLE SAT in the bedroom and rubbed her chest. There was a dull ache where she'd had the surgery. That was supposed to be the end, wasn't it? One treatment after the procedure and done. Yet, here she was on her second round.

But she wasn't healthy. Still on chemo. The problem was that was all she knew. Elliot had kept information from her, the doctor giving only the barest of details.

Bastard.

They were in the other room, Manuel and Elliot moving things. Tammy had been trying to read—some novel about an Irish hitman in the Bronx—but the words kept blending together. Whenever she blinked to focus her eyes, she pictured Kenneth.

"Elliot," she said.

After a sharp *thunk* in the other room, he came to the door. His face was red and sweaty, and the T-shirt he wore was drenched. He caught his breath as he leaned on the doorjamb. Always leaning.

"When is my next treatment?"

She didn't look forward to chemo, the needle, the boredom—the endless time thinking about death.

"Tomorrow. We have to get everything out of here and go to the next spot. We'll move tonight, in the next few hours, and then once we're set up, I'll call Dr. Haskins."

stared at each other for a few seconds, then Elliot said,
"How are you feeling?"

Jimmy realized her hand was still on her chest. She snapped it back to her side.

"Tired," she said.

"Does it hurt?"

She shook her head. "Not today."

Elliot came in the room and took her hand with his clammy right. He went down on one knee and smiled at her. She remembered when he proposed, and he refused to get on one knee.

"It's going to be okay. Just a few more weeks."

"What did the doctor say?"

"Once we get to Cuba, you're going to be fine. I promise."

"You think Kenneth will agree to this?"

Elliot pursed his lips. "I think he still loves you."

A shudder went through her. Kenneth was a flowers guy: tulips, roses, and hydrangeas. Whatever was in season. Any time they completed a job, he'd get her a bouquet. Their little apartment would smell like a garden, even though it made him sneeze. He had the worst allergies, but wouldn't let that stop him from making her smile and helping her celebrate. When they found out they were pregnant with Matt, he got her eight different bouquets.

Elliot never did anything like that. No thought, just bare walls. Always on the move, always ready to run. Kenneth never wanted to run. That was why he got caught. It was why she was with Elliot.

"How can you afford another safe house?" she asked. "You don't have the money."

"These were bought and paid for a long time ago."

"And Dr. Haskins?"

"He owes me a favor."

Always vague. Never telling the full story. It drove her nuts. But she learned a long time ago not to ask follow-up questions. Elliot cared, but he had a nasty streak. Not that he hit her, but the yelling, the sharpness of his tone would last days. Told her she was stupid and to trust him.

She never saw him treat Kenneth that way.

But Manuel took the brunt of it. Anything for money, she guessed. But now that it was drying up?

"We're at the end," she said. "This can't go on."

"It won't. Next month, you'll be getting healthy and then we

can sip Moscow Mules on the beach." Elliot exhaled.
back to work. Why don't you read for a while?"

She patted his hand. "Okay."

He grinned at her, leaned in and gave her a kiss on the
His gray five o'clock shadow scratched her cheek. They we
twenty-five anymore, but she got a chill when his face touch
hers.

"I'm too young to die," she said.

"You won't. I won't let you."

"Kenneth better not let us. And what about Donne, do you
trust him?"

Elliot didn't answer. He left the room, and she tried to
remember what she knew about Jackson Donne.

Allegedly a badass. A cop killer, an assassin. Seemed like too
much for one guy. And probably unstable. Not the kind of person
you could trust on a big gig. But if Kenneth needed him...

It was the only way to live.

She scratched her cheek where Elliot had kissed her, and then
picked up the book.

"This is not how I die," she said out loud. The words caught
her by surprise, meant for internal monologue. She waited to see if
Elliot had heard her. There wasn't a response, just more furniture
behind lugged. Slamming into the walls. Occasionally, she heard
Manuel apologize.

It was probably still Elliot's fault.

Matt had been here. She heard him, felt his presence, but she
feigned sleep. She wasn't ready to face that moment. That would
break her. Her left eye teared. She wiped at it. The words blurred
on the page again.

Never supposed to have a kid.

Never supposed to get cancer.

It was supposed to be a fun, freewheeling life. They loved
Warren Beatty and Faye Dunaway, that movie they saw in their
teens. No pressure except hiding from the cops. Time to do
whatever you wanted.

It didn't work out that way.

Matt made her happy for a hair over eighteen years.

She put the book back down again. When she married Elliot,
she did it out of panic—they had to hide and she needed a new
identity. At least a new last name. Kenneth knew, he even blessed

ot was a good man. She did love him.

it. A he didn't trust him at all. And that meant keeping both

ey en until Cuba.

CHAPTER 18

IIIIIIIIIIIIIIIIIIIIIIIIIIIIIIIIIIIIIIIIIIIIIIIIIIIIIIIIIIIIIIIIIIIIIIIIIIIIIIIIIIIIIIIIIIIIIIIIIIIIIIIIIIIIIIIIIIIIIIIIIIIIIIIIIIIIIIIIIIIIIIIIIIIIIIIIIIIIIIIIIIIIIIIIIIIIIIIIIIIIIIIII

FIFTEEN IN A row. What a waste of a workout.

They'd been in the gym about an hour. Sarah was doing a stations routine in the weight room—and not a state of the art weight room—leaky pipes, low ceiling and a very musty smell. Donations only went so far at St. Paul's High School, but it got the job done. Meanwhile, Herrick was working on free throws and three-point shooting. And the best he'd made was only fifteen shots in a row.

That sucked. He wasn't leaving here until he made at least twenty.

Sarah came out of the weight room, drinking water and drying sweat from her hair with a towel.

Herrick took a free throw and it clanked off the rim. He cursed, retrieved the ball and laid it into the hoop.

"Tough workout?" Sarah asked.

"We're not leaving until I make twenty in a row." Another free throw, back rim, in the cylinder and then it bounced out.

"Will they leave the lights on that long?"

Herrick shot Sarah a look, and forced a smile. A tickle at the back of his neck spread into his shoulders.

"Sorry," Sarah said. "Talk to me."

Talking was the one thing Herrick could always do with

Sarah. He tried not to keep secrets from her. His parents had hidden things—he didn't know they were thieves until high school. He took Yankees tickets from his uncles without asking questions. Christmas gifts, birthdays. Everything was bought with stolen money, and they never told him. They kept secrets, and he promised himself he wouldn't.

"I saw both my mom and dad."

Sarah took a step toward him. But not before he could take a shot. Swish.

"Your mom?"

"Been a long time. I haven't seen her since I got back from the Middle East. Other than that picture of her being 'saved,' I haven't known anything about her." He went and got the ball. "And I didn't expect to see her today, that's for sure."

"Did you talk?" Sarah was standing at the three-point line now. Close enough that he could feel her presence without looking, but far enough away that he still had his space.

"No."

Another free throw. Banked it in. He shrugged. Counted it anyway. Sarah didn't have to ask why they didn't talk.

"She was asleep. She's sick." He got the ball again. This time stepped out to the three-point line. Swish. Talking to Sarah was helping. "Cancer."

"Matt, I'm so sorry."

He shrugged. Made another three. And another. The ball bouncing off the wooden floor echoed across the gym.

"Yeah, it didn't really make my day." Another make. He was finding his rhythm now.

"Your dad, he wanted to see you. He and Jackson—did they want to talk to you about your mom?"

He was up to ten in a row now. Maybe they'd make it out of the gym before dinner.

"Seeing my mom has something to do with why they're out. My mom's husband, Elliot Cole, he used to work with my parents as a thief—their partner. And from what I can tell, he's out of money. The first person I went to talk to was my 'uncle,' he used to fund them and now he's out of the game."

Sarah took a step forward. To Herrick's eye, it was like a defender coming off a screen to help. He ignored it and swished another basket.

"Are you trying to figure out what they're up to?"

Swish.

"Or are you worried about your mom?"

"Can it be both? Elliot needs money."

Fifteen in a row. Five more and they could go get a drink. A nice glass of Bulleit. Maybe some sushi. Sarah would get a white wine. And then they could go back to the apartment, and he — swish — could get back to work. But he still had to make four more shots.

Sarah said, "If it's money Elliot wants, why did he spend what he had on buying your dad and Jackson out of prison?"

He went back to the free throw line. This should be easy. He could feel the heaviness in his legs from jumping, and the sweat starting to trickle into his eyebrows. Swish, retrieve, swish, retrieve, swish, retrieve. He lined up the last shot.

"That's a question that keeps sticking out to me as well," he said. "They could have used the cash on treatments."

"How can you get an answer to that?"

Swish. That was easy. Why wasn't it coming earlier? He exhaled. Because he wasn't talking before. Because Sarah was in the other room, and he was too busy with his own thoughts to focus.

"I'm going to have to go talk to Uncle Elliot again."

Sarah smiled. "Uncle?"

"Force of habit." Herrick shrugged and went to get a towel. "I know where he is. He isn't hiding. Might as well try to go back. I can see my mom awake this time."

"You never told me why you went into the military instead of going to college," Sarah said. "I looked you up, you know. When you first came here to coach. According to some news articles, you should have been a college ball player. You had a bunch of offers. Even UConn."

Herrick sat on the first bleacher and wiped the sweat off of him. Sarah came over and sat next to him. She put her head on his shoulder.

"I'm gross," he said.

"I don't care." He felt her smile. "But you never answered my question."

"Getting away to college wasn't enough. I had to go far, far away. Afghanistan was as far away as I could imagine. My dad was on trial. My mom had run off with...his partner. Life was weird."

"You could have died."

Maybe I wanted to, he thought. But he didn't say it. He could talk to Sarah about anything, but those words just wouldn't come out of his mouth. They weren't true anymore. He learned that the day the boy tried to blow them all up. However, weird things crossed the mind of an eighteen-year-old kid.

"But I didn't," he said instead.

CHAPTER 19

||||||||||||||||||||||||||||||||||||||||||||||||||||||||||||||||||||||||||||||||||||||||||||||||||||||||||||||||||||||||||||||||||

I F YOU DIDN'T have any money, there wasn't much to do in New York City after the sun went down. Donne and Kenneth were in Alphabet City somewhere, passing some old bars. Donne craved a drink — beer, preferably. But he wasn't going to use cash from the wallet Kenneth had stolen.

He still had his wallet, the one they'd given back to him when he left prison this morning. Maybe the credit cards still worked. They wouldn't have an address to send him the bill, at least. His old New Brunswick home was probably trashed, sold or rented to some frat boy.

The world had changed so much.

Kenneth turned to him. "Okay if I get some time by myself? I'm going to check us into a hotel."

"You can afford that?"

He nodded. "We've been walking around for hours, but..." He pointed at his head. "I'll figure it out."

"I'm gonna get a drink, then."

"You need cash?"

"Nah."

"Holding out on me? Meet back here in an hour. We'll have a spot by then."

Donne said, "Have a good walk."

He turned and headed to the bar, some hipster joint he hoped had a good beer list, and found a seat at the bar—a small miracle on a Saturday. For some reason, this place was pretty empty. Maybe hipsters didn't show up before eleven. It was only just after seven. *The Shining* played on a grainy TV screen over the bar, but the soundtrack was drowned out by The Jam Live on the jukebox.

Donne passed his credit card over when the bartender placed a pint of Brooklyn Lager in front of him. He held his breath while the card was run. The bartender didn't say anything, so Donne took a sip. Falling back into old habits already—beer, beer, beer. It was amazing how the craving came back the moment he knew he was allowed to drink it.

An older guy took the seat next to him and ordered a scotch and soda. The bartender nodded.

With a slight Russian accent, the guy said, "Next one for this guy is on me too." He pointed at Donne.

The bartender nodded again. Donne took another sip of beer to hide the burning sensation in his cheeks. His fingers were covered in sweat from the glass.

"Do I know you?" Best Donne could come up with.

"We have mutual friend. I'm Adrik." He stuck out his hand, but Donne ignored it.

"I'm just trying to enjoy my drink here."

"First one when you get out is the best, right?"

It's not my first.

Donne exhaled and put his beer down. "I appreciate the extra beer, but I really just want some time to myself here."

"We should talk. It will make Kenneth feel better."

Donne blinked. Didn't answer.

"Kenneth and I, we were very close." He took a sip of scotch and grimaced. "Tammy and Elliot, I was very close to them. I helped them."

Donne waited. Drank some more beer.

"Tell me about yourself." He knocked back some more drink. "You see, Kenneth is going to try to do this job. And without someone he can trust, it will be difficult to accomplish anything."

Donne finished the beer and the bartender brought him another. Adrik finished his drink.

"Our life is a dangerous one," Adrik said. "But these two, Elliot and Kenneth, they can't let it go. Can't live without the risk.

Not without…" He pointed at his temple with his index finger and made a circle motion. "I say too much."

"What about Tammy?"

Adrik drank and grimaced again. "She is what keeps him somewhat grounded. But maybe this is not all about her."

"You know what his plan is?"

Adrik smiled. "Even though I don't help anymore, I am still in the loop."

"I should have stayed in jail."

"That's not what I want to hear, Jackson. I want to know you're all in on this. Trust is very important in our situation. And your past, what you did to your partners…I'm not sure we can trust you."

"Who's to say if I help him out we will survive?"

The Shining ended and the screen went black. The bartender ignored it and cleaned glasses instead. A few guys with mustaches and flannel came in and went over to the jukebox. Whatever replaced The Jam was unrecognizable to Donne.

"No one can say you will survive. But I think you are changing. You may not see it yet, but you're definitely not the man you were when you entered prison."

"You just met me."

Adrik grinned. "But I have heard so much about you."

"How did you find me?"

"It's not hard to figure out."

"I can walk away right now. I don't owe anyone anything." Donne polished off his beer.

"You owe Kenneth. How long has he kept you alive?"

Donne didn't answer.

"I've read up on you, Mr. Donne. You requested to go to prison. You are a nasty man. A man like you can be very helpful in our situations. But not if we have to worry about you."

"You don't know me at —"

Adrik cut him off by putting a hand on his forearm. Donne wanted to snap it in half.

"I need to trust you. To give Kenneth the okay."

Donne took a deep breath. "That thing you talk about, when I was a cop. Bill Martin was my direct partner. Not just one of the guys, but the guy I worked with day in and day out for years. And he was probably the most corrupt. When I turned in the division, you know who I didn't finger? Bill Martin. Because he was my partner."

Adrik flared his nostrils. He threw some money onto the bar and stood up from his stool.

"That is what I want to hear."

He left Donne there, staring at a blank television screen. Donne wanted to run, track down Jeanne and start over again. Their own fractured little family. If she would have him.

What was wrong with him? It would never work. And he didn't even know where to start looking.

Meanwhile, Kenneth had gotten him through so much. He wouldn't be alive without the old man's help.

Donne closed out the tab as the bartender picked up Adrik's cash.

Two hours later, he was in the hotel room Kenneth had booked. And his boss had given him an assignment for the following morning.

CHAPTER 20

THE MOVING TRUCK rumbled along Route 78. It was early, before the rush hour, a time Cole had gotten used to. Of course, it was Sunday, so even rush hour wasn't a problem. The sun was just starting to peek out of the horizon behind them, squeezing between the buildings of the Newark skyline. He checked the news headlines quickly via his phone.

Haskins' eyes were on the road in front of them. Cole would have preferred Manuel drive, but he was on assignment.

Tammy had been sleeping in between them, head resting on Cole's arm. But they'd hit a few bumps in a row, and she'd opened her eyes. Tammy yawned and stretched her arms as much as she could considering she was stuck in the middle of a small truck cab.

Haskins gave her a quick look. "You should really try to sleep some more. You need your rest."

Tammy gave him a quick look and then turned to Cole. The butterflies he felt whenever she looked at him were long gone now. Instead, he just felt exhaustion. He needed the finish line to be near. The two of them together on a beautiful beach.

"Do you remember the picture?" he asked her.

She smiled. "Of course."

"That afternoon, did you ever think we'd be here? You and me?"

The smile left her face. "No. I didn't think I'd ever get sick like this. Cigarettes do you in. And no. I thought our last job would be with Kenneth."

Cole wiped his nose. "I saved you that day."

"You also took me away from Matt."

"He's back now."

"And you're taking me from him again."

The world sped by them at seventy miles per hour. Haskins was going just fast enough to get to their new place this century, but also slow enough that the cops wouldn't pull them over. The sides of the highway were lined with trees, and mountains peaked over the sides of the road. The radio signal kept going in and out.

This was the part of New Jersey no one ever talked about. Cole loved coming to this house. It was quiet, secluded. A little piece of Kansas or West Virginia only an hour away.

"I'm trying to save you," he said.

Tammy rubbed her forearms as if she were cold. "That picture always bothered you, didn't it?"

Cole took out his phone again. This time he looked at his bank statements. Just a quick peek. He smiled.

"Why do you say that?"

"Because no one ever knew it was you. Wasn't that always the problem? You drove the car. You planned the score. But it was never you."

Cole's heart rate picked up. Sweat formed on his brow, but he didn't wipe at it. He felt Haskins glance in his direction but ignored it.

"I did my job. Back then, that day. My goal was to get the money and make sure you were safe."

"What about Kenneth? What about Matt?"

"They were both fine. It took a while, but we saved Kenneth too."

"Didn't you like being unknown the past ten years? You could walk anywhere. You plucked Manuel out of a gang and got him on his feet. You went to see Kenneth monthly and no one batted an eye. You made friends with the warden."

Cole sniffled. "Fred Aguilera isn't exactly Jesus Christ. He's no saint. He and I have worked—you know what, you don't need to know that stuff. Neil is right, you need to rest."

"No. I want to keep talking."

Cole shifted in his seat. "Fine."

"When Kenneth was away, when you went to see him, did you rub it in?"

Cole thought about the first visit, when he told him that Tammy and he had gotten married by some Kansas judge a year earlier. It didn't matter that it was probably illegal. Everything they did was illegal. All that mattered was Tammy's gaze wasn't on Kenneth anymore. She didn't think about him as much.

"I took care of you," he said. "I'm doing that now too."

"Shit," Haskins said.

Cole looked at him. He was looking in the side mirror.

"State cop just pulled out. He's behind us."

"We'll continue this later if you want, Tammy," Cole said.

Tammy grinned. "Maybe."

Haskins took his foot off the gas, and Cole felt the deceleration in his body. He watched the speedometer slow to sixty.

"If he got you, slowing down won't help," Cole said. His old heart couldn't take this shit. Plotting a heist? Sure. But the cops on his tail brought back too many memories.

"If I slow down, he'll be forced to pass me. At least then we'll know if he's after us."

Cole nodded, but refused to say, "Smart move." Haskins didn't need any more credit. He was already doing enough.

The state cop hung behind them for a tenth of a mile. Then he quickly threw the car's left blinker on, changed lanes and accelerated. As the cop passed, he looked out his passenger window, staring up at the U-Haul. Haskins exhaled.

"You used to deal with this all the time?"

Tammy said, "He ran in between the cops and my ex-husband to save my life. And they didn't even get his face on camera."

Haskins shook his head. "I can't handle that."

"Elliot always loves a headline."

Cole couldn't argue with that. "What good's a headline if they don't know your name?"

Haskins said, "If they don't know your name, the chances are better that you'll get to live."

Instead of cursing Haskins out for the logic, Cole went back to his phone. Tammy knew him all too well.

CHAPTER 21

"**W**HAT HAPPENED TO you?"

Herrick had barely made coffee the next morning when Mack was at the door. Sarah had gone to get bagels and would be back any minute. Herrick stepped out of the way and let Mack in.

He offered him a cup of Joe, but Mack shook him off.

"No one calls it Joe anymore."

"My girlfriend went to get bagels, if you want."

Mack shook him off again. "Stop offering me stuff and tell me where the hell you went yesterday."

Herrick went over his rules again. Secrets got you in trouble. "My dad and Donne, they showed up. Dragged me down to the PATH station."

"God damn it. I was right here. Your girl wouldn't buzz me up. You should have told me."

Herrick turned back to the coffee and mixed his with cream and sugar. He breathed through his nose. Mack was right. There was an opportunity to learn more about what was going on, and having an officer there could have coerced his dad to talk. Or it could have gotten him to run.

"I hadn't seen my father in ten years. I wasn't thinking clearly," he said.

Mack nodded.

"Are you even supposed to be on this case anymore?" Herrick drank coffee.

Mack arched an eyebrow. "You've never had something catch your interest? Maybe a hobby?"

Herrick walked over to the couch and took a seat. "So this is all off the books?"

Mack leaned on the counter top. Herrick tried to figure out when Sarah would come in, and he'd have to explain who this guy was. Not that it was a big deal, but he didn't really want Mack here. Too much other crap swirling around in his mind. He was going to go talk to Elliot Cole again today.

And see his mom. Mack didn't need to know that.

He shouldn't be privy to all this family drama.

"I don't want to create too much smoke. Other people will wonder where the fire is. Could bring some undue attention on me from the top. These guys took money to let Donne and your dad out. That's big time suspicious."

"What do you want from me at this point?"

Mack crossed his arms. It felt like they'd had this conversation before, and he was showing it to Herrick.

"Why did someone want your dad out of jail so badly?"

"I don't know."

Herrick took out his phone and texted Sarah that Mack was there. Then he said, "I talked to Adrik Vavilov. I talked to Elliot Cole. I didn't get any information. I have a job to do at school and real cases to work. I haven't talked to my dad in ten years. I can't be doing you a favor. Otherwise, I can't pay for this apartment."

Mack spread his hands. "I can't make you do anything you don't want to, but you and I both know this smells sour."

Herrick shrugged. "I can't do this for you. My dad—he's not my family. Not anymore."

"You just saw him yesterday."

"Not anymore." The meaning was clear from his tone.

Mack exhaled. "You hear anything, you call me."

Herrick sipped coffee.

Mack left. Herrick felt the tension in his shoulders return.

CHAPTER 22

HERRICK DROVE DOWN a street in Paterson, past several other row houses, until he found the one Manuel had dragged him out of. He parked, grabbed the ASP nightstick out of his glove compartment and took a deep breath. Seeing his mother again. Life wasn't supposed to sneak up on you like this, even though — for Herrick — it often did.

He stood on the sidewalk, the ASP bopping off his hip, clearly visible. If a cop were to pull up to him now, that would be a big time problem. ASPs, retractable nightsticks, were illegal in New Jersey, but for a private investigator who hated guns, they were invaluable. When you hit someone with it, it hurt like hell. They stayed down.

Usually.

After five steps to the front door, Herrick knocked. The knock sounded hollow, as if there was only the void behind the door. Herrick knocked again, and this time the door swung inward. Herrick pulled the ASP from its holster and with a snap of his wrist had it extended to its full length. The hallway was empty, not even a dust mote.

Herrick stepped inside and a bead of sweat trickled down the back of his neck. Without thinking, his muscles coiled, released and sent him in a sprint down the hallway. He hung a right into the room where his mother had been only to find it vacant. The entire house was empty like an abandoned house on a realtor's list.

The wind went out of Herrick and he sat down. It was an odd sensation being both disappointed and finally feeling human again at the same time. Herrick hadn't realized how much seeing his mother again was weighing on him. There'd been times over the last ten years, mainly when he was in the sandbox, when he dreamt about reuniting with her.

In his mind's eye, she was always healthy and strong. The Bonnie to his father's Clyde, including the cigarette hanging from the corner of her mouth. Seeing her sleeping, looking like she'd stopped eating months ago, shook him. And now that she wasn't here — was she dead? — was both a relief and a disappointment. He didn't have to face her, but he wouldn't know how she was.

Herrick forced himself up and did a quick sweep of the house. The rooms were immaculate. Picked clean, swept and vacuumed. If not for the lack of smell, he would have suspected it was even re-painted. The question now, why did Elliot Cole leave? Too many people had been in this room. Donne, his dad and himself. Maybe Cole needed to keep moving. He stood in the kitchen staring at the spotless oven, pondering possibilities.

"Thought he'd be out of here."

Herrick whirled and raised the ASP, only to find his dad standing in the doorway. As quickly as it had gone, the fist clutching his insides returned.

Kenneth Herrick had his hands up, and was grinning.

"Easy, son."

"What are you doing here?"

Kenneth shrugged. "Knew you'd come here eventually."

"I've already been."

"Yeah. I've heard. Elliot gave you some good advice."

Herrick worked his jaw. "I don't want to see you."

Kenneth nodded. "I know, but I need you."

"For what?"

"To save Mom."

Herrick's heart thumped hard in his chest, struggling to break from of the fist crushing him. The sensation was familiar, but one he had rarely felt since he got back from the sandbox. Since he worked everything out with his therapist — whom he hadn't seen in five years.

Might be time to go back.

"What do you mean save Mom?"

"It's the reason I'm out. And I need your help."

Herrick shook his head. "You have Jackson."

"Not enough."

Herrick wished there was a chair in the room. He retracted the ASP and put it back in his holster.

"I don't know what you're talking about. How are you going to save her?"

"What am I good at, Matt? The only thing I'm good at. The thing that makes me really damn happy?"

Herrick opened his mouth, but before he could answer, Kenneth held up a hand. The silence hung in the air like clothes on a drying line. Herrick tried to breathe through the anxiety, each exhale pushing a little bit out of his system. He didn't want to hear his father explain himself, but he still had to know.

Kenneth took a step forward and pointed at the holster. "I'm glad you put that away."

His dad didn't look as old as Mom did. He was virile and healthy, cut and chiseled. All those hours working out in a prison yard must have done wonders for his physique. Yes, there were gray hairs and wrinkles on his face, but it was still the dad he remembered. The guy he told his friends could beat up anyone when he was hanging out in the school yard.

"I'm going to leave," Kenneth said. "But I want you to think over what I said. We can save your mother. You, Jackson and me. We can do it. But I need your help. I need you."

"You're a thief."

Kenneth shrugged again.

"You think I'm going to risk my reputation for you?"

Kenneth said, "I think you'll risk it to help your mother. We don't have much time. I'll be in touch."

He turned and sauntered out of the room. A few seconds later, Herrick heard the front door open and shut. He leaned against the counter and caught his breath. He literally had ten minutes of feeling like himself. Now there were pins and needles, pressure in his chest and air didn't feel like it was making it all the way to his lungs.

That was okay. He could deal with it until it passed. But he was going to be running his father's words over in his head for the rest of the night.

He pulled out his cell phone and texted Sarah he was coming home.

Sunday Funday my ass, he thought.

CHAPTER 23

||

H ERRICK FROZE AT the door.
He missed something. He must have. No one could leave a room completely empty, let alone a townhouse. Standing in the doorway, Herrick felt the breeze from the street pour over him and into the hallway. He closed his eyes and took a few calming breaths.

Refocus and find what you're missing. Everything, even something minor, could be a clue. He turned back to the hallway and tried to slow down. It wasn't about the motes or the shiny floor. It was about what wasn't there, what was unusual about this room.

Times like these, it was good to go back to the sandbox. When he was in Afghanistan, out on a convoy, sweeping the road for an IED, everything that seemed out of place was considered out of place. It deserved an extensive investigation, even if it would delay the convoy an hour or more.

Another deep breath.

So, what in a completely empty building was out of place? Answer: the fact that it was completely empty. That was impossible. Something was always left behind, even a scrap of paper. A crumb. Something that could help him track down Cole. Something left behind.

He started with the ceiling—drywall and smooth. Nothing

stood out there. He walked the entire row house, staring at the ceiling like some deranged Brian Wilson impersonator.

Nothing.

What goes up, however, must come down. So he tried the floorboards, spending the next fifteen minutes staring at the hardwood beneath his feet. Scanning back and forth. His eyes were expecting to come up empty, but his gut said otherwise.

And then he entered his mom's room, and caught the molding on the floor, pulled apart from the wall just a hair. If he hadn't been so focused, looking for anything in disarray, he wouldn't have noticed it. Herrick kneeled down and pulled the piece of wood away from the wall a hair more. Behind it was a piece of paper, the size of a receipt. There was handwriting on it.

Herrick stared at the words.

Matt, Kenneth, Whomever:

I have heard Vernon Valley is nice this time of year. Though not as nice as Long Valley. Maybe you would want to look at both.

Mom/Tammy.

Herrick's breath caught at the back of his throat, but the fist in his chest did not pull tighter.

This *was* a clue.

He didn't have to be Sherlock Holmes to figure that one out.

CHAPTER 24

COLE STARED ACROSS the table at Kenneth Herrick. The rabble in McDonald's as people filled up on breakfast would be enough to cover their conversation. The Egg McMuffin was still wrapped in paper in front of him. Kenneth fiddled with a hash brown.

"A lot has changed in the past ten years, it seems like. But damn, these are still the same," he said.

"Yeah, the food is still terrible for you."

The corner of Kenneth's lip crooked upward. He exhaled. "You took her from me."

Cole sat back and looked over Kenneth. The scrawny kid from Seton Hall Prep who used to love to steal thumb tacks from the nuns when they weren't looking. Such a minor crime, and it was hilarious when they found all the volleyballs popped in the gym. No one ever knew it was Kenneth. Anything to play more basketball.

And anything to try to get away with doing something wrong.

"She wanted to be with me," Cole said. "After you went away, she couldn't be alone. And I was there for her. You knew that might happen."

"I knew you always hated that she cared more about me."

Cole shifted in his seat. Felt the heat on his cheeks. Like the spotlight during the first curtain call on opening night. What play was it? *Twelve Angry Men.* The applause washed over him like warm water. The best feeling, almost as good as when he directed *Peter Pan* in college, and the cast brought him on stage for the final curtain call.

"Your plan," he said. "It's led to some dicey times in my home."

"Tammy doesn't want to be in the game anymore." Kenneth flared his nostrils.

"We're getting old. She's —" Cole looked at the front counter. A cop sauntered in and the cashier waved at him. "Sick."

Kenneth nodded. "But I'm working on Matt. I just saw him at your place."

"I'm not there anymore."

"We're going to get caught if we keep meeting like this."

"Once this is over with, we can go on our merry way."

The cop ordered a cup of coffee, stuck his thumb in his belt and looked around the restaurant. After the cashier handed over his coffee, he left.

"Imagine this. How famous we will be. The ones who pulled off the greatest heist of all time."

"They never caught the people who stole the Iraq money." Kenneth took a bite of a hash brown. "They aren't famous. They're rich."

"The Turkish government did it, I'm sure. People will know our names. And they still won't get to us. We'll be in the wind."

Kenneth nodded.

"Why do you trust Jackson Donne?"

Kenneth said, "He's my puppet. I kept him alive. He owes me. Adrik can vouch for him too. I do my background work. I vet."

"He worries me. He's been in the paper too much."

Grinning, Kenneth said, "Yeah, living out your dream. Front page news."

Digging into the McMuffin, Cole chewed to cover the frustration burning inside him. His muscles tensed like they wanted to tear through his skin and pull Kenneth through the table. No one talked to him that way.

"It's not the same," Cole said after swallowing.

Kenneth finished the hash brown and turned to his coffee. The restaurant was thinning out, with only a few senior citizens left over. Probably finishing breakfast before mall walking. Cole nearly choked on his sandwich when that thought passed. He and Kenneth were senior citizens too.

"You came to see me a lot when I was away," Kenneth said. "They're on to you, I'm sure. We're probably being watched now. The cops, the Corrections Department, they notice that shit."

Cole shook his head. Aguilera would make sure no one was on to him. The money was too good.

"We're fine," he said.

"How can you be sure?"

"Trust me."

Cole stared at him over the rim of the coffee cup. He took a long pull. Steam rose in front of his eyes.

"You don't trust Jackson. I can see it in your eyes. How can I give you that courtesy?"

The air in the restaurant had the heaviness and odor of the french fries or—at this time of day—maybe hash browns. The grease stink would be caught in Cole's nose for hours after this. They should have met in a Starbucks. But Kenneth thought the cops would use a McDonald's drive-thru. Not walk in. He was wrong.

Kenneth was wrong about Donne as well.

But Kenneth kept talking before Cole could vocalize that thought.

"I have an idea. We work the plan, you and me, together. But the rest of the prep is separate. You train your guys. I take care of Jackson and getting Matt on board."

Cole squinted his eyes. "Your recruiting is terrible. Two private eyes. A former military brat and a former cop."

"Your group ain't exactly Al Capone's crew. Times change. Old-fashioned thieves are hard to come across. You ask me, I prefer to trust family."

Cole laughed. He couldn't resist. "I don't know why. Your family doesn't have the best track record. Your wife walked to me ten seconds after you went away."

Kenneth Herrick went red as ketchup. "You got me out."

"I did."

"So I won't kill you."

"If I were you, I'd worry more about Jackson Donne than me. About Matt. From what I've heard, he's not so fond of you either. Again, you and your family don't have the best track record." Cole wiped his nose. "Be careful with the choices you're making."

Kenneth stood up. "From now until go time, try to stay off the Time Square Billboards."

"Dreams do come true, Kenneth. But I'm one you can trust. None of that will happen until the job is done." He exhaled. "But Jackson is going to be a problem. Maybe your son too."

"Fine," Kenneth said. "You're so worried about it, we'll keep separate until game time. You get your men busy and keep an eye on Tammy. It'll be easier for me to plan if the police aren't looking for coincidences like the two of us meeting up."

"My men are already busy. You'll see," Cole hissed.

Kenneth didn't say anything. He turned on his heel and walked out of the place. Cole finished his sandwich and got another coffee. No hurry.

Just waiting for confirmation from Manuel that Jackson Donne was dead. That should be going down soon.

Until then, a little cream, a little sugar and some grounds.

In less than a week, he'd be on billboards everywhere. And it wouldn't matter, because he'd be in the wind by that point.

Gone.

But not forgotten.

CHAPTER 25

JACKSON DONNE SAT in the stands of the high school football field, on the top bleacher, binoculars in hand. He didn't look at the track team making their way through their dashes, though. He wasn't even looking at the field.

Behind him, the traffic on Route 17 buzzed by. One of New Jersey's busier highways during the week, it was quiet on a Sunday. Bergen County still abided by blue laws, closing everything that didn't sell food. But Donne wasn't eyeing the traffic either.

No, he was looking to his left, across an entrance lane to the highway, and directly into the Federal Reserve Campus. Technically, the building was called the East Rutherford Operations Center, an arm of the New York Federal Reserve. No one called it that. It was just the Federal Reserve building. Some people liked to say "the one in New Jersey." Or, after having read the article Kenneth had given him, "The one that lost the money in Iraq."

The campus was locked down, of course. A short metal, spiked fence surrounded the block, save for gated road entrances. Beyond a few armed guards dressed in military gear, there wasn't much action.

Kenneth had called this an initial scouting mission. Donne wasn't supposed to take down any notes. No routines, no information. Just get a lay of the land. The building was only a few stories tall, boxy and gray concrete. The rest of the campus was tough to see, as he had to look between a car dealership and corporate bank to get a view. The high school bleachers did not go high enough.

Donne exhaled. What was he doing here? It wasn't the first time he asked himself that question. Kenneth had left him for the day, saying he was going to "work on" Matt. Donne could have left him right then, disappeared. He was out of prison, against his will, and not on the run.

But, if he stayed with Kenneth, he would be a part of a major crime. One that had nearly no chance to succeed. You didn't go up against the military and expect to get away scot-free. That didn't seem to matter to Kenneth, however. All that mattered was getting the money to Elliot Cole.

Staying with Kenneth, Donne was likely signing a death sentence.

The thought didn't send a chill through him. It passed without any kind of biological reaction. It was funny; Kenneth kept him alive in prison, and now would likely be the cause of his death on the outside.

Donne took another look at the campus through his binoculars. Nothing stood out. It was just a bland, big building. Like the prison. Kenneth wanted to break back in.

An armored car drove out of the campus and no one made a peep. It turned left and then merged onto the highway.

After replacing the binoculars in their case, Donne stood and made his way down the stairs of the bleachers. A coach blew his whistle, and a few of the students started running. Sunday practice — not something Donne expected to see. He nodded at the coach and exited the stadium.

The bus stop was up on Hoboken Street about half a mile away from where he was, but Donne wasn't ready to go back to the NYC hotel they were staying in. Neither he nor Kenneth wanted to be in that dinky room longer than absolutely necessary. The little cash they had landed them a place that smelled like rotted meat and had walls the shade of mold.

Instead, he walked to a pizza restaurant about a block away from the stadium. Restaurants were allowed to stay open even under the blue laws. It was starting to hum with a lunchtime crowd. Donne considered going in to try and bum a beer off someone, but didn't. Instead he turned right and walked toward the Federal Reserve.

This wasn't his neck of the woods. If he had to be out, he wanted to be in New Brunswick, or even better, Vermont — the two places he'd lived the longest. Instead, he was shuffling from Manhattan to East Rutherford to Paterson and back, all for some ham-fisted idea of a plan. If there even was a plan.

He walked the length of the Federal Reserve campus, the back of the building. Besides a vent, the building was completely bare. No windows, and nothing but concrete. The fence was solid except for one wide gate with a dirty road that led around the side of the building. A sign indicated that was for the fire department.

He wondered how thick the concrete was and what the people who worked inside looked at. Seemed claustrophobic, and if the walls were extra thick, could even a bomb blow through there? If they blew a hole in the wall, he wondered how much time they'd have to get in and get out before their bodies were bullet ridden. If not by the MPs guarding the place, then by the police and SWAT team that would undoubtedly show up minutes later.

Donne didn't have a mind for this type of stuff. He saw no way in, and he didn't even know how much cash they had on hand. Wasn't it all digital now? Maybe Kenneth planned on walking in with a thumb drive and leaving with millions. He hung left and climbed a big hill toward Hoboken Street.

The bus squealed to a stop in front of him.

The ride into the city was a quick one.

It seemed that no one in the world wanted to be outside today. Donne spent the rest of the afternoon wandering the city.

To him, each step signaled another minute closer to the end. No, he intended to tell Kenneth this was useless. There was no way to escape and no way to get away with the money clean. Again, no reaction to the thought of death. His hands didn't shake, sweat didn't form at his brow. Death was inevitable. Why worry about it? He'd been surrounded by death his entire adult life. This was just another day.

He wasn't sure how he'd lived this long anyway.

Donne looked around the bus. Over his shoulder, the big man from Elliot Cole's house stared back at him.

CHAPTER 26

TAMMY STRETCHED HER arms out and felt the dull pain across her chest. She yawned and focused on the wall, the one with the painting of the fisherman on the Manasquan lagoon, until the pain subsided. She wished for a window instead, but the painting would have to do. The beach painting was nicer than the forest reality anyway.

She pushed herself out of bed, the same recliner she was in in Paterson, and walked across the room. Her stomach rumbled and she smiled. Hungry for the first time in a week. Across the room was a full-length mirror, but she didn't dare look at it. Her damaged and thin body wasn't how she wanted to remember herself. At least not until chemo was over with.

Instead, Tammy walked to the waist high bookcase. When she got there, she rested her hand on top and caught her breath. As a twenty-five-year-old, she could run from the cops like she was running the New York Marathon. Now she could barely keep from throwing up, despite the hunger. She leaned down and skimmed through the titles. Nothing she recognized, but they were all true crime. Her favorite genre. She pulled a book off the shelf and started to read the back cover copy.

"Amazon does wonders for a book collection."

She shook, startled at the words. It was Elliot, his voice calm and cool like an evening breeze. She hadn't expected him. The momentary jitter sent some pain back into her chest. She counted to five until it subsided again, and then turned to face him.

"How can you afford all these books? How can you afford to buy two men out of prison, but you can't get us to Cuba?"

Elliot sat on the bed. He smiled at her.

"First of all," he said, "those are all used. They cost me, like…a penny a piece. Amazon has this weird used book sale. Next, please don't worry about money. The stress will only wear you down. Come sit."

She shook her head. "I just got up. And you haven't answered my question. We're running around. You have a place in Paterson. A place—" she waved her hand around "—wherever the hell we are. Long Valley?"

"It's pretty here, isn't it?"

"You're infuriating."

"Part of my charm."

Elliot got up off the bed and walked over to her. He put his hands on her hips. Tammy could smell the Axe body spray. Ages ago it was the finest cologne, now it was Axe. He smelled like a frat boy. Maybe he couldn't afford the good stuff anymore. She missed that scent on him. She put her hands on his.

"I can't tell you everything," he said. "I don't even tell Manuel."

Tammy turned and faced Elliot. "I'm your wife."

"What do you want me to say? I'm a private person, you've always known that about me."

Fire burned through Tammy's stomach. "I'm your wife and I'm dying. You have me hooked up to that chemo machine every day. According to you, going to Cuba can save my life, and you don't want to keep me informed of your plans? How callous are you?"

Elliot's phone rang, and he let go of her to check the call. He held a finger up. "I have to take this."

Tammy went back to the bed and sat down. Her breath was now ragged and her chest ached like a rhino was sitting on it. The scar from her surgery throbbed. She wondered if, eventually, she'd be able to tell when it was going to snow.

In Cuba, she wouldn't have to.

She could hear Elliot, who'd moved into the hallway, talking to Leon, Manuel's partner.

"I sent him out for business. I'm sure he's fine." Elliot coughed. "He's working, Neil, that's why he's not picking up his phone."

Tammy went back to the true crime novel. The style was devoid of voice, and if it didn't pick up and sing soon, she'd find another book. Life was too short.

"Okay, okay, Neil. I'll call him." There was a beep, and then Elliot ended the call.

He poked his head back into the room. "I have work to do."

"We will continue this later. I will not forget."

Elliot nodded. "You think I don't know that about you?"

He disappeared into the hallway, his feet clomping against the hardwood floor. Tammy read another sentence and then threw the book across the room.

A prisoner. She was a damned prisoner.

CHAPTER 27

ONNE GOT OFF the bus in Port Authority and took the elevator to the first floor near Heartland Brewery restaurant. His stomach cried out for him to stop, and Donne took a deep breath, seriously considering it. His consideration ended when he turned left and saw Elliot Cole's bodybuilder buddy approaching him.

"You got on that bus later than I thought. I figured you would have gotten on the first stop by the stadium," the guy said.

"What's your name again?"

The guy squished up his face like he smelled a bad fart. "Manuel."

"Right." Donne turned away from him and started walking toward the street.

"Whoa, hold up. You ain't walking away from me that easily."

Donne kept heading toward the doors, but slowed his step so Manuel could catch up with him. "What if you missed me?"

Manuel sucked his teeth. "There'd be other chances. I'd find you. Even in this city."

"It's New York, there's always a witness."

"I learned from a guy who doesn't care about that sort of thing. We'll work it out."

Donne pushed the door open and stepped out onto the pavement. The smell of dirty waters dogs wafted in his direction.

Manuel was right behind him.

"What do you want?" Donne asked.

Manuel put a hand on Donne's shoulder and squeezed the muscle tightly. It forced Donne to stop his pace. They stood on the corner, and Manuel leaned in closely. His breath was hot against Donne's ear.

"Well, since I found you, I'm going to kill you. Today. Right now." The words had a tone not unlike someone ordering lunch.

Donne's stomach went cold, the remnants of breakfast.

"Usually, when someone says that to me, they jam a gun in my ribs. Or, at the very least, a knife."

"Like you said—witnesses. Walk with me." Manuel's grip got tighter and he directed Donne downtown.

Donne did as he was told and followed. Had he even been out of prison forty-eight hours yet? Already his life was in jeopardy. They pushed through the light Sunday afternoon crowd, and Donne wondered where you took someone you were going to murder in a city like New York. They turned west and headed toward the Javitz Center.

"Are we going to a convention?"

"Shut up," Manuel said. He'd taken his hand off Donne's shoulder, but now it rested on his back, gently pushing him along.

"I don't know how much Cole spent getting me out of jail, but isn't killing me a waste of time and resources?" Donne's breath was even, his heart rate a drum keeping time.

"You're sunken costs, man. You were never part of the plan. You're a wild card and we don't need you."

Donne didn't respond. Why bother? Nothing he could say would change this scenario.

There wasn't a convention today, and Javitz was quiet. The afternoon was beginning to turn into evening. A few of the local pubs were blaring music and gathering crowds of people who didn't want to give up the weekend. They passed them and continued heading toward the shiny glass convention hall. The Hudson River odor wafted toward them—wet birds, salt and garbage.

"How are you going to do it?"

Manuel said, "You got a preference?"

They came around the corner of the Javitz Center. There was a loading dock for trucks, and then across the pavement, just the river. No one was around. Donne looked out toward New Jersey and tried to pick out Weehawken landmarks. If he was going to die here, he at least wanted one last look at his home state.

Fuck New York.

Donne took a deep breath and wondered if death was warm or cold. Manuel wouldn't be able to tell him.

Before Manuel could make a move, Donne whirled and caught Manuel with a left jab to the gut. It was like punching a rock, but Manuel gasped for air and took a step backward anyway. Donne didn't let the pain in his hand slow him. He moved closer and caught Manuel with a right cross.

Manuel jerked backward and reached for his jaw. Donne moved in close and caught the beast with two more shots to the stomach. Manuel went down to one knee. It wasn't supposed to be this easy.

But it was.

Donne hit Manuel one more time, hard in the jaw. A hiss went from him and Manuel slumped to the concrete. Donne waited for him to get up, but the only thing rising was Manuel's chest as he breathed. Shallow, slow breaths. Manuel's eyes rolled back in his head. He was down.

"Fuck you too, Manuel." Donne spat the words, and then tried to catch his breath.

Donne walked to the nearest pub, threw his credit card down and ordered a shot and a beer.

Just another day.

CHAPTER 28

THE BEER AND shot sat in front of Donne. He stared at them while realizing his heart had slowed and his breathing was normal. The usual tension in his neck and back weren't there.

How many people had he fought in his life? And how many times had he desired a drink after it was over?

Not today. He'd had enough. Donne took a breath and watched the head of the beer dissipate.

"You okay, man?"

Donne looked up to see the Irish bartender standing over him. The guy pointed at the beer.

"You been staring at that for, oh, near five minutes. All okay?"

Donne blinked. "I'm fine."

The revel of people behind him was starting to fade. The bar was emptying as people realized the weekend was over. On the TV above him, Sunday Night Baseball was entering its third inning. Time went fast when you beat the shit out of someone.

"I'll let you enjoy your drink, then. Let me know when you need another."

Donne exhaled. "I don't think I'm going to drink this."

The bartender shrugged. "I'm still going to have to charge you."

Nodding, Donne said, "That's fine. It's just—"

He thought about the Olde Towne Tavern. Artie would have just poured the beer down the drain. But Artie wasn't here, and Donne wasn't sure if he'd ever see him again. His best friend, and Donne had gotten his bar blown up. Artie never visited him in prison, and Donne couldn't blame him. Always how it happened with him: Jeanne, Karen, Bill Martin and Artie. Someone always died. Someone always got hurt.

Donne stood up from the bar and asked the bartender to close him out. The bartender came back with a receipt, and Donne left a generous tip. It wasn't like he'd actually pay the credit card bill, but Visa wouldn't realize that until next month. Hopefully.

Out on the street, it took a minute for Donne to regain his equilibrium and figure out where he was. He started the long walk toward the hotel. On 58th, a police car, sirens roaring, zoomed past him. Donne barely flinched. He wondered if they'd found Manuel already, or if he gotten up and stumbled off.

It didn't matter. Not at the moment.

All that mattered was moving forward. He swung around the corner and came up on the hotel. Maybe Kenneth was back already. Donne walked through the doors and nodded at the woman behind the front desk. She barely noticed him.

He took the elevator up and got off at their floor. Each step down the hall felt like it was in slow motion. Usually, he'd be running. He was always running. But now, it was time to continue the job.

After unlocking the door to the room, he stepped in. Kenneth was sitting on the far bed, taking off his shoes. He looked up and caught Donne's eye. He grinned at Donne.

"Matt is getting closer to joining us," he said. "We're going to have a team. I know it."

Donne didn't return the grin. Instead, he said, "We're fucked."

And then let the silence hang over the room.

PART II

NOBODY RUNS FOREVER

CHAPTER 29

HE WROTE VERNON Valley first, so that was where Matt Herrick went. Vernon Valley was popular in the winter. There were a couple of ski resorts. One of them turned into a water park in the summer, but the park had an awful reputation. Like the kind of reputation you got when you put a dummy down a water slide to test it and it came out without a head.

So, the area was quiet. After the ninety-minute drive from Hoboken was over, Herrick stopped at a gas station. While the attendant filled his tank, Herrick texted Sarah. She didn't respond right away, and, on a Monday morning, he expected her to be in a meeting. But it was always nice to say hi.

The gas attendant handed Herrick back his credit card, and Herrick asked him who would know things about the town.

"I don't know what you mean," the attendant said.

"When things happen in small towns like this—new people move in, dirty scandals, you know stuff people don't talk about. Who would know about it?"

The attendant shook his head. "Man, these days everyone knows everything. Facebook and Twitter."

Herrick nodded. "But I don't."

"Maybe you don't need to."

"It's my job. Who can I talk to?"

"The police?"

Another car pulled up next to them and the attendant started to turn away. Herrick cleared his throat.

"A barber? A bartender?"

The attendant said, "I have no idea. It's not 1965, man. The bar over on Park, the Everstone Inn, people go there."

Herrick thanked him and started the car. He put the name of the bar into his GPS app and followed the directions. Ten minutes later, he was there.

The Everstone Inn looked like it had been built during the Revolutionary War. The foundation was cobblestone, and red siding started at about waist height. A small sign with an image of a horse and the name of the inn hung above the heavy wooden door. Herrick pulled mit open and walked into the dark pub and took a seat at the bar. No one else was there. The place smelled like soap and old beer.

He texted Sarah again, *I am in a bar. Day drinking on a Monday,* and added a smiley face emoji.

This got a quick response. *Better not be. Not without me.* Winky emoji.

There were rules, and not drinking on the job was one of them. Herrick didn't do it. He wondered how Donne was able to function. When Herrick had visited him in prison a few times, Donne had told stories of old cases. Nearly all of them involved some form of booze. Herrick would spend all of his cases napping if he drank at work.

The bartender, a heavy guy in his sixties, sidled up to him.

"Early start today?" He put a menu in front of Herrick. "What can I get you?"

"A club soda, a corned beef sandwich and information."

The bartender tilted his head. "I'm sure I can help with two of those."

Herrick placed his PI license on the bartop. The bartender looked it over.

"Let me get you your food, and then we will talk."

Herrick agreed and flipped through some news articles on his phone while he waited. Slow news day. He thought again about his father's visit. Why did Kenneth need him? How could he help? There wasn't really a way — unless Herrick was willing to risk his entire life.

He wasn't.

The bartender came back and put the sandwich in front of him.

"Has anyone new moved into town?" Herrick asked.

"Do I look like a realtor?"

Herrick pursed his lips. Then he said, "I mean—have you heard any rumors of anything odd sticking out? A rushed move? Shady people come to town?"

The bartender shook his head. "Not that I know of. I mean, people come in here and talk, but nothing's come up. People are worried about the Board of Ed giving out those new contracts for teachers. Not worth it if you ask me. Bunch of overpaid, lazy know-nothings. The board should say no."

Herrick took a bite of his sandwich. "My girlfriend is a teacher, and I didn't ask you."

The bartender shrugged.

"No gossip?" Herrick tried one more time.

"Sorry, but I haven't heard anything at all."

Herrick nodded and finished his sandwich. Next stop was the supermarket. People always gossiped in supermarkets. He hoped they wouldn't be whining about teachers.

The glamorous life of a private eye.

CHAPTER 30

ERRICK DROVE TO the supermarket, a ShopRite that shared mini mall space with a Dunkin Donuts, a liquor store and a pizza place. Across the two-lane street was a gas station. Beyond that there was nothing else but large spaces of grassy land. Vernon wasn't the busy commuter town of Hoboken or hustling suburb like Cedar Grove. This was one of the areas where New Jersey earned its Garden State nickname.

After pulling into a parking spot, Herrick checked his phone. Nothing. Not that he was expecting any messages, but pressing that button to check the home screen had become a habit. He got out of the car and headed toward the entrance. The lot was mostly empty, a few people pushing carts out of the building. Maybe this was a dumb idea, but his mom's note did not give him much in the way of good ones.

He stepped through the automatic doors and was immediately smacked in the face with the odor of produce. A few people sorted through cantaloupes and broccoli. Herrick didn't spot a friendly face. The corned beef sandwich rumbled in his stomach, and he reminded himself to have a vegetable with dinner tonight.

He strolled over to the Starbucks stand near the front door. Smartest grocery store idea ever. Buy a coffee and stroll the aisles. So, Herrick did. The barista looked at him crooked when he asked if she had heard any good, recent Vernon gossip. Herrick shrugged. After mixing some cream into his coffee, he took his cup and started walking the store.

While perusing the meat section, a guy with a military haircut approached him. The guy had his chest puffed out and appeared to be in attack mode. Herrick had left his ASP in the car. Didn't expect to need it while talking to someone in dairy. He rested his coffee cup on the edge of the meat case.

"You're wasting your time," Haircut said.

"Starting to feel like it." Herrick rubbed his nose. "At least until you showed up."

"No, I mean, you know how this is going to end, so you might as well join in."

Herrick tilted his head. "Not sure I know what you're talking about."

The haircut put his hands in his pockets. "I think you do. You're not going to find anything out asking random people in a supermarket. And if I was able to track you down this easily now, then I can do it any time."

Herrick's stomach gurgled, a combination of nerves and the sandwich.

"So here's the deal," Haircut continued. "You should go back to your little Hoboken apartment, call your dad and tell him you're going to help him. Your dad is trying to help your mom. But you don't have a relationship with her or him."

Herrick bit his lip. Tried to think of a retort. Stuck with silence.

"You know your dad. Or at least you did, when you were a kid. Do you think he's going to give up? Jackson Donne fucked up last night. That's going to hurt your dad's little team. Let Elliot Cole solve everything. Or you can help your dad out."

The guy was a trip.

"Think you're this big man, trying to run away from your past, Mr. Herrick. Forgetting your family. Going to Iraq and all the bullshit that happened over there. Yeah, you're a PI, but you want to just think of yourself as a basketball coach. You're not. Blood runs deep with your family. Nobody runs forever. Not from their past. They need you."

"You know all the talking points," Herrick said. "Who are you, anyway?"

Haircut shook his head. "Certainly not a friend. Maybe I'm just your conscience."

"Like Jiminy Cricket?"

Haircut spread his hands. "If that's what you want to call me."

Picking up the coffee, Herrick took a big sip. Play it cool.

"Think about what I said. Think about what your dad is saying. Think about it really hard.. This isn't about you. This is about your mom and her health. Elliot will fix it."

Jiminy Cricket turned on his heel and started walking away. He turned right at aisle ten and headed toward the cash registers. Herrick didn't follow him. He took a deep breath.

He pulled his phone out and texted Sarah. *We have to chat about dad.*

She didn't respond right away. After Herrick counted to one hundred, he walked out of the supermarket. No one attacked him.

But maybe Jiminy was right.

He couldn't run. Not from his dad. But maybe this was the out, how to stop him. By joining in.

Time to find out who Jiminy Cricket was.

CHAPTER 31

JIMINY CRICKET EXITED the supermarket fifteen minutes later, long after Herrick was supposed to be gone — back on Route 23 heading toward Hoboken. Herrick, however, had other ideas and stuck around. Sometimes you had to force things to happen, and Cricket had given him a chance to do that.

Cricket made his way to a Ford Explorer two parking rows over. He took a look around the lot and then got in the car. Herrick watched him back out and then counted to fifteen. And then the tailing began.

Herrick wasn't very good at tailing people. When he was in the sandbox, it was all open land. You weren't following bad guys — you were keeping your eyes open for IEDs. In America, on the highway, tailing was tricky because of traffic and quick speed changes. On open side roads, like he was on now, tailing was tricky because, well, there was no one else around. But Herrick tried as best he could. Cricket hit Route 23 and headed south. Herrick followed suit.

They traveled, and Cricket seemed to know Herrick was on his rear. Cricket weaved through traffic and Herrick did his damnedest to keep up. Of course, if Cricket was actually on to him and still couldn't shake Herrick, there was no guarantee he'd drive to his original destination. Didn't matter, Herrick decided. He was going to follow anyway.

They merged onto Route 46 and then Route 3 and then the Garden State Parkway south. The New Jersey way: highway-to-highway-to-highway. A spider web. Traffic was light at this time of day, and Cricket fell into a cruising speed. Herrick stayed about two car lengths behind. Cricket merged onto the Turnpike, another major New Jersey artery, and Herrick's heart started pumping harder. Where the hell was this guy going? They'd been on the road for over an hour already. Was he just trying to drive Herrick into the ground? He checked his gas gauge and realized he'd be okay for at least another one hundred miles.

Herrick had expected Cricket to lead him to his mother and Elliot Cole. That was the easy guess, but their direction didn't line up with where the man was driving. They stayed on the Turnpike for another five miles and then Cricket put his blinker on. The first polite move of the last ninety minutes. He exited at Exit Nine, the exit for Rutgers, New Brunswick and a whole mess of Middlesex County. Jackson Donne Country. Or at least it used to be before Donne decided prison was the spot for him.

What a week.

Herrick kept on Cricket's tail through the EZ Pass toll and beyond. They stayed together for the next mile or so — still heading south. At this point, Cricket didn't seem to care that Herrick was still around. And, as the big set of brick buildings came up on their left, Herrick knew why. This was the end of the line for the private investigator.

The National Guard base Cricket pulled into was ultra-secure. A gated community with armed guards at the entrance. Cricket pulled up and slowed at check-in. Herrick had no choice but to keep going. At the next intersection, he pulled a U-turn and passed the base again, just in time to see the Ford Explorer disappear inside the complex.

Herrick exhaled and headed back home, his brain swimming with questions. Number one of which was: who is Jiminy Cricket? Not an easy answer to it either.

Heading north on the Turnpike, it was a straight shot back to St. Paul's High School. He could be back in time to work out a few of his kids for some of the coaches who were in town. He called Sarah and let her know he was on his way, in case the guys were looking for him. Sarah sighed. She told him she had appointments to keep and that he could call the principal for that.

"Not after last year."

"You're lucky you still have a job."

"You keep telling me that."

"See you soon." The line disconnected.

Acid burned in Herrick's gut. Newark Liberty Airport passed on his left, and he prepared to exit. This was getting bigger all the time. The National Guard was involved. Maybe Uncle Adrik could tell him more, but it seemed unlikely. A phone call never hurt though.

As Herrick pulled into St. Paul's fifteen minutes later, his head was nearly spinning. He couldn't pull the pieces together and have them make sense. Of course, his father was the key to all this. An idea for a happy medium wasn't there yet, but Matt Herrick was going to have to reach out to Kenneth.

As he walked through the doors into the gym, the sound of dribbling basketballs started to calm him. There was always a solace to be found. Even with all the questions. One of his players yelled out a hello to him.

Herrick faked a smile back and told the kid to keep shooting.

CHAPTER 32

"I DON'T UNDERSTAND THIS at all." Kenneth Herrick rubbed his hands together.

They hadn't left the hotel since Donne'd come back the night before. The TV played CNN at a minimum volume. They were reporting on early stock market returns. Donne would have preferred SportsCenter.

Kenneth wanted to sleep on what Donne had told him the night before and did. Donne wondered how he slept, if it was full of nightmares and guilt, or if it was a sound rest. Donne was dead to the world all night, his muscles recovering from the workout they'd gotten.

The only reason either of them had even left the room this morning was to get coffee, Kenneth bringing two cups back. He passed one to Donne, and then sat on a chair on the opposite side of the room. He put the coffee on the table. Donne watched steam waft into the air and dissipate.

"I told them I needed you," Kenneth said.

"Clearly they disagreed."

"But why?"

Donne shrugged.

"You really beat the shit out of Manuel? Jesus."

Donne thought of a few wisecracks, but passed them up. He

was no Sean Connery.

"He's not dead. That's a problem. You wimped out."

A tremor ran through Donne.

"I'm gonna call Elliot," Kenneth said. His voice was wobbly.

"No," Donne said. "Don't you dare."

The words were so sharp, Kenneth's head snapped up.

"We don't know what his game is yet. And he may not know yet. We go about our business, and if you want to plan this heist, you'd better get to work. No distractions."

Kenneth shook his head. "I need Matt involved."

CNN moved on to a story about the Middle East. Donne glanced at the stock shots of the desert.

"Then get busy, damn it."

Kenneth stood up. "Seems like someone woke up."

Donne stared at Kenneth. "My turn not to understand, I guess."

"For a year in prison, you sat there like a proverbial duck. Trying to make friends, and lean on me for protection. People coming after you every ten minutes. Bring me the head of Jackson Donne. And I kept you alive, didn't I?"

"You did."

"But you were a damn mope. Sitting around doing nothing."

Donne stood up and walked over to the window. Their room had a spectacular view of the brick-building wall next door. Nothing else.

"I was in prison," he said. "Not a *Mary Poppins* revival."

"So, I'm glad this incident with Manuel woke you up. But we need to be smart, and not killing Manuel wasn't smart."

"I've done dumber things and I'm still here."

"Good for you, Half Measure. I'm calling Elliot."

Donne nodded. "I don't think it's the right play. Call Matt instead."

Kenneth took a deep breath.

"Think about it," Donne said. "We have a finite amount of time before Elliot figures out I'm still alive. We don't know why they don't want me in the picture, but if you're going to save your wife — or whatever the hell she is to you now — then you need to get working."

"You used to feel bad when people died. When I had to kill someone to save you. I should have known you'd hold back"

Donne exhaled. "Times don't change."

"They should." Kenneth slammed his fist into his own thigh. "God damn it, Jackson."

Donne stood up and walked to the other side of the hotel room. He wanted to go outside.

"When I cased the joint yesterday, I noticed something."

"Was it the fact that you said 'case the joint'?" Kenneth's words were sharp.

Donne wiped at his nose. "Place looks like Rahway Prison. We just got out of there, and now we have to go back in."

"You didn't want to leave Rahway." Kenneth scratched his cheek.

"This is different."

"You keep saying that."

"What is your problem?" Donne asked.

"Maybe because you should have killed a guy yesterday. You just made things so much harder for us. You..." He trailed off.

Donne didn't respond. Pushing Kenneth to finish the statement would only cause more tension. Unnecessary.

Outside, bus brakes squealed. Donne looked at his fists. He didn't answer Kenneth and instead got up and left the room. He needed to talk to Matt.

CHAPTER 33

ER ROOM WAS cold.

Tammy walked through the house slowly, wrapped in a blanket, looking for the thermostat. Elliot had gone out in a panic, something he couldn't talk about. She hadn't seen Manuel or the other one recently. Just Elliot. And now he was gone. Since she'd spent so much time sleeping, eating and reading in her room, she hadn't taken the time to learn the layout of the house. But the thermostat had to be around here somewhere.

She was always cold.

Ever since that day, a year ago, when they got the diagnosis. Tammy sat on the sticky leather bed. She'd already pushed the white paper out of the way, hating how it scratched her legs. Elliot leaned against the wall of the office, across from the cabinets. They'd been waiting for about twenty minutes, and Tammy's heart was doing the jitterbug in her chest. There was sweat starting to form at her hairline. She was just about to ask Elliot where the doctor was when there was a knock at the door.

She and Elliot made eye contact before he said the doctor should come in. Dr. Rosenberg, white jacket and all, strode into the room. He didn't look at Tammy, instead grabbing the stool with wheels all doctors owned, and pulled it over to an area between Tammy and Elliot. Elliot could see over the doctor's shoulder, but

Tammy couldn't. She wanted Elliot to come over to her, but he remained against the wall.

Rosenberg cleared his throat, and Tammy felt something catch in hers. He fiddled with some paperwork as Tammy coughed. She wanted to beg him to *get on with it*, but the words wouldn't come. Elliot could see the paperwork, she knew he could. He had shifted off the wall and was squinting. He never squinted.

"I'm afraid," Dr. Rosenberg said, "that the news is not good. The results of your biopsy are in, as is your blood work. I'm afraid you have cancer."

The doctor held up an X-ray result, and the light swathed through it, except for the dark mass in the center. The mass looked huge. That was when the room temperature changed. It felt like everything iced over. The sweat on her forehead felt cold to the touch. She shivered.

Doctor Rosenberg was talking, yacking away, but the words didn't connect with her. A wave of ambient noise filled her ears, and her vision went to shit. Air clogged her lungs and her balance was giving out. Then Elliot was there, finally. His arms were around her. He helped her lie backward. The doctor brought her water. Elliot and the doctor were still chattering, like her teeth. And the words weren't clear. All she heard was surgery and chemo.

Then began the process she was still going through. Six weeks until the surgery. Then recovery. And then chemo. Still with the damn chemo. Low dosages because that was what the doctor told her she needed. Low dosage over a prolonged period. So she felt exhausted, and cold. Always cold.

And she still couldn't find the damn thermostat.

Now, she rounded the corner of the hallway, and shrugged the blanket tighter around her shoulders. Her breathing was ragged, and all she wanted was to get back to bed. Today's session had been exceedingly exhausting.

Elliot's office was in front of her, at the end of a short hallway. Maybe she'd find the little temperature dial there. She shuffled forward, inhaling the smells of breakfast from the kitchen behind her. The toast and butter odor made her fight vomit back into her stomach. Last thing she wanted to even think about now was food. The chemo had destroyed her palette to the point where even simple foods turned her stomach.

She walked into the office and closed the door. To her left was the thermostat, just beyond Elliot's trashed desk. Usually this room was locked. Whatever had caused him to fly into a panic and leave made him forget his routine. Thank God. Tammy just wanted to feel some warmth.

The white thermostat was set for sixty-five. Too cold. She pressed the up button four times, and heard the furnace kick on with a muted *thunk.* Tammy exhaled as steam hissed from the radiator in the office. She stepped over to it and put her hand close, feeling the warmth exude. Now, back to bed.

As she turned, her eyes caught a glimpse of the paper disaster that spread over Elliot's desk. One of those items was an X-ray, looking very much like the one the doctor had held up a year ago. She blinked. And reached over, picking it up. On the bottom, it had her name and the date of her diagnosis. But there was something different about the actual X-ray.

There was no large mass in the middle of it, only a very small one. Not the same tumor Rosenberg had blathered about. Tammy's internal alarm started ringing loudly. She started spreading out the rest of the papers on the desk, sorting through them. There was another paper, this one a report. It had her name on it as well. It was the blood test she'd gone through.

Tammy scanned through all the results. The words "Stage 1" and "treatable" were typed on them. She sorted through more paperwork. The final one was dated the day after her initial treatment after her surgery. It said she was free and clear. She dropped the paper.

And the blanket.

For the first time in a year, sweat formed at her hairline. Her heart did the locomotion. And bile caught in her throat. She ran from the office and found the bathroom. Once she hit the toilet, everything in her stomach — which wasn't much — came back up again.

No cancer.

Not anymore.

But she still endured another chemo cycle. And a promise of a Cuban cure.

Good God, what was going on?

Tammy wasn't sure she wanted to find out. Elliot would be

back soon, and she was going to have to talk to him.

Not until she calmed the heat in her ears and the throbbing in her temples. She needed to know more.

CHAPTER 34

HOBOKEN WAS HUMMING.

Donne always pictured the town to be a rush hour town, crowded from six to nine in the morning and five until the bars closed at night. But today, at lunchtime, the town was bustling. It was one of those great spring days in New Jersey, in the seventies with a breeze coming off the Hudson and spiraling up Washington. People were having liquid lunches outdoors or wandering the street while chomping on pizza slices. Donne's stomach growled just watching them. But he ignored the feeling and wandered over to Herrick's apartment.

The buzzer wasn't needed as someone entering the apartment building held the door for Donne. Once inside the lobby, Donne closed his eyes and tried to remember Herrick's room. It'd been a long time since he'd been upstairs, that night he got back from Vermont. They got back from Vermont, with a killer on his tail.

Donne exhaled and remembered the fourth floor. He took the stairs, and exited into the hallway that smelled like an old pizza box. Donne took to the hall and started eyeing up the doors. Four-oh-three seemed like a good place to start, so Donne knocked. And then he counted to thirty. If Herrick didn't live here, he could ask which apartment was his. Herrick seemed like a sociable guy. The kind who'd talk to neighbors and make friends. Donne used to have a friend. Artie. But now who? Kenneth? Maybe.

When he got to twenty-seven, he heard someone approaching the door.

A stroke of luck. Herrick answered. And then nearly slammed the door in Donne's face.

"We have to talk," Donne said. He caught the door with his foot, like a stereotypical encyclopedia salesman.

Herrick gave the door one more push. The move sent a shockwave of pain as far up as Donne's knee.

"My dad already chatted with me. We really don't have to."

"No. Fuck that. Things have gotten worse."

Herrick eyed Donne, who remained as stony faced as he could. *Don't break. You're a goddamn salesman today. Be calm and be excited.*

"Oh no," Herrick said. He stepped aside to let Donne in. "My dad?"

"No," Donne said. The apartment smelled like some sort of berry. "My fault."

Herrick didn't offer Donne anything, but Donne took a seat on the couch anyway.

"What happened?"

"You know that guy, Manuel? Big guy, works with Elliot? Kind of crazy?"

Herrick nodded.

"He tried to kill me so I beat the crap out of him."

Herrick stopped mid-step. His face turned red. Donne looked away from him to the magazine on the table. He picked up and flipped through it. Something about Pottery Barn. It was a catalog, not a magazine. They had nice tables, though.

"Had to be done. He was going to kill me."

"Why?"

Donne shrugged. "Not sure yet. But it's put us on the clock big time."

"What are you getting at, Jackson?" Herrick sat down on the chair in the corner of the room. The cushions creaked under him.

Herrick crossed his legs and arms. That was the point—make this as uncomfortable as possible. They needed Matt in on this if they were going to have any chance at success.

"Listen, Matt, it's taken me a while, but I've learned something. In our business, people die. Sometimes it's the good guys and sometimes it's the bad guys. But I want to keep breathing for a long time. And I wasn't going to let some two-bit henchman take me down."

"But you didn't kill him. He can come back."

Donne shook his head. "Probably. Maybe your dad was right."

"You're crazy." Herrick's voice wobbled. "This doesn't worry you?"

Again, Donne shook his head. "I'm surviving. And to keep surviving, I need you. Because Elliot is going to be up my ass. On my case. However you want to put it. And your dad can't do this alone. I'm going to have to be helping from behind the scenes."

"And what is it you're doing?"

Donne grinned. He was putting on a show at this point. No matter what, sell Matt Herrick. This was the moment to do it. And to sell him, he was going to be flat out honest.

"We're robbing the Federal Reserve. That place on Route 17 that looks like a prison. We're going to steal a lot of money and get your mom down to Cuba to get treatment. Save her life. It's a good cause. Like March of Dimes."

Herrick put his head in his hands. "Jesus Christ."

"Yeah, I know. It's not the basketball Tournament of Champions, Matt. But we need you."

Herrick shook his head. "This is stupid."

"You can help your dad. And your mom. And figure out what the hell Elliot Cole is up to. What do you say?"

There was a beat. A moment of silence where Donne could only hear Herrick breathing and the hum of his own blood pumping through his ears. Herrick looked up. The red in his face was gone.

"Okay," he said.

Donne clapped his hands. *Always be selling*. "Hot dog. Let's get to work."

"Jesus Christ," Herrick said one more time.

CHAPTER 35

ERRICK FOLLOWED DONNE to the PATH train, then into the city. Through the streets full of people to some small hotel somewhere uptown. They had been walking too fast for Herrick to keep track of the streets.

When they entered the hotel, Herrick's hands started to shake. He balled them into fists to try and slow the tremors, but to no avail. His dad was upstairs. Had to be.

Donne pressed the button to summon the elevator and looked Herrick up and down.

"You're okay?"

Herrick nodded. "Seems to be my body's general reaction now that my dad is back in town."

Donne shrugged. The elevator dinged. "If it makes you feel better, he's happy to see you again."

"Nah."

They got on the elevator and with each passing floor, Herrick's breath got shallower. He tried to slow his breathing. Long, deep breaths. Four seconds in. Four seconds out. Imagine the stress leaving you. That was what his shrink told him to do after he left Afghanistan.

His father brought back his PTSD.

Great.

The elevator doors opened and Donne led him out. They walked down the hall. Herrick spent so much time focusing on their journey he hadn't even begun to think about the news Donne had dropped on him.

Donne used one of those magnetic hotel room keys to unlock a door and they both entered. Kenneth Herrick was sitting in a chair staring out the window at a brick wall. He turned and grinned when he saw them.

"Matt!"

"Dad, are you insane?"

Kenneth stood up. "Matt, I—"

"You're essentially trying to break into a prison. Into Fort Knox! You're not Goldfinger."

"Calm down."

Donne stepped in between them. "Matt, this isn't helping. We need you."

Kenneth looked at Donne. "Did you tell him?"

"Just about everything."

Kenneth said, "Jesus."

Herrick said, "Just about?"

Donne shrugged. "The days in Rahway were pretty rough. You don't want to hear about them. I don't need to tell you everything. And you told me your dad was a good guy who made a mistake. Not John Fucking Dillinger."

"Shut up!" Kenneth shouted. "Everyone just shut up."

Donne and Herrick turned toward him. Kenneth rolled his shoulders and cracked his neck.

"We're going to rob the Federal Reserve," he said. "But no one said anything about breaking into it."

CHAPTER 36

COLE OPENED THE door to the house and helped Manuel to the couch. The bruises on his friend's face had swollen up and closed an eye, despite hours of icing the wound. Manuel was coherent and had been able to talk Cole through the events behind the Javitz Center in great detail. Including Donne's apparently fantastic right cross and left jab.

Manuel groaned as he sank into the couch cushions. He put his head back, and his breathing trailed off into sleep.

"Wouldn't have happened if you'd done your job," Cole mumbled.

Before he could go to the kitchen, he heard movement in the back room. Padded, soft footsteps moving toward the living room. Cole straightened up and waited for Tammy to appear. He expected her to be sleepy, bleary eyed and wondering what the noise was.

Instead, he got someone who looked like she'd just finished her third cup of coffee.

"Where have you been?" she asked, her voice louder than it'd been in weeks.

Cole scratched his chin. "New York City, and then one of the houses in Jersey City. I couldn't move Manuel too far after he called me. So we holed up for the day to try to get Manuel back to moving around. This is the best I can do."

"What happened to him?"

"Accident." Cole shrugged.

"That's no accident. Someone beat the shit out of him. I've been around too long, Elliot."

Cole walked over to her and pulled her close. It wasn't always like this. Ten years ago, she was stronger, sinewy like a runner. He remembered how, after a successful gig, when they'd hidden out in a Jersey Shore town in the summer, she'd go for long runs in the morning. Ten miles up and down the beach. When she got back, Adrik would have brought Matt Herrick down to their hideout, and she'd take him out for breakfast.

The breakfasts stopped ages ago. The running? Three or four years ago. She got tired.

"Everything ended," she told him when he asked why. Sometimes you just had to move on.

"Don't worry about what happened, Tammy. You have to recover." He pulled her closer and felt her palms against his chest. "We wanted to get back in time for your next treatment."

Tammy gently pushed away from him. He tried to hold her still, but the push grew stronger. He let her go.

"There won't be another treatment," she said.

A stalagmite grew in Cole's chest. "You need to recover. And until Cuba—"

"Shut up, Elliot. I know."

Cole blinked. "Know what?"

Tammy shook her head. Her eyes glistened. "How could you?"

Cole stood there, silent. He wasn't sure where Tammy was going with this. What she knew. Or thought she knew. Better to let her talk it out, and he could react afterward.

"I found your paperwork. The X-rays. The doctor's notes. The cancer is gone. I don't need chemo."

Cole took a step forward and saw his way out. "Sweetheart, you can't read a doctor's paperwork. It's all gibberish. Nonsense words. Do you have a medical degree? Trust what the doctor told us. You need more treatment. Or you'll die."

Tammy looked like she'd swallowed bleach. The rock in Cole's chest crumbled a little bit.

"No!" Tammy shouted. She turned her back on him. "I know what I read. The cancer is gone, Elliot. If it was ever there."

Manuel snapped his head off the couch, suddenly wide awake. "What? What are you talking about?"

Tammy turned toward him. "Your boyfriend told my husband I am cancer free. Yet he still hooks me up to the IV every single day. Pumps radiation into me. My hair is falling out in clumps."

Manuel touched the bruise at his eye and winced. "Neil wouldn't lie."

"He didn't," Tammy said. "Elliot did."

Manuel turned to Cole. "Where is Neil? We have to verify this."

Cole shook his. "You will all play your roles. We need the money and we need to get Tammy back to full health. We need to get out of here.

"Where does Matt live?" Tammy asked.

The question caught Cole off guard. "What? Why?"

"I'm leaving. I'm going to see my son. To fix things. It's been too long. I'm not a part of your life anymore."

A burst of flame shot up Cole's throat. "You are my wife! And you will do what I say."

"No. I am not defined by you. Tell me where my son lives. He is a good man. I believe that. He will help me."

Manuel forced himself out of his chair. "Wait." He tried to catch his breath before speaking. "Wait until Neil gets here and we will figure this out."

Tammy seemed to sink in a little bit. She wasn't getting past Manuel, punch drunk or not. Cole counted to ten, waiting for the jangle in his nerves to settle.

"I am not lying to you, Tammy. I love you."

Tammy shook her head. "You love money more. You love the game more. You love the spotlight more than you ever loved me. This all started because you got the wrong kind of credit back when Kenneth got caught. You weren't the villain, but the hero. Well, faking cancer? Fuck you, Elliot."

She clutched her nightdress tight at the collar and turned back toward her room. Cole breathed deep.

"Thank you," he said to Manuel.

"You shouldn't have lied to her. Or me. I'm going to talk to Neil about this."

Cole nodded. "First you need to rest. You have work to do. And, I promise you, when we get the chance, I'm going to let you kill Jackson Donne."

Manuel grinned. With a groan, he sank back down into the couch. Cole stood and waited for him to fall completely asleep, the rhythm of his breathing only interrupted by the occasional snore.

Satisfied, Cole went to his office, pausing and listening at Tammy's door. He could hear the quiet weeping. He wanted to go wrap her in his arms and hold her until she cried it out.

But it was him she was crying about. Going in would only make it worse.

Once in his office, Cole found all the paperwork Tammy had sorted through. Cole pulled out the metal garbage can next to his desk and dropped it in. He then used the lighter for the grill to burn away the evidence.

CHAPTER 37

THE TEARS DIDN'T last long. Tammy rested her head on the pillow, willing herself to calm down. She counted in her head, first up to eleven and then back down again. The second time she did it, her breath came back to normal and the ache in her chest eased a bit.

Her eyelids were so heavy. Counting to eleven was like counting sheep. She could figure out her next step tomorrow morning.

As the world started to fade, a knock came at her door.

She rolled on her side, away from the IV hanger, and opened her eyes.

"Go away, Elliot."

The door opened a crack.

"It's me," Manuel said.

Tammy adjusted herself on the bed, trying to sit up a little bit. The bruise on her arm ached as she pushed on the mattress. That damn IV. The one she never, ever needed.

"Come in, Hon," she said.

The door opened all the way, and Manuel's huge body filled the frame, backlit by the hallway lamps. He came all the way in the room, pulling up a chair. He left the door open.

"Close the door and put on the lights," Tammy said.

"No. I don't want you to see me like this. My face. It was like —
"

Usually, Tammy would rub Manuel's shoulders and let him talk about the past. The days when he was a gang member just trying to get by. Before Elliot pulled him out of the neighborhood. Out of that life. Put him in the National Guard.

Manuel would be dead if it hadn't been for Elliot. There was so much he was able to do because he wasn't identified on that photo ten years ago.

Of course, the way Elliot would tell it, he was a hero. And the more notoriety he'd had, the more he would have done.

Was that right? Tammy wasn't sure. He took such pains to hide in Kansas those first three years. But Elliot was always talking, sometimes on one end of the spectrum and other times another. Maybe it was the illness that was confusing Tammy.

"I just want to say," Manuel said, "I had no idea. I thought you were sick."

Tammy let those words sit for a minute, processing them. Manuel wasn't someone you wanted to come at half-cocked and angry. He could fly off the handle at any moment.

"Really, Manuel?" Tammy chose her next words. "Neil never said anything to you? He was my doctor, you know. He was the one who was supposed to keep me healthy."

Manuel shook his head. "Never said a word. Can you believe that? I love him, but he keeps quiet about the medical stuff. Always says I wouldn't understand it."

"You're smart about other things. How is your face?" She didn't want to know what happened.

"I've had worse. Back when."

The words dissipated into the ether and they both sat in the dark for a while. Tammy stared at the ceiling, hoping her eyes would adjust to the dark, but the light streaming in from the hallway made her head hurt.

Manuel finally said, "Do you remember when I first came here? After my discharge."

Tammy nodded, but realized Manuel probably couldn't see her. "Yes, I remember."

Manuel continued anyway. She knew the story he was going to tell, but let him go on with it. His deep voice, with the slight accent, was soothing. Maybe she'd fall asleep.

"He was so scared about getting older. So worried about losing his edge. Remember? And he asked me how many pushups they'd have me do when I was training. And he'd try to do one more. And how far we would run. And he would try to do that extra mile. You were so worried about him having a heart attack, Tammy. We didn't know you were going to get sick."

"I'm not sick," she said. It was still unbelievable to hear out loud. "Not anymore."

"I know. I know." Manuel leaned back, the chair coming off its front two legs. "The first time, it went great. Elliot did the workout no problem, even though you said he was sweating like a bull." He laughed. "I always liked that. Like a bull. Not a pig. You were so careful how you spoke to him."

Tammy didn't respond.

"But the next time, he told me he wanted to do more. That I was going easy on him. And when I told him I wasn't lying, he slapped me. Open hand, pop, right on the cheek. And I didn't do anything at all. I wasn't lying."

"I know, Manuel. I remember. You don't have to say anything. It's just nice for you to sit here."

They were quiet for a moment. Somewhere in the other rooms, Tammy heard thunking and clunking. Elliot was searching for something. Or working off steam, or both. He never was able to do things quietly in the house. Plan a crime and no one would know. Look for the ketchup in the pantry and wake up the neighborhood.

Of course, after the robbery, he wanted everyone to know anyway.

"I want to tell you, Tammy. Please. It feels good to talk about stuff like this."

"Go ahead," she said, exhaling the words. She just wanted to sleep, but Manuel—somewhere inside of him was this sweet man. A boy who'd been ignored or sent down the wrong path.

What could have been.

"After he slapped me, you came to him. Remember? Ran to him. You looked so young to me at that moment. You grabbed Elliot's arm. I've never seen anyone stand up to him like that. You told him to stop. He had to remember how much younger I was than him. He couldn't push me like that anymore."

"That's not all I said," she whispered.

"No. It wasn't. You told him he couldn't treat me like that. That

I owed you my life, yes. But I wasn't his stress ball. He couldn't take his anger out on me. I always wondered what he was angry about."

Tammy slid down the bed a little, into a more comfortable position. She hoped Manuel would get the hint.

She said, "He didn't like being bested. He doesn't like knowing how old he is or that the end is near. It's getting closer for us, Manuel. We are getting old. But Elliot doesn't like to hear that or think about that. He loved the old days, when he would plan and drive us away. But now. I don't know. He needs that thrill."

Maybe that's what this was about. When did he first broach the idea of this crazy heist to her? Before she knew she had — thought she had — cancer. After some day trip he took. Told her he'd been thinking about the good old days. He always had. And they should do one more job and retire.

She told him no. Those days were over.

"Do you think Elliot likes Neil, Tammy?"

The world was starting to fade again. She was so exhausted.

"I do. He using him, isn't he?"

Manuel must have leaned forward because the legs of the chair clunked against the floor.

"Do you like Neil?"

"I like when you're happy, Manuel."

"I swear I didn't know."

Tammy closed her eyes. She wanted nothing more than sleep. To figure things out in the morning.

"I believe you."

"I promise you this. If you ever need help, I will help you. But I owe Elliot. He got me out. He saved me. I owe him. But I owe you too."

"Good night, Manuel. Thank you."

She felt his big paw around her wrist, a quick squeeze. He said good night, and then walked out of the room. When he closed the door, she welcomed the darkness.

Sleep came only moments later.

CHAPTER 38

|||||||||||||||||||||||||||||||||||||||||||||||||||||||||||||||||||||||||||||||||||||||||||||||||||||||||||||||||||||||||||||||||||||||||||||||||||||

HERRICK FOUND HIMSELF back in his apartment, alone. The sun had set. The streets were quiet. *Sarah should be home soon*, he thought. He stared at the iced tea in front of him. He was thirsty but had no desire to drink.

The fact that Donne and his dad let him even leave New York was shocking. He said they wanted him to continue his life, keep working and keep showing up to school. Nothing out of the ordinary. He wondered if they knew Mack had been in touch with him.

Herrick tried to will himself not to think too much. The TV played an NBA game, but he couldn't focus on it. The tremors were starting, running through his hands. His chest vibrated.

Not now.

Inhale for four seconds. Exhale for four seconds. Breathe the stress out. Herrick could do this. He knew he could.

At that moment, he heard the key in the door. He squeezed his eyes shut and counted. The door opened at six.

"Are you okay?" Sarah was breathless.

"I..." He squeezed his fists tight. Tried not to slam them into the couch cushions. "I'm fine."

He heard keys and her purse drop to the floor. The keys bounced.

"No, you're not." Her footsteps tapped against the wooden floor. Her arms wrapped around him.

And then Herrick let it all out. He shook as she held him. His breath became shallow. He clutched her shirt. He fought the tears.

"What happened?" she asked. "What happened?"

His breathing started to slow. The tension throughout his back and his arms eased. Sarah rubbed his back.

Finally, he pushed away.

"I'm sorry," he said.

"Please. Don't apologize. You did this last year too. After Donne went away. I get it."

"Yeah—but your apartment building blew up. Not mine. I should be tougher."

Sarah smiled. "You know it was more than that. But I got to move in with you."

"To make sure I didn't die in my sleep."

"Seriously, are you okay?"

"It's my dad. It's everything that's going on." Herrick rubbed his face. "Jesus. I feel like I just left Afghanistan."

"This is the second panic attack you've had since this all started." Sarah pulled one leg up onto the couch.

Herrick nodded. "That's not good."

"Maybe you should see someone."

He looked away from her.

Sarah didn't push him for a response. He liked that. He liked that she lived here. The insurance she pulled down from the explosion meant she could have gone anywhere, but when he asked, she decided yes, she'd live with him full time. They were in shock when it first happened, and didn't have time to react or do anything but try to grin their way through the hell he'd put them through. But within a month it became second nature.

Things were just fine.

And had been for a year. Now, he wondered if she would stick with him through his family reunion.

"My dad needs me and I'm going to help him."

"Your dad is a thief."

Herrick nodded. "When I'm done—when we're finished— he'll be back where he belongs."

"What about your mom?"

"Getting healthy."

"And Jackson Donne?"

Herrick exhaled. Another tremor rolled through him, like the aftershock of an earthquake.

"I don't know what to do about Donne."

"You'll figure it out?"

Herrick nodded again. "I'll play it by ear."

"That's not your best decision. Maybe you should come up with a plan for him. Play it by ear is not a plan."

"It's really all I have right now."

Sarah leaned into him and rested her head on his shoulder. "When will you start?"

"I already have," he said. "Thank God it's not basketball season."

CHAPTER 39

IT STARTED WITH Jiminy Cricket.

Herrick was back on the highway, cruising south on the Turnpike. This was part one according to Kenneth. Figure out who the National Guard guy was who threatened Herrick. It would have been the first step for him too, but his dad was insistent.

Traffic was slow, the beginnings of rush hour starting to clog the roads. But Herrick pumped the rock station and tried to enjoy the drive. He followed the same route as the last time, exiting at New Brunswick and swinging around the winding roads down to the base. Instead of driving past it, he pulled into the entranceway, right up to the guy with the loaded weapon.

The guard held a hand up to slow him down. Herrick obliged.

"Can I help you, sir?"

"I'd like to talk to someone in charge," Herrick said. He liked the feeling of being back on a base, which surprised him.

"Right now, until I tell you otherwise, I'm in charge, sir."

Herrick nodded. He held up his PI license and his military discharge papers.

"Does this help?"

The guard took the two pieces of paperwork and studied them. He whispered something into the walkie-talkie attached to his uniform. He looked at the paperwork some more. Herrick hummed along with the song on the radio. The music was loud, but Herrick was respectful and didn't drum on the steering wheel. The humming kept him occupied, so he barely noticed that this entrance looked almost exactly like the one on the base in Afghanistan.

Behind them cars whizzed past on the road, paying no attention to anything else. Their days just went on. The guard passed Herrick's paperwork back to him.

"I'm going to raise the gate. When I do, pull just beyond it. A car will come meet up with you and escort you to your parking spot. You will then meet with Major John Christenson."

The guard stepped back and pressed a button. The candy striped gate in front of them raised and Herrick drove through. He was careful to do as he was asked, immediately pulling over and waiting. Nearly two minutes later, a green military Jeep pulled up in front of him. The driver waved for him to follow. Herrick did.

They took two left turns and parked in front of a two-story brick building. Herrick got out of the car and nodded at the Jeep driver, who drove off. He entered the building and found a man with the nametag Christenson standing at the front desk waiting for him.

It wasn't Jiminy Cricket.

The major didn't hold out his hand for a handshake. Instead his arms were folded and he looked like he was about to scold Herrick. The memories started to rush back to Herrick and he quickly balled his fists to try to suppress the tremors.

Not here. Not now.

"What can I do for you?" the major asked.

Herrick surveyed the room. It was plain and dated, as if constructed in the seventies. The walls were wood paneled. A ratty old couch, the kind you'd find in a fraternity house, was pushed up against the far wall. In front of it was a table with old magazines on it. Other than Herrick, the major and a man behind the reception desk doing paperwork, there was no one else in the room. The air conditioner was blowing so hard it made Herrick shiver.

"I'm looking for someone."

The major didn't respond.

"I am working a very important investigation. A few days ago, I was up in Vernon asking questions when a man came by to talk to me. He threatened me."

Herrick watched the major's reaction. There wasn't any.

"When we were done talking, he thought we went our separate ways. But I followed him. All the way down here. He pulled in through the gates, and that's when I 'lost' him. I'd like to talk to him today."

The major nodded. "You get a name?"

"No. He referred to himself as, um, my conscience. In my head I've been calling him Jiminy Cricket." Herrick smiled.

The major didn't. "Let me get this straight. You drove all the way down here to talk to a guy you followed from Vernon. And you're calling him Jiminy Cricket?"

Herrick nodded.

"You're wasting my time. You know that, right?" The major's voice sounded like coffee going through a grinder.

"I'm just trying to get some information."

"This is ridiculous. Go home."

Herrick opened his mouth about to say more, to try to convince the major to talk to him.

Before he could utter a word, the alarms on the base started going off. Without missing a beat, both the major and the man behind the reception desk bolted out into the parking lot. Herrick had to fight the nerves down again.

The alarm got even louder. Outside, people were scattering, running, trying to figure out just what the hell was going on.

Herrick watched through the window, trying to force himself to join them. He'd left his ASP at home, but if there was a security issue, at least he could be an asset. He glanced at each face as they sprinted by.

And then he saw him. One man not running, but walking like he was out for a late night stroll.

Elliot Cole's buddy. The one Donne said he beat the hell out of.

Manuel. With a big ass black eye.

CHAPTER 40

ERRICK SPRINTED OUT the door toward Manuel, who was casually getting into a Jeep. One of those deep green Jeeps with a star on the side of it. An instant later the engine roared to life. The alarm bells still clambered, and military men were running toward the entrance.

Herrick wished he didn't leave his ASP home. He ran hard. The Jeep backed out of its spot, turning away from all the running guards. Herrick leaped for the Jeep and grabbed the door handle. He pulled hard and it opened, but nearly ripped his shoulder out of its socket. The Jeep braked and with his free hand, Herrick reached into the car and grabbed Manuel by his shirt. Pulling Manuel toward the open door, Herrick hoped he would slam on the brakes and stop the Jeep completely.

Instead, Manuel punched Herrick in the face. Herrick's head snapped back and he lost his grip on the shirt. He stumbled backward and the Jeep accelerated away. Herrick rolled in the dust, his shoulder screaming in pain.

Herrick turned to find three guardsmen aiming rifles at him. They screamed to freeze and to raise his hands. He tried to do both. The alarms stopped ringing, but left a buzzing in Herrick's ear. He counted to ten in his head and prayed no one had an itchy trigger finger. Loud alarms tended to set people with guns on edge. He didn't want to find out how good the guards' aim was.

No one took a shot.

Christenson suddenly appeared, and stepped to the side of the guard, not in front of them like you'd see in a movie. The major wasn't an idiot, and wasn't about to get himself shot by some hair trigger. But he did yell out that they should lower their weapons.

He had to yell it twice before they listened. Christenson shook his head as they did. Once they lowered their weapons, he walked over to Herrick. His face was as red as a British soldier's uniform.

"Come with me," he said. "Damn it."

THEY WERE IN a room much like an interrogation room at a police station. Herrick hated rooms like this, and it was the last place he wanted to be. Not while Manuel was getting away.

Again.

"Are you going to let me go?" Herrick asked. It was a pain in the ass to waste time here.

Christenson shrugged. "Depends on what you have to say. You know attacking a military vehicle raises some eyebrows."

Herrick frowned. "I was hoping you wouldn't tell anyone."

"Maybe you shouldn't have come."

"I'm a private investigator. It's my job."

"You carrying?"

It felt like a shadow crossed over Herrick's face. They had already searched him.

"First off, I don't do guns," he said. "Second, you're really wasting my time."

Christenson nodded. "While we had you in here, I looked you up."

Herrick rubbed his chin. He figured that was what they were doing while he stewed for an hour. Thank God he didn't have to take a piss.

"You know about what I did in the sandbox, then?"

Christenson sniffled. "You shot a kid."

"One strapped with a bomb, who had already killed one of my best friends and was going to kill the rest of us."

"You did your job."

Herrick's turn to nod. "And I'll never shoot anyone again."

"Never say never."

Herrick balled his fists.

"I have big time respect for a man like you, Herrick. But you swung at a Jeep with one of my guys in there. Probably a reason for that."

"That was someone I know."

"Jiminy Cricket?"

"No, actually. But they're probably connected."

The silence hung in the air. Christenson looked up at the ceiling.

"Fuck," he finally said.

Herrick waited. Behind Christenson, the walls were bland, a faded beige bordering on white. Herrick wondered why these rooms were always so boring. No pizzazz. Maybe because the more bored you were, the more likely you'd be willing to talk. Herrick wasn't in the mood to spill the beans on his dad, Cole and Donne, but he worried he wouldn't have a choice.

"Why are you looking for him?" Christenson asked, as if Herrick hadn't already answered that question nearly two hours ago. Probably just stalling for time.

Herrick reminded him of the answer. Then asked, "I wasn't. But why was Manuel?"

"I don't need to tell you anything. You walked in here and broke government property."

"You know about me. You said so yourself. I'm a good guy. I'm not here to mess around. You also know Manuel probably set off the alarms so he could get away. I mean, you all went running to the front gate and he waltzed out the backdoor essentially."

Christenson flared his nostrils. "Manuel is — was — one of ours. But...the name Neil Haskins mean anything to you?"

Herrick shook his head *no*. The last name sounded familiar, but he couldn't place it.

"No idea why it would. He's faceless. Lifelong Army brat who didn't like the real thing. So he took the weekend job with us. He met Manuel Parada here. They fell in love. I don't know much about Neil. Before he came here, his dad moved him around. Bruce Haskins was his dad, I think. I'm trying to remember from his file. I think he went into medicine."

And that's when Herrick's stomach turned to ice. He took a deep breath. The name Neil Haskins wasn't a familiar one. But Bruce was.

Herrick stood up. "Can I go?"

"What? No. We're not done."

"I need to get out of here."

"What's the matter? I don't understand."

Herrick couldn't explain. Not until he talked to his dad. Because Bruce Haskins was the world's biggest psychopath.

Someone even his dad wouldn't work with. In fact, Herrick had only heard stories.

And all of them ended with someone dying.

CHAPTER 41

||||||||||||||||||||||||||||||||||||||||||||||||||||||||||||||||||||||||||||||||||||||||||||||||||||||||||||||||||||||||||||||||||||||

DONNE HAD HIS own mission.

Kenneth had sent him out for supplies. It was an odd feeling, not worrying about using his credit card. Not worried about being followed. At least not by law enforcement.

Because Herrick's girlfriend, Sarah Cullen, had been trailing him for about two blocks now. He checked the time in the window of the bank as he strolled past it and saw it was after three o'clock. He wondered what time she got out of work.

And how she found him.

He shook his head absently at Herrick's carelessness. He must have told her. Of course it was his fault.

Donne walked another block and then turned into a Starbucks. He got in line and waited. He wondered how much she wanted to be seen, and if she would just keep walking. She didn't. Less than sixty seconds later, Sarah walked in. Donne exhaled. He turned toward her.

"Hi, Sarah," he said.

She frowned. "You're not surprised."

"I was surprised about three blocks ago. I got used to it. Want a coffee? I'm gonna get one."

"We have to talk."

Donne nodded. "Coffee first."

Sarah sighed, gave him an order and went and took a seat at a table across the room. Minutes later, Donne joined her.

"I want to talk to you," she said. "Not Matt, not Matt's dad. You."

Donne took a sip of his coffee. Sarah did the same with her latte. They didn't speak. Donne waited. He didn't really have time for bullshit. He had computers to buy.

"Why are you dragging Matt into your world again?" Sarah finally asked.

Donne sat back. The Starbucks chair creaked under his weight. "I'm not dragging him into anything. His dad needs him."

"For what? His dad is a criminal—"

"*Was* a criminal. He's out of jail now." Donne realized he had no idea what she knew. He wasn't about to let even simple verb tenses get himself into trouble later. Donne had slipped up enough in life. A guidance counselor wasn't going to get him into more trouble.

Not today, at least.

"When I was a kid," Sarah said, "in—I think—ninth grade, my friends and I used to go to the movies all the time."

Donne sighed. He didn't have time for this shit.

"Anyway, we used to movie hop, right? Buy a ticket for one movie and then see a second. You have to time it just right, but—"

Donne said, "I know what you're talking about."

Sarah fiddled with her coffee cup. "Anyway, one of the girls who came with us, her name was Lisa. She liked to steal candy from the concession too. We lived in a small town and, well—"

"Wait a minute. Are you trying to sell me some bullshit about your past to keep me from using Matt?"

Sarah drank her coffee. She didn't say anything.

"You work at the school, don't you, Sarah?"

"Yes."

"Think you're a little out of your league in this conversation?"

Sarah tilted her head and squinted. "And you aren't? Matt told me about you. You gave yourself up to the cops as some form of penance. And you think you can handle dealing with the people Matt's dad deals with?"

Donne's coffee steamed as the cup rested on the table. "What do you do at the school? A teacher?"

"Guidance counselor."

Donne nodded. "So you deal with kids in trouble. Troubled lives and all that?"

"Poor kids. Abusive parents. Gang members. I've heard it all. I worked kids through a lot of bad shit."

Donne leaned across the table. "I've seen worse than any of them. And Matt? You know Matt's story—he's seen, and done, bad shit too. So why are you worried about them?"

Sarah put her cup down hard. "You don't get it. Where's your sense of humanity? Matt is just getting his feet back under him. Things are really, really good between us. He has people—kids— who depend on him. And you're helping him throw it all away."

"Matt's a big boy."

"So are you."

"We need him."

"Why?"

Donne didn't say anything.

"What happened to you, Jackson? Last year, Matt, he believed in you. I know you can help him get out of this. I don't care about his dad and I don't even care about you. But you have a soul."

Donne worked his jaw. The low rumble of crowd noise behind him turned to static in his ears. He turned his head and looked out the window, watching traffic go past.

"I'm a different person."

"Jail changed you?"

Donne nodded.

Sarah stood up. "It took me a long time to re-build my life too. My friend Lisa? She got us both arrested the night she wanted to steal a car. I spent two years in juvie. You don't hear about that with kids from Ridgewood. But it's true." She took a breath. "Matt doesn't even know that."

Donne watched her hovering over him, cheeks red.

"I've seen shit too. I know jail can change you. It's funny, isn't it? How people can end up in the same circle? You, me, Matt's dad—all circling around Matt's life. Things happen for a reason. I don't know why you are here, but I want him to survive this. There's a future for us. Don't let what happened to you and me happen to him too."

She stormed off. Donne counted to fifteen after she left before he started drinking his coffee.

CHAPTER 42

KENNETH LOOKED OVER the computer monitor at Jackson Donne. Donne had to use his second credit card as Visa had finally shut down the one he'd been using. But the computer store, a dinky place on the East Side, accepted the second one and passed the laptop over. Once he got back, Kenneth took it, set it up and started typing. Donne waited until Kenneth looked up.

"At any given time," Kenneth said, "the Federal Reserve could have up to sixty billion dollars in cash in its walls."

"That's crazy." Donne rubbed his face. "Don't they just keep all of that on a computer chip?"

Kenneth ignored the comment. "In 2003, twelve billion dollars earmarked for Iraq went missing. Some say it ended up somewhere in Lebanon, but the government wasn't able to track it down. That's what I'm working on. How did that cash—real, live hundred dollar bills—go missing? Because if we can figure that out, then thirty million dollars is a drop in the bucket. They'll never be able to find us."

Donne rubbed his face. "I don't buy it. Thirty mil is a ton of money."

Kenneth shook his head. "Like pocket change to these guys."

He went back to tapping away at the computer. Donne walked over to the other side of the beds and stared out the window at the brick wall across the street. He listened to the ambient sounds of traffic and wished he was anywhere else. The city was overwhelming, a shadow hanging over everyone's head.

But this was where Kenneth wanted to set up. Away from Elliot and out of the perimeter of the Federal Reserve. You could hide in New York. Or so he thought. Donne didn't remind Kenneth about Manuel, nor did he tell him about Herrick's girlfriend.

Someone knocked at the door.

Kenneth slowly closed the laptop, and Donne went over to the door and looked though the peephole. On the other side was Matt. Donne exhaled and pulled the door open.

Herrick stormed into the room. Looked at Kenneth and then to Donne.

"Come walk with me," Herrick said. "I need to talk to you."

"I think we can both stand to hear what you have to say."

"You're gonna want to hear this alone."

Donne shook his head, and Herrick took a step toward him. His cheeks were flushed and a sheen of sweat appeared on his forehead. Donne didn't flinch at the approach. His hands were in fists before he realized it.

Kenneth stood up. "Go. I don't give a shit. You can tell me later."

They stepped into the hallway and Donne closed the door. Herrick counted to three, long enough for Donne to raise his eyebrows.

"Manuel's a National Guardsman," Herrick said.

Donne's stomach felt like it was going to crawl up through his throat.

"He's in love with Jiminy Cricket."

Pressing his fingers against the bridge of his nose, Donne said, "Who?"

"Haskins. His name is Neil Haskins."

The name meant nothing to Donne.

"The National Guard guy?" he asked. "What are you talking about?"

"Jiminy Cricket," Herrick said. "Neil Haskins is Jiminy Cricket. He's Bruce Haskins son. And he's dating Manuel, who apparently heals quickly."

"Between your dad and Cole, there's a lot of military people being recruited for this job."

"And it doesn't seem like the Cole side wants you involved."

Donne slumped against the wall. He slipped up, not eliminating Manuel. Knocking him out was a half-measure.

Herrick talked about visiting the National Guard base that afternoon. And then he talked about nearly getting arrested after trying to catch Haskins. None of this made much sense to Donne, but he didn't interject. Silence was always better when people were ranting.

He said, "Bruce Haskins was a psychopath. My uncle used to use him to do some dirty work when Elliot and I needed information. I don't think my dad was comfortable with the trail of blood that led to his front door. The cops would catch up with them eventually."

Donne's neck muscles tightened. Was that how Kenneth ended up in prison?

"So, Haskins threatened me the other day. Told me I should be working with you guys."

Herrick shoved his hands in his pockets.

"We should follow up on the military stuff."

Donne turned his back and ran his hands through his hair. "We can't worry about ancillary stuff."

"Being threatened isn't ancillary. Jesus."

Donne laughed this time. "Your dad got me out of prison. I owe him."

"You're being stupid. You're a detective, or used to be. Come with me. Let's talk to my uncle and find out more."

In another hotel room, a glass crashed to the ground. Both Donne and Herrick stopped to listen to the resident cursing about it.

Herrick said, "There's something more going on here. I can't tell if my dad and Elliot are on opposite sides or working together. Elliot bought you two out, but then Manuel tried to kill you."

Donne nodded. "Lots of complications."

"As always."

"Let's go," Donne said.

CHAPTER 43

ERRICK'S CAR IDLED outside Adrik Vavilov's house. Donne fidgeted in the seat next to him, staring at the front door. Herrick wanted to tell him to cool it, but didn't. There was something different about Donne—Herrick noticed it on the ride up here.

"Nervous?" he asked.

Donne shook his head. "You are."

"The guy up there could crush us both with the force of his money." Herrick gripped the steering wheel. Then reached down and turned the key off. "But he's also my uncle."

"Blood?"

"No. One of those friend type deals. Kind of like a Godfather."

"Damn." Donne rubbed his thighs. "They don't usually kill blood relatives. But Godsons?"

Donne grinned, and Herrick forced a laugh.

Then Donne opened the passenger side door, got out and slammed the door shut. Herrick counted to four while watching him make his way up the front lawn. Herrick turned the engine off and followed Donne's lead. By the time he reached the front door, Donne was already leaning on the doorbell.

Bastard was going to get them both killed.

They sat in the giant living room, and this time Herrick couldn't smell any food cooking. Vavilov stood over them, arms crossed and nostrils flared. He stared directly at Herrick.

"You bring him here?" Vavilov uncrossed his arms for a moment only to point at Donne.

Herrick shrugged. "You know he's involved."

Vavilov's eyes widened. "But I'm not."

"You sure?" Donne asked. His voice was tight like a laundry-shrunken sweater.

Vavilov sniffled. "Your kind, you act like the good guy, but you're not. You're a killer. The news says so. You assassinated a politician, didn't you? You're a prisoner out on a whim. You are a dangerous man, Jackson Donne."

Donne shifted in his seat. Spread his hands. Smiled.

"And here I am, in your house."

"Enough," Herrick said. He got up from his chair and stepped in between Vavilov and Donne. "You and I have to talk, Uncle."

After shaking his head, Vavilov said, "There is nothing to talk about."

"Then why did you let us in?"

No reply.

Someone else in the house whistled. It wasn't a song Herrick recognized. He waited a few bars before speaking again.

"Why do Elliot and my dad need so many military guys?"

No reply again.

Herrick watched Vavilov's body language. Always a good poker player, there wasn't a tell this time either.

"Bruce Haskins' son. Neil. And he threatened me into working with my dad. You always kept his dad employed. The connections are easy to spot."

Vavilov exhaled. "You know nothing about me. As for Neil? He is a bit rash, but sometimes he can be useful."

"What was his use this time?"

Vavilov shook his head. "This time it wasn't me."

"Then who? Uncle Elliot?"

Donne pushed himself out of the chair. "Stop talking in circles."

Herrick's muscles tightened, and he turned to Donne—half expecting him to be charging at Vavilov. Herrick tried to shoot him a "calm down" look.

"Matthew," Vavilov said. "Shouldn't you be worried about your mother? She's sick, and your dad can help save her."

"He's working on that."

Vavilov held up a hand. *Listen.* "I understand this is a huge risk for you."

"You told me you weren't involved."

Vavilov shook the hand he held up. *Listen!* "If there ever was a time to take a risk, it's for family. That's what you should focus on now. Help your father. Help your mother. And get Jackson Donne out of my house."

Herrick worked his jaw and tried to think of the right thing to say. Nothing would come.

"He's in," Donne said. "You don't have to worry about that now. He's going to lose everything to save his mother. Like me. I've lost everything. He's going to find out what that's like. They couldn't leave him out of this, could they?"

"Damn it, Jackson."

Donne moved behind Herrick, but Herrick didn't turn toward him. Didn't want to see his face. He focused on the bookcase over Vavilov's shoulder. Tried to read the titles on the spines. But he couldn't. Too far away.

Somewhere a door opened and closed.

"It's true, Matt. Sorry, but it is. You and Sarah could have had something, but if you keep going down this path...you might already be too far."

Herrick spun around. "Don't you mention her."

Vavilov laughed. "Like I don't already know."

"She came to talk to me today, Matt. She's worried about you. You haven't seen your mother in how long? Your dad? Think about your priorities. I can handle what your dad needs help with. We can do it. Not you."

Herrick ran a hand through his hair. Words were not coming to him. The sun blinked through the window, the last rays of light before nightfall.

"Sarah went to see you?" The words did not leave his mouth easily.

Donne nodded.

Then his eyes went wide.

Herrick whirled around. Elliot Cole stood in front of him, gun in hand.

"I heard some of that. Real interesting talk, Mr. Donne."

Vavilov spoke through gritted teeth. "Not here."

"Shut up." He turned the gun toward Herrick. "Matt, you're going to have to work with your dad. I'm sorry about that. Jackson talks a big game, but he's coming with me. He and I have some business to settle."

"Because your big man couldn't do it on his own," Donne said.

A shadow crossed Cole's face.

"Not here," Vavilov said again.

"Donne, come with me." Cole waved the gun in the direction of the kitchen. Herrick reached for his ASP.

Donne held up a hand.

"I got this," he said. "Get back to work. I'll see you soon."

He started to walk toward the kitchen. Cole kept the gun on him the whole time.

"You're an asshole," he said. Donne shrugged.

When they were gone, Vavilov sighed. "I had to drag this out until Elliot got here. I'm sorry it's come to this."

Herrick said, "Me too."

And punched his Uncle Adrik square in the mouth.

CHAPTER 44

DONNE LOOKED INTO the side mirror of the car he was in. They pulled down the street, using every last bit of horsepower the Altima had in it. He watched Herrick give chase on foot for maybe fifty yards before slowing into a trot. Donne shook his head. Herrick should have gone for his own car.

Cole sat in the backseat, gun still pointed in Donne's direction. He didn't recognize the driver, but the military haircut and rest of him matched the description of this Haskins character Herrick had been talking about. Donne wished he'd used his credit card to buy himself a gun when he got out of prison.

Like it was that easy in this part of the country.

He stayed silent. No use in talking. Might as well let them drive him around before they killed him. Or explained their cunning plan to him.

Whatever.

Cole and Haskins didn't speak. The car rumbled into to the night.

Long Valley, New Jersey was an area of the state Donne knew nearly nothing about. It was secluded off Route 78, well before the Pennsylvania Border, but miles away from the congestion of the Turnpike and Parkway. It seemed to be a bunch of small towns tucked into a gigantic forest.

They exited Route 78 and wound through roads without streetlights until they found a small cabin at the end of a cul-de-sac. Haskins parked and got out of the car. He walked to the front door. Never made eye contact with either of the them.

Donne waited for instructions.

Behind him, the door opened and shut, and Cole came around to the passenger door and opened it.

"Get out," he said. The gun barrel was close to Donne's cheek.

After undoing his seatbelt, Donne did as he was told. The driveway they were parked on was paved with asphalt so brand new, he expected his feet to stick.

"I should probably just kill you," Cole said.

Donne shook his head. "Everyone says that. They never do it. Even Manuel."

"Maybe I have a good reason." Cole pointed to the front door. "March. There's someone I want you to meet before you die."

"Seems like a wise plan." Donne started to walk. "I mean, you're a cunning thief judging by what I hear. So dragging me into a house with a gun to my face can't possibly go wrong, can it? Never mind that I've killed a small army during my life. But okay."

"A small army. But not Manuel. You pulled your punches that time?"

Donne didn't respond.

The house was less bare boned than the Paterson place. It was decorated with pictures of beaches, new furniture and fuzzy carpet. It smelled like Thanksgiving. Manuel sat on one of the couches, and noticeably tightened his posture when Donne walked in. Haskins stood off to the corner with a glass of water. Donne felt the gun barrel jammed into his back.

"I want you to give Manuel another shot," Cole said. "That is Neil, Manuel's boyfriend. His lover. They are going to get married in a month. So, maybe this is my wedding gift to them."

Manuel's voice was strong. "Step into the light."

Donne stepped forward and felt the light from the lamp on his face. The gun barrel moved with him. His back would certainly be bruised tomorrow.

Air caught in his throat.

If he even saw tomorrow.

Arrogance was no guarantee Cole would screw up. But it

usually led to Donne having some form of advantage. No one expected aggression against a gun.

"You should have killed me," Manuel said, his face twisting as he fought his rage down.

"You're right," Donne said.

The sentence made Manuel flinch.

"I should have broken your neck with my bare hands and dumped you in the Hudson River." Donne kept his words even. "We were behind the Jacob Javitz Center, overlooking the water. No one would have found your body. Not for days."

Donne gave Manuel credit. He didn't leap out of the chair. He played with the ring on his left hand and his mouth twitched. Out of the corner of his eye, he could see Neil's tremors.

"You son of a bitch," Manuel said. His voice wasn't as strong now.

"Before you call me that again, let me ask you a question." Donne rolled his shoulders and dislodged the gun barrel from his skin. "Do you know why I didn't?"

"Careful," Cole hissed.

"Do you?" Donne repeated.

Manuel licked his lips. "Tell me."

"Because I'm stupid. In jail, with Kenneth, I was soft. Sat around and waited for people to come and get me. I have a lot of enemies. But Kenneth saved me. And you know how? He killed a man. Broke his neck. And I sat there and let him. I felt guilty about it. But next time I see you? I'm not going to screw up. I'm done feeling guilty."

Manuel grinned. "Bring it."

"You know I will. And when I do, how will Neil feel? He'll be alone without you. Walk away, you two. Go live your life."

"Don't speak for me," Neil said. "I'm enjoying this."

"That's a mistake. But it doesn't make Manuel a better killer, does it?" Donne expected a tremor to go through his body as he spoke. It didn't.

Donne stood there. Waited for Manuel to make the next move.

"You're going to burn," Manuel said. "I hope you enjoy the last few minutes of your life."

Donne smiled. "I promise you this: I have some time left. To make up for a mistake."

Manuel leaped out of the seat toward Donne. Donne held his

ground, and Neil caught Manuel before he could get any further.

"Not here," Neil hissed. "We'll take him somewhere else."

"You're going to die. You *will*." Manuel's words came in fits and gasps.

Donne walked over to him and leaned in close to his ear. Both Manuel and Neil could hear him. But he didn't think Cole could.

"Let me tell you something." He said each word slowly. Donne's vision clouded at the corner of his eyes. "You missed me the first time. You fucked up. And I fucked up by not finishing the job. But I am in your life now and this is what happens. I am a tornado. A hurricane. I swoop in and mess everything up. I'll leave one of you to pick up the pieces. Ask my sister. Ask Jeanne Baker or Artie or Jesus Sanchez. Ask anyone I've come close to. But threaten me? You know how many times I've been threatened? I always win. I'm finally learning."

"I know you. The people you've killed: self-defense."

"I think I'm over waiting for that point."

Manuel's body shook like an earthquake victim.

Donne felt the gun against his head, behind his ear.

"Let's go," Cole said. "Outside."

"Let me," Manuel said. Haskins nodded. "You promised."

"And let you screw up again? You're like a dead leaf right now. Work the plan," Cole said.

Donne turned slowly. Not many options now. He walked toward the back of the room, and then into the hallway. A back door waited at the end of it. Donne looked for something to use as a weapon, but the hallway wasn't decorated like the living room was. He walked forward. To the right was another door. It was closed.

And then it was open.

A woman stood there — Kenneth's ex-wife? Donne thought it was her.

"Back inside, Tammy," Cole said.

She shook her head. "No. I have to talk to him."

Pointing at Donne, she said, "Alone."

CHAPTER 45

"**Y**OU'RE OUT OF your mind, Tammy," Cole said. "I'm not letting him out of my sight."

Tammy grabbed Donne's wrist. Her grip was tighter than he expected. "Give me a break, Elliot. This man knows my son and my ex-husband. I want to talk to him before you kill him. I need to know more about Matt and Kenneth. For my sanity. They're my family."

Cole said, "I'm coming in there too."

"Oh please. You can stay right outside the door. You have a gun. Where is he going to go? Out my window? You know what's out there. Nothing. He's not going anywhere. Stand here, and when I'm finished with him, you can have your way."

Cole shifted his feet. The gun lowered an inch. Donne kept his eyes trained on Cole's, looking for him to blink.

Tammy gave Donne's wrist a tug. With her free hand she touched her chest. "Please. You *owe* me."

Cole blinked. "You seem better today. Are you feeling better?"

Tammy's grip on Donne's wrist got even tighter. "Better than I have in a long time. No thanks to you."

"Ten minutes." Cole took out his phone, opened an app. He set a timer.

"Thank you, Elliot. We won't even need that much."

She pulled Donne into her room, and closed the door. She didn't lock it. Donne waited for his eyes to adjust against the darkness. A desk lamp in the corner near her bed was the only illumination.

Most people, Donne assumed, would allow this delay in death to cause more anxiety. Donne, however, felt the air come back into his lungs and his muscles relax. The longer he was alive, the longer he had to figure a way out of this mess.

Tammy was a blessing. One worth ten minutes. He started running over different survival scenarios in his head. Each of the first two ended with him getting shot.

"Sit down."

Donne acquiesced and went over to the bed. It was a bit lumpy.

"Thank you," he said.

Tammy shook her head. "Don't have time for that. We have to find a way to get you out of here."

Not exactly what Donne expected her to say. "Why are you helping me? He's your husband."

"And he's a psychopath."

"I'm not going to argue with you there."

Clearly the show Tammy put on in the hallway had taken a toll on her. She walked over to the bed and sat next to Donne. She seemed to deflate into her seat. It was like some of her soul had left her body.

"For a long time," she said, "I've been sick. Aches in my chest. Doctor appointments. Chemo. They told me I had lung cancer. We went to a doctor, the best Cole could find. They showed me X-rays. They put me on treatment."

Her voice caught in her throat. Donne had an idea where this was going, but he didn't interrupt. Still trying to figure out a way to get out of this cabin alive.

"The whole reason for this heist—for breaking you out of jail and for breaking Kenneth out—was to get to Cuba. For some experimental treatment. Elliot promised me I would get healthy. But it's not true. That's not why. I just found out. I don't have cancer. After my last round of chemo, I was cleared. But I've been hooked up to that contraption. He's been sedating me with radiation."

Donne looked at Tammy. Her face was wrinkled like leather. Her eyes were sunken and she was as thin as an antenna. Not the adventuring, swashbuckling, grinning Bonnie Parker Kenneth had talked about both in prison and since he'd gotten out.

"In fact, I had a treatment this morning," she said. "Elliot's been lying to me."

Donne scratched his chin. She was on chemo as early as this morning? Jesus.

"Why?" he asked.

"Hell if I know. But I want to find out. You have to help me. This isn't some charity heist."

"It never was," Donne said. "You don't rob from where we are targeting and call it charity. But I don't understand the motivation, then. I don't at all."

"You need to get out of here and go talk to Kenneth. No—talk to Matt. Don't trust Kenneth."

"He went to jail to save you," Donne said. "He saved my life time and time again. We can trust him."

"No one dives into a job like this so easily."

Donne looked at the true crime book on the nightstand. He played everything over in his head.

It felt wrong. Very wrong.

"Tell Matt that I'm not sick. But tell him I need help."

"How can I get out of here?"

Tammy shrugged. "Out the damn window. I think it is about a thirty-foot drop into the forest. Probably where Elliot was going to shoot you."

"In the middle of the night?"

"It's not even ten p.m. yet. I'd be asleep if it was."

Donne took a breath. "Okay."

Tammy tilted her chin toward the door. "That bastard lied to me. I want to know why."

"Can you handle more treatments?"

She looked at the ground. "It gets harder every day. I already called Elliot on his bullshit. He won't question it anymore."

"We'll come back for you."

"No. Tell me where Matt lives. I'll get there on my own."

Donne paused for a minute, thinking it over. He gave her the address.

Tammy patted Donne's shoulder. "Okay, tough guy. Go out the window. I can kill five minutes and give you a head start."

"Come with me."

"I'll be fine. I need to stay here. For now."

Donne stood up and walked over to the window.

"You should have killed Manuel," Tammy said.

Donne nodded.

"He was a nice man. To me. He was gentle." Tammy tapped her fingers on her leg. "But you don't leave a man like that alive."

"I won't make the same mistake twice." Donne opened the window. A warm breeze kissed his cheek.

Tammy nodded. "You live, you learn. Right?"

Donne climbed out the window. A second later, Tammy screamed. He heard the door burst open. As he scrambled down the hill, he heard Tammy saying Donne pushed her to the ground.

"That bastard!" Cole shouted. "Did he hurt you?"

Donne moved into the darkness, shuffling as fast as he could without tripping over the bramble.

CHAPTER 46

HERRICK WENT BACK inside. His Uncle Adrik sat on the couch with an ice pack pressed against his nose. Herrick leaned against the doorjamb, arms crossed.

"You put your hand on me," Adrik said.

Herrick said, "Yup."

"Men have died for less."

"You going to kill me, Uncle?"

Adrik shifted on the couch and put the pack of ice down on the table. His nose was turning a fine shade of purple, and it was swollen like a clown's.

Herrick walked over and sat next to him on the couch.

"Call Elliot Cole and tell him not to kill Donne."

"No."

"Uncle, you know my dad needs him. This would make the job that much harder.

Adrik put a hand on Herrick's shoulder. "Why do you think you're still alive? Two are better than one when it comes to bank heists."

"You know this is more than a bank heist."

Adrik stood up from the couch and picked up the ice pack. He walked across the room to the bookcase and stared at the bindings.

"Essentially, that's what it is. Just a lot more money involved."

"Why didn't you tell me about this when I first came to see you?"

Adrik took a book off the shelf and looked at the back cover. Herrick couldn't tell what it was. Adrik re-shelved it.

"Why should I? What advantage does that give me?"

Before Herrick could answer, a telephone rang. Adrik smiled. "Here's the good news."

He walked over to a landline on a table and pressed a button. The speakerphone.

"Tell us, Elliot."

There was a static-y breath and then, "He got away."

Herrick's chest tightened. Adrik's eyes widened.

"The asshole got away. My wife wanted to talk to him. Tammy wanted to—she's not right. It's the chemo."

"Your age is turning you into a fool." Adrik exhaled. "Tell me what happened."

Cole told them through short, raspy breaths. "He jumped out the window. Haskins and Manuel are out looking for him, but they won't find him. Not tonight anyway."

Adrik glanced at Herrick, who stood up and brushed off his pants. Adrik picked up the phone and started talking. Herrick texted his father that Donne was probably on his way and then left the room.

He wanted to talk to Sarah. He missed her.

And he wanted to know what she told Donne.

CHAPTER 47

HERRICK WALKED INTO his apartment forty minutes later and wanted a tumbler of bourbon. But there wasn't time for that. As far as he was concerned, he was on the clock twenty-four seven now. He called out Sarah's name, and she returned with a hey babe.

He settled down on the couch and checked his phone. His dad wrote back a quick *okay* from the burner phone he was using. Herrick put the phone down on the table and sat back, waiting for Sarah. His stomach churned both with hunger and nerves.

Sarah came out of the bedroom in her pajamas, drying her hair with a towel. She sat next to him and put her free hand on his elbow. Herrick left it there. Her fingers were warm against his skin as she traced circles on it.

"You talked to Donne today."

Sarah's hand didn't pull away, but she stopped tracing.

"I did," she said.

"Why?"

"Because I don't want you to ruin your life."

Herrick shifted in his seat, careful to keep Sarah's fingers on his arm.

"I got this," he said.

"Don't get tough with me."

Herrick closed his eyes and forced his body to unwind. He

wanted nothing more than to fall asleep with Sarah next to him. The world could fade away around them like some teenage love song. But that wasn't going to happen.

"It's not toughness. It's my job."

Sarah sat up, and suddenly the skin to skin was gone. "It's not a job. You're not getting paid. You're working with your *dad*."

Herrick opened and closed his hands and felt the blood run through them.

"It's about my mom," he said.

"A mom who abandoned you."

"And she's sick now." Herrick wiped his face. He couldn't figure out what to do with his hands, but they wanted to move. "So none of that other stuff matters."

"Remember last year? When a monster blew up my apartment building?"

Herrick turned and looked at her. "Of course."

"Didn't it seem odd to you that I didn't freak out? That I just moved in?"

Herrick exhaled. "Do we really have time for this right now?"

"You wanted to talk. You started this."

Sarah turned away from him, and her wet hair snapped at the motion. A droplet of water caught Herrick's nose.

"So, tell me. Yes, it was weird. But you were—I wanted you here, so I didn't ask."

"You never asked. You just went with it."

Herrick took a beat and stood up from the couch. "Do you— did you want to be here?"

"Yes. Then and now. I love you."

"I love you too. Except you were going to add a but—"

"There's a reason that explosion didn't faze me. I've seen some shit."

Herrick waited.

"I've been to prison. Like Donne. Before I got my job, before I got my life turned around. I've seen a girl kill another girl for stealing her corn muffin at breakfast. Jammed a shard of plastic in her eye. I don't shake easily."

"Is this one of your 'when I was a kid' lies you tell the students?"

"No. My friend got me to help her steal a car. We got caught."

The words tore through Herrick's body like a shockwave. "But you're normal now."

"Normal is a terrible word, Matt. You know that. It took a long time getting here. And I'm sitting here watching you have panic attacks about your dad and your mom. You aren't in any shape to make good decisions."

"If I can help him, Maybe—"

Sarah turned back to him. "Maybe what?"

"Maybe I can stop him. Maybe I can get him to turn his life around."

Sarah shook her head. "Let him work with Donne. Stay out of it."

"You know I'm in too deep now."

"This is the same mistake my students make. Your players, Matt. They come to me with this stuff. Not you. Remember kicking Andrew Harmon off the team?"

"It's not the same."

Sarah opened her mouth, but before she could speak there was a knock at the door. More like a pounding. They both turned to it. Herrick ran over to the door and opened it.

Jackson Donne stood there, face scratched and completely out of breath.

"We have to talk," Donne said.

"Seems to be the theme of the night," Herrick said.

Donne stepped into the room and gave Sarah a half wave.

"It's about your mom," he said. "She's not sick."

CHAPTER 48

ERRICK BLINKED. AND then he stepped back. And then he was on the couch. Sarah had her arm around him. The edges of his vision were blurring as Donne was talking.

Not again, he told himself. *Enough of this bullshit.*

"Sixteen, fifteen, fourteen, thirteen."

"What are you doing?" Herrick thought it was Donne asking.

"Twelve, eleven, ten, nine, eight."

"You're okay, Matt." Definitely Sarah this time.

He finished counting down. By the time he had, the world had re-focused and he was in his apartment again. Not some twisty, whirly version of that room. He gritted his teeth and counted back up to sixteen, this time in his head.

When he was finished, he said, "What do you mean she's not sick? I saw her."

"Cole is fucking with her. She's been doing chemo, she had a segmentectomy…but according to the paperwork she saw, the cancer was clear after the surgery and one quick round of chemo."

Herrick put his head in his hands. "Jesus Christ."

Donne paced the room. Herrick wondered what he was thinking.

"We have to get her out of there," Herrick said.

Donne shook his head. "I think she can take care of herself."

"You've met her twice."

"I can read people pretty well. Like your girlfriend here. She can—"

"Shut up," Sarah said. "Do you know how messed up that is? Matt, your mom's life is a lie and she's just finding out now. She needs to talk to someone. You're right. Get her out of there."

Donne said, "She told me not to worry about her. That she'd be fine for now."

The silence in the room hung there for a moment. Sarah's body language sagged into the couch. Herrick counted his heartbeats, and felt it slowing down. There was work to be done, and that always distracted him from the panic.

"The big question—do we tell my dad?" he asked.

"No. Let him play it out straight. If he knows, it would complicate things even more."

"They want you dead."

Donne walked over to the window and looked out. There was the usual rumble of partygoers on the street. The squealing of bus brakes.

"Been there," Donne said. "I'm going to have to stick in the background. I'll still help."

Sarah said, "That means Matt has to do more."

"Yeah," Donne said.

Herrick looked at her, but couldn't read her expression.

"I have no choice," he said.

"Yes, you do. Now that you know your mom is okay? Why do you have to do this? Your job with the kids, it'll be gone."

Herrick turned toward her and pulled her in tight. He didn't say a word. Sarah pulled away.

"You're an idiot."

Herrick finally said, "I have to fix this."

"Fix what?" Donne asked. "We're going to rob a—"

"No, we aren't. We're just going to act like we are."

Herrick felt a wave ride through his gut. He thought of Haskins, and his connection to the National Guard. So much money went through the Federal Reserve. They lost billions that should have gone to Iraq in the early part of the century. He needed to know more about Cole. Not just the stories his mom and dad told when they were younger.

"No. There's more to it than that."

"You'd better be right," Donne said.

"I am."

Donne moved toward the door. "Then get some sleep. The next few days are going to be busy."

He left, the door clicking shut behind him. Sarah went over and locked it.

"I'm not going to be a criminal," Herrick said.

"Then what are you doing?"

Herrick took a deep breath.

"Trying to be a hero."

CHAPTER 49

ORMALLY, DONNE WOULD stop for a beer. There were plenty of Hoboken bars to stop at, and he still had a credit card that worked. But he hadn't had a beer since Manuel tried to kill him. For some reason, the alcohol wasn't calling to him.

And he didn't mind.

Instead, he hopped on a train to New Brunswick, his old stomping grounds. He considered looking up Artie again, but after last year it wasn't worth it. He wasn't in the mood for an argument or an icy glare. So he used the burner phone he bought with the computer and left a message on a familiar number. He was happy to hear it was still in service.

If there was a man who had information on local thieves, drug dealers or hitmen, it was Jesus Sanchez. The former cowardly corner dealer grown into big time New Jersey crime lord had connections Donne had since lost during his time hiding in Vermont and stewing in prison.

Forty-five minutes later, Donne got off the train and walked through New Brunswick. It was still early for a college town, just cresting ten p.m. The streets were buzzing with college kids gossiping, stumbling or walking with a purpose. It was a warm spring evening so the bars were jumping even for a Monday night. Donne strode past them and walked into Papa Grande, a BYOB place that served exactly the kind of food college kids wanted. Burgers, burritos, tacos, fries.

Donne was seated by the hostess who put a menu down in front of him. He took the seat facing the door and didn't look at the menu. When the waitress came over, he ordered an iced tea. He kept his eye on the door.

Ten minutes later, and halfway through the iced tea, three men came in and cased the room. Donne shifted in his seat, sliding the butter knife off the table. He held it at his side. The three men took a look around, and then stared long and hard at Donne. Donne nodded at them. They nodded back. One left the restaurant.

When he came back in, he brought Jesus Sanchez with him. Sanchez saw Donne and lit up in a grin. The new — at least new to Donne — scar on his chin burned red, but the rest of him looked exactly like Donne remembered.

"Yoooooooo!" he said, holding the word out as he skipped through the restaurant. Donne stood up and put the knife back on the table. He let Sanchez wrap him up in a huge bear hug, even though Donne had six inches on him.

"I heard you was in prison," Sanchez said. "What happened?"

Donne shrugged. "I got out."

"This is great news. Great news! My man survived." Jesus punched Donne in the arm lightly.

Donne grinned and sat down. Same old Jesus.

"I need help," Donne said.

Jesus nodded. "It's rough when you first get out. You need a little taste to get you back on your feet? I got money, and I won't even charge you interest. Pay me back whenever."

Donne shook his head. "That's not what I need help with."

"My man, already back on his feet. I like it."

He should have taken the money.

"You know Elliot Cole?"

Jesus tilted his head and knit his eyebrows. "Yeah," he said slowly. "Heard of him. Been a while though. Thought he was out of the game."

"He had a guy. Big, tough, burly dude named Manuel. Kind of the muscle for the operation."

Jesus nodded. "Manuel Parada was in a Passaic gang for a while. Tried to encroach on me down here. Good guy, could bust some heads. Wasn't made out for drug dealing though. So he joined the National Guard. I have some friends there, they talked about him. Smart to move to muscle with Cole. Why?"

"He tried to kill me," Donne said. His voice didn't waver.

"That's nuts."

"I should have killed him." Donne whispered it, but Jesus sat back anyway.

"You just got out." Jesus wiped his nose. "That ain't you anyway. Not if you can help it."

"It is who I am. Maybe it's time to embrace it."

Jesus looked at the three men who escorted him in. They were standing at the front door, staring down two college kids who came in to pick up their take-out.

"Why you telling me this? Why you want to meet up with me?"

"I need information. I want to know what Cole and Manuel have been up to the past few years. This whole situation is weird."

"Tell me what you mean." Jesus's voice had lost some of its bounciness.

"It has all the makings of 'one last job,' except Cole is hiring people to pull the job. He could have done it himself."

"Including you?"

Donne shook his head. "He didn't want me on the job. He tried to kill me."

"Maybe he doesn't trust you. I wouldn't."

Donne didn't any anything.

"I am going to have to look into this some more. That phone you called me from. It's a cell."

"Burner."

"Keep it for a little while. I will get you some information."

"That's what you do, Jesus."

"This time, though—you're gonna owe me."

A waitress came over again, but Jesus waved her away. The restaurant was strangely quiet. Donne expected more chatter, but Jesus' men were keeping that clamped down.

"How?"

Jesus shrugged. "We'll talk about that when I get you your info."

"There are a lot of loose threads here. Keep an ear out for a man named Haskins too."

Jesus leaned across the table. "Oh, Jackson. What have you

gotten yourself into this time?"

"Nothing I can't handle."

"Story of your life?"

Donne didn't respond. Jesus threw a twenty on the table. Then he got up and patted him on the shoulder. Then he walked to the front door.

"I'll be in touch very soon," he called. "Maybe, don't even leave."

The bell on the door rang as he opened it.

Donne finished his iced tea.

CHAPTER 50

COLE WASN'T SCARY. He never was. At one point in her life, Tammy actually loved him. After Kenneth went away, Tammy would curl up in Cole's arms and just lay there. No sex. No kissing. No talking. Just warmth and quiet. She *loved* him. And, she was sure, he loved having her.

But now?

As Cole towered over her, face contorted in rage, waving his gun in the air and ranting, Tammy didn't flinch. She stared at him.

"He's gone! You just let Donne climb out the window and run?"

"Elliot."

"How could you? He's going to ruin everything! He's out there doing God knows what."

"Elliot!"

"You ruined everything! You did." The gun barrel was directed at the ceiling and Tammy waited for him to put a bullet in the plaster.

"Elliot," she said.

"What?" he screamed.

"Why did you tell me I still had cancer?" She didn't shout.

"What?" he repeated. This time not as loud.

"I saw the reports on your desk. I am cancer free. Tell me why you did this to me."

Cole opened his mouth and closed it. He lowered the gun to his side. A shadow fell across his face.

"There's always been a plan," he said.

"Maybe you could fill me in on it." Tammy didn't move as she spoke.

"Because," he said. "Because…" His nose scrunched up.

Tammy waited.

"Because how else would I convince him to do this? How else?"

The air went out of Tammy. She sat back down on the bed and waited until her lungs—what was left of them—filled again. This wasn't about her. It never was. What the fuck? It was about some long time ago brotherhood. And Cole screwed with her over that. Lied to her.

Put her through hell.

"You need to let me go, now," she said.

Cole tilted his head.

"Now. I'm out."

He lifted the gun.

"You're going to shoot me, Elliot? After all this?" Tammy spread her hands. "Go ahead. I have nothing left."

Cole held the gun steady. Tammy took a deep breath and stood up. Walked into the gun, pressed the barrel against her chest. She felt it hard against the surgical scar.

"There is nothing else you can do to me, Elliot," she said. "You've pushed me far enough."

The barrel made a mark in her skin. She could feel it.

Cole stared at her.

Tammy looked over his shoulder at the books on the bookcase. Which one would she take with her?

"Let me go," she said. "You've lost me now. And you know it."

The gun remained pressed against her chest. The pressure from the barrel hurt more than the incision did. Tammy's breath was even. The air was cold.

"Or shoot me." Tammy waited a beat. "Either way, make up your mind."

Manuel wasn't there. He promised he would help. But she picked the wrong time. Now she was counting on Cole having some sort of conscience. She held her breath, waiting for the shot to come.

Cole put the gun down.

"Where was Donne going?" he asked.

"I have no idea."

Tammy walked out the room. She kept walking, nightgown and all, until she was halfway up the road.

CHAPTER 51

HERRICK FOUND HIMSELF in Manhattan, in his dad's hotel, just as Kenneth was leaving. And not just for the afternoon. The totally packed up kind of leaving. Herrick spotted Kenneth in the lobby with three black duffel bags, struggling to avoid people trying to check in as he headed toward the door. He couldn't stay out of Herrick's way, however.

"Can I carry one of those for you?" Herrick held out a hand. "Come on, Dad."

Kenneth looked up at him — Matt had him by six inches — and scowled. Then handed over a duffel bag. It was light and didn't clack when it moved, so it had to be clothing. The other two bags rattled with each movement Kenneth made. Herrick assumed those were the computers.

"Where are we going?" Herrick asked.

"It's time to get things started."

Herrick refused to reference *The Muppet Show*, and followed his dad out to the street. His dad stuck out a hand and hailed a cab. A yellow car screeched to a halt in front of them. Synchronicity.

They got into the taxi.

"Where to?"

"Hoboken," Kenneth said.

"That is eighty bucks." The cab driver said it through gritted teeth.

"That's okay. My son can take care of it."

Herrick didn't respond. Instead, as the driver pulled into traffic, he said, "We're going to my place?"

"Don't you remember how this worked when you were a kid?"

Herrick shook his head. "No, I think my nose was in all those basketball strategy books you used to give me when we went on road trips. You didn't want me to know."

Kenneth shrugged. "Had to keep you occupied. I think you always understood what was going on, though."

Herrick stared back at him. He didn't speak.

"You stage at one place, and then when it's time to go, you move on. Don't want the cops to catch up to me."

"That really works? Cops are smart."

They wheeled through traffic toward the Lincoln Tunnel. Herrick tried to make sure the cabbie wasn't taking the long route. He didn't seem to be, and he was managing to avoid red lights. Any time Herrick drove in the city, all he hit was the color red. The shows were getting out now, Manhattan's nightlife switching from the older crowd to the younger folk out for drinks.

Even on a Monday, New York never, ever slowed down.

"We are setting up shop at your place. It's close to the event, and no one is staking it out."

"What about Cole? He knows where I live." A sliver of ice ran down the back of Herrick's spine. He dared not mention Sarah.

"We're doing this *for* Elliot. For Tammy."

"Dad, this doesn't feel right."

"We're going the day after tomorrow."

The cabbie glanced at them in the rearview mirror.

"Oh, fuck you. I'm not a terrorist," Kenneth said.

The cabbie blinked, then hung a quick right. Into the middle of a traffic jam. Dad should have kept his mouth shut. This was going to cost an arm and a leg now.

"And then what?" Herrick asked. "What happens when you're done? Assuming you live through this."

Kenneth sniffled. "I'll be out of your life forever."

"You're blind if you think this is going to work." Herrick shifted in his seat. "Dad, I'm asking you to be smart."

"I need to save your mother."

"Mom isn't sick."

"Don't screw with me."

Herrick hated to drop it on him like that. "Mom doesn't need chemo. Elliot lied to her."

Kenneth cracked his neck. "No. You're lying to me. You think telling me will make me stop."

"I want you to be smart. You got out of jail. You're free, and you're running right back into the muck. Mom doesn't need help — not in this way. We need to save her, but not from cancer. She doesn't have it."

"Stop lying!"

"Dad —"

Kenneth turned toward Herrick. "You've never accepted me or Mom. You needed those books as a distraction from who you are. You went into the Army —"

"Because you got arrested and I had nowhere else to go!"

Kenneth pressed his lips together.

"I had no choice. Mom ran off with Cole. You went to prison. I didn't want to be around for your trial. I didn't want to be in this country. I couldn't handle it. I can teach, Dad. I do it well. And I shouldn't have to teach you that armed robbery is bad. Isn't this a lesson you should have learned a long fucking time ago?"

The cabbie took another turn and suddenly the Lincoln Tunnel's mouth was in front of them — a dark abyss.

"You can run, son. You're a Herrick. This is what we *love*."

"I don't want to run. I want you to be smart."

"You've run from me all your life."

They drove into the tunnel.

As the radio staticked out, Kenneth said, "Day after tomorrow, you earn your last name. We're going to be rich, and we are going to save your mother."

Matt Herrick put his head in his hands and didn't speak until they got to the apartment. Kenneth got out of the cab without even looking at the driver. Herrick paid him with every piece of cash he had.

Herrick let his dad into the apartment, all the while trying to come up with the words to change his mind. They ignored the elevator — too many people were waiting for it — and took the stairs. But they did so in silence. The only sound was the thunk of their shoes on the metal staircase.

They pushed the door open and walked down the hallway.

Herrick took his keys out. He opened the door only to see Sarah standing on the other side.

And his mother lying on the couch, her face pale and ashen.

She said, "Hello."

And Kenneth sank to his knees. The duffel bags clunked to the floor next to him.

"You can't be here," he said.

"Too late," Tammy whispered.

CHAPTER 52

ONNE FINISHED HIS burrito and wanted to lick the empty plate. The owner, a tall guy with a five o'clock shadow and football player build, stared at him. Probably recognized Donne from all the hell that had broken loose a few years ago — the stuff with Bill Martin.

Didn't matter. There was nothing this guy could do about it. Not anymore. Donne didn't really have a chance to think about his freedom. Too much running around with Kenneth; too much worry about Matt Herrick. But right now, Donne was a free man and didn't have the cops on his tail. It was a new feeling. Like someone had moved things out of his way.

Maybe he should take off.

The bell at the entrance jingled, snapping Donne out of his reverie. He looked up and saw Jesus walk in. This time he was alone. He nodded at the owner, who winked at him. Donne checked the window and saw Jesus' entourage standing on the sidewalk, hands in their pockets.

Donne's back muscles tightened up like a snare drum.

Jesus took a seat on the other side of the table and took his phone out of his pocket. He looked at it for a few seconds while tapping the screen. Donne breathed through his nose and out through his mouth, as if running a 5K.

"Neil Haskins is a doctor, no?" Jesus tapped on the screen some more.

Donne shrugged. "I know nothing about him."

"He's a doctor, oncology. But off the record."

Donne didn't get it. "I don't get it."

"It's not our thing, my guys and me. We have our own health insurance, but Neil Haskins worked for the National Guard for a long time. I talked to some of my buddies out there. They said he's good at what he does."

Donne said, "Okay." Like *move it along.*

"He was kind of crazy. Some misdiagnosis with some of the guardsmen—said it was stage five testicular cancer. Wasn't. Crazy too. General said he was 'aloof.' So they let him leave a little early. They also didn't like that he fell in love with Parada."

Donne shifted in his seat. Kind of started to see where this was going now. Tammy. He should have seen it a while ago, but he was a step slow these days.

"This guy, I guess Cole hired him next."

Jesus nodded.

"Yes. I guess Cole's wife had cancer. Cole found him through Manuel—since they were lovers, you know."

"You talked to some of Manuel's former gang buddies too?"

Jesus shrugged. "I talk to a lot of people.. No Dr. Haskins, administered some chemo and spread the word of how great Cuban medication was."

Donne asked, "Neil. Is he cheap help?"

"Fuck no," Jesus said. "None of these guys are cheap. He cost an arm and a leg."

"Cole was supposed to have used his last dollar to bust us out of jail."

Jesus started laughing. "His last dollar? My boys say Cole is worth a pretty penny. Still."

Donne tilted his head. The gears were starting to click into place. He tried to remember what Kenneth was like in prison. What he talked about. It was always stories. The glory of the job.

And how Tammy wanted out.

Donne stood up.

Jesus' head snapped up. "Where you going? I ain't done."

"I have to go talk to my partner."

"You got a partner? Shit, you been busy since you got out."

"I need one more thing, Jesus. Guns."

Jesus laughed. "Oh, yeah. Hold up. I got that right in my trunk."

Donne waited.

"Get the fuck outta here, Jackson. I don't have that. You know what my thing is. You want that stuff, you know who you should talk to?"

"Who?"

"Your old buddy. The one who was in Nam. He's got friends. Isn't that how you first met?"

Donne ignored Jesus and headed for the front door. Artie wasn't the guy to see about this. He wondered if he missed the last train to Hoboken.

They weren't trying to save Tammy. That wasn't what this was about. This was about Elliot Cole and Kenneth Herrick making one last go of it. One more job. For the record books.

And Donne was right in the middle.

As usual.

Donne burst through the front door and Jesus' entourage stared at him.

"Thanks for the help," he mumbled. They nodded back at him.

Donne pulled the burner phone and scrolled through the few saved numbers he had. He almost clicked on Kenneth's cell but ignored it. Instead, he went for Matt Herrick. His finger hovered over the call button, but stopped there too.

No, there was one more number he kept. The one he kept since he was in the coffee shop.

He dialed Sarah Cullen. She answered after two rings.

"Are you alone?"

Sarah said, "Who is this?"

"Jackson Donne."

"Oh, I didn't recognize—"

"Are you alone?" Donne found himself running, but didn't know why. There wasn't anything he could do at the moment, but the adrenaline pouring through his veins propelled him.

"No. They're all here. Both Herricks…" She paused to chuckle. "And Tammy. You lose their numbers?"

"No," Donne said. "But you gotta separate Matt from the group. I have to talk to him privately."

"Is that Donne? Why didn't he call me?" It was Kenneth in the background. "We need him here."

"Hold on," Sarah said. "Can you just get up here?"

Donne shook his head. What other choice did he have?

"I'll be there as soon as I can."

"Good," Sarah said. "Maybe you can talk some sense into them. Like we talked about."

Donne ended the call. He hoped he could do better than that. The coolness of the air made his sweat feel like ice. The train station was empty. On the board was a schedule saying another Hoboken train was due in fifteen minutes. The air in Donne's lung caught. A stroke of luck.

His burner phone rang again. This time it was Kenneth. Donne answered.

"You on your way?" Kenneth asked.

"Yeah. Be there in an hour and a half."

"Good. We need you." There was a moment of silence. Then, "You made me step away from my family to call you. You made me walk away from my work."

Donne didn't say anything. His prison days made him want to apologize, but he kept his mouth shut.

"Also," Kenneth said, his voice lowering into a whisper. "You were lucky to leave when you did. Elliot talked to a few people today. Paid a couple of guys. They just took care of your friend Jesus."

The phone call ended. Then it buzzed with a picture message. Donne opened it. Jesus Sanchez and his three men were lying on the sidewalk, bullet ridden and lifeless, outside Papa Grande.

PART III

SLAYGROUND

CHAPTER 53

ERRICK SAT NEXT to his mother, arm around her. She leaned against him, her eyes fluttering and her breath soft and even. Herrick gave her a quick squeeze. Sarah was in the kitchen making tea. Kenneth had stepped out to call Donne. On the TV, two NBA teams went at it, running way more isolation plays than Herrick could tolerate.

Tammy was quiet. Herrick wasn't sure she'd said more than six words in over an hour. But that was okay. She was here.

That was different.

He expected to go into full PTSD mode when he first saw her—the shakes, the heavy breathing, the sweats. A true panic attack. But that didn't happen. In fact, the usual adrenaline surge went away when he hugged her, some instinct from his childhood kicking in. He felt safe with her around.

And he wanted to protect her.

Kenneth stormed back into the apartment. He slammed the door so hard, Tammy shuddered in Herrick's arms. Kenneth slapped the phone down on the table and started pacing the room. He was the one going through PTSD, that was for sure.

"Cole is going to come for her," Herrick said. "He's going to track her down."

"No, no, no." Kenneth kept pacing. "No, he's not."

Herrick gave his mom another squeeze and then gently eased his arm from around her.

Herrick walked away from the couch over to the window, forcing his dad to follow. Outside the window, a bird fluttered its wings as it searched for food on the ledge. There didn't appear to be anything to eat waiting for him, but the bird walked back and forth anyway. Herrick tapped on the pane and it flew away.

Kenneth stood next to him. They didn't make eye contact.

"He loved Mom and she ran from him. He's crazy. He's going to want her back. We are going to have to hide her."

"No. We do the job. As long as Cole has the money, he won't care."

Herrick shook his head. "Why did he lie to her? That's cruel, even for Cole."

"When Cole told me about the job, he told me about Tammy's illness. And how it could save her. Get her to Cuba. This place, they've lost money before. Billions that was supposed to go to Iraq. But we need you."

Herrick shook his head. "Or Neil Haskins. Or Manuel."

"What do you mean?"

"You need a military guy, don't you? I'm retired, and Haskins is in the National Guard. I don't know what you're going to use one of us for, but you need us."

"Haskins was never part of the plan. You were."

Down on the street, Herrick saw Donne crossing Washington and approaching the apartment.

"Why?"

Kenneth shook his head.

"Dad, secrets time is up. Lay it all on the table. You want me to help you with a crime that could get us put away for life. Or worse, the death penalty."

"You don't have to worry about that."

"How the hell do you know? Jesus. Spill it, Dad. The whole plan. What's going on?"

Kenneth tilted his chin toward the window. "Jackson's here. I'm going to go talk to him on the street."

"Dad."

Kenneth walked to the door. "Take care of you mother. It will all become clear soon. Promise."

"Like hell," Herrick said, but the door clicked shut before Kenneth responded.

Sarah put the tea on the coffee table, and Herrick considered bourbon instead. She walked over and gave him a kiss on the cheek, and then looked at Tammy.

"How are you feeling, Mrs. Cole?"

Tammy sat up, leaned over and picked up the tea with two hands. She took a long sip. "Call me Tammy. Please. And I'm tired. I need to sleep."

"You can have the bed, Mom. Sarah, you don't mind the couch tonight, do you?"

Sarah smiled. "Where are you going to sleep?"

"I probably won't. Not tonight."

Tammy said, "You have to rest."

"No, Mom. I need to think."

Tammy pushed herself off the couch and headed toward the bedroom. "Elliot said he lied to me to get your dad involved. But that—I don't know. It feels wrong. There's more. But I can't focus right now."

Herrick watched her go into the bedroom. And then he turned to Sarah.

"You going to work tomorrow?"

Sarah nodded. "Kids need me too."

"Can you get her out of here first? A hotel or something. Some place comfortable that has room service."

Sarah smiled. "I got your credit card number."

Herrick turned back toward the window.

"Matt," she said. "I'm worried about this. Be smart."

"I'm trying," he said.

"Come on. I'm not going to leave you alone. I'm staying."

Sarah left the room, and Herrick's phone buzzed. He looked at the caller ID and saw it was a number he didn't recognize. He answered anyway.

It was Christenson.

"Herrick. The media is going to go with this in an hour, but I wanted you to know first, since you're involved."

Herrick sucked in air.

Christenson continued, businesslike. "The day you were here, when the alarm went off, we lost a rocket launcher. And some other guns. MPs are going to come talk to you in the morning. But you were with me the entire time. We were looking for your buddy. Got me?"

Herrick dropped the phone.

CHAPTER 54

DONNE SAW KENNETH leave the apartment building, looking directly at him. Donne broke into a sprint, and brakes screeched as he crossed the street. Kenneth didn't flinch or run. He stood there grinning.

Grabbing Kenneth by the shirt, Donne said, "I should kill you."

Kenneth spread his hands, leaning back so Donne was holding him up by his shirt.

"Uh-huh. You keep saying you should have. You're too weak. Prison broke you," he said. "And let's say you do. What happens then?"

"We can go back to our lives."

Kenneth brushed Donne's hand away. Donne flexed his hands into fists. But didn't step forward. Kenneth brushed a winkle out of his shirt, something Donne had seen him do a thousand times back in prison.

"What life is that, Jackson?"

Donne didn't say anything. A couple of onlookers stopped, and then, when Donne didn't throw a punch, kept walking.

"Come on, tell me," Kenneth said. "What life?"

Donne breathed in through his nose.

"Yeah. That's what I thought. I'm all you've got. Without me, where are you going to go? You can't go back to New Brunswick.

You're not going to be able to get a real job or go back to Rutgers or do any of that stuff you told me about before Kate died." Kenneth's grin grew. "That's right. Don't you remember all that down time? All the shit you told me about your life? I know you, Jackson. I know you better than anyone knows you. I know you better than I know my own fucking son."

Donne cocked his fist back. More onlookers stopped. One took out a cell phone. Donne gritted his teeth so hard his jaw hurt. Kenneth didn't move. Donne exhaled. He put his fist down. The cell phone guy booed. The crowd dissipated and they were alone.

"You killed a friend of mine," Donne said.

Kenneth shook his head. "I didn't. Elliot Cole didn't. Could have been anyone."

Donne turned around and stared at the traffic. He should have saved the image on his phone, the burner. But the shock of the blood and the eyes without vision shook Donne and he deleted it immediately. Now, he realized, as the adrenaline peeled away from him, how stupid that was. Evidence gone. A signed text message with images of a dead body on it.

You're slipping, he told himself. But then wondered if actually he was. Maybe the ties to Kenneth were right. How many times did he have to save Donne's life in jail?

"Have you been playing me this entire time?" Donne asked.

"I don't understand what you mean."

"Since Matt gave me your name, you protected me. You kept me alive in jail. You broke Luca Carmine's neck in front of everyone. And still you got out. And you brought me with you. Since you got my name, have you been planning on bringing me with you?"

Kenneth came up next to him. They both stood on the curb watching traffic stop and start. The one-way streets of Hoboken that intersected with Washington were clogged with cars waiting for green lights. Washington was packed with cars looking for parking. The Hoboken way.

"I have known about Cole's idea for a long time. But we didn't have a plan until I met you. Until my son was involved. A stroke of luck, I guess."

Donne said, "Yeah. I have the best luck."

Kenneth said, "You have no life now, but imagine what you could do when we finish the job. What just a million would buy you. You could track down that woman—what was her name? Jeanne? You could find her. Make things right."

Donne felt the emptiness in his stomach. He didn't want Jeanne back, though a part of him wanted to track her down again. He wanted Kate back, and that would never happen. Maybe he could return to Vermont.

But a heist of this size was a death sentence, nothing less.

"What about Tammy?"

Kenneth didn't respond.

"Did you know? Did you know her results were faked?" Donne said the words, but didn't want to hear the answer.

Kenneth rubbed his hands together.

For an instant, Donne's stomach muscles relaxed. He though Kenneth wasn't going to answer.

"Know?" Kenneth put his hands back in his pockets. "It was my idea."

The air went out of Donne and his stomach turned. He coughed to cover up the physical reaction of flinching.

"How do you think we would get her to agree to be an accomplice? While I don't think she enjoyed seeing me go to prison, she loved her new life. She wasn't my Bonnie anymore. She was a *Real Housewife of New Jersey*—once she wasn't hiding anymore. We needed to find a reason for her to go back to the old ways. She was sick. We just extended her illness."

Donne burned inside. "You put her through that?"

"She could have stayed with me." Kenneth worked his jaw. "But she let me go to prison."

Donne turned toward Kenneth and pushed him. Pushed him again. Kenneth scuttled backward along the curb.

One more push, Donne thought. One more and Kenneth would trip into the street. Someone looking for a parking spot wouldn't see him and run him over. That was all it would take. And Donne could move on with life.

Kenneth knew it too.

"You won't do it."

Donne paused.

"You're a *chicken*. You couldn't even kill Manuel, and he was fodder for you."

"A test?"

Kenneth nodded.

"I chose to go to jail. It was me. I pled guilty. It was the only way to keep my friends safe. And then you expect me to kill someone? Death is what I'm running from."

"It's the only way to fix a problem. Of course, killing me won't stop anything. Everything is already in motion. I'm just a cog. Not the entire wheel. Alive or dead, this goes down morning after tomorrow."

Donne put his arms down and Kenneth straightened up.

"Why did Manuel come after me?" Donne asked.

Kenneth cracked his neck. "Elliot thinks you're too much of a wild card. He didn't trust you. I did. But I wanted to see what you were made of."

"Maybe you and Cole should stop playing games."

Kenneth shook his head. "But that's the fun! Elliot loves the spotlight, the planning. And he thinks he's better than me."

"I'm leaving," Donne said.

"If you go, you're a dead man." Kenneth pulled open his jacket to reveal a pistol. Donne also caught glimpse of a piece of yellow paper sticking out of his jacket pocket.

"I don't care about the witnesses. I'll shoot you right here on the street. That's the difference between you and me. I'll do it."

"You're crazy."

Kenneth shook his head back and forth as if to say, "Maybe."

"You will stay with us and you will keep Matt on the straight and narrow until this is over."

Donne said, "Matt is your son and you're going to force him to lose everything."

Kenneth grinned. "But now he has his family back."

CHAPTER 55

THEY MOVED AWAY from the curb, and moved close to the apartment building wall. The heat pulsated from the bricks — which had been holding it all day like a pizza oven. Sweat started to soak Donne's hair. It was only April.

Kenneth leaned in. "Don't you see? This is about putting the past right and getting my family back together. The people I lost when I took the fall for Cole."

Donne flared his nostrils. "And you dragged me along. Almost got me killed."

Kenneth shook his head. "That's Matt's fault. He could have stayed quiet, never told you about me."

"And then I'd be dead in prison."

Kenneth laughed. "And, judging by your demeanor, happy about it."

"Shut up," Donne said. "This is insane. It always has been insane. You can't rob a federal building. Not one like this."

"I have a plan."

"I'm not a criminal. Your son is not a criminal."

"How many people have you killed, Jackson?"

Kenneth went straight to the dagger. Years ago, a question like that would have sent Donne spiraling. He would have lost days in the bar, drowning in beer. All the blood on his hands that took hours to scrub clean from his skin. The bruises. The powder burns. All those reminders that he was a murderer.

This was who he was.

"Doesn't matter."

"It doesn't?" Kenneth looked out at the traffic, then back to Donne. "You're telling me all those bodies you piled up don't matter? That it's not worse to kill tens of people over stealing money from the government? After all they've taken from us? From you? Years of our lives behind bars. Millions in taxes. Our rights. The government closes its fist around us every single day, and you're telling me taking a little from them is worse than what you do? Think about it, Jackson. How many have you killed?"

Donne chewed the inside of his lip. "I'm out of here."

"Then I'll call the police."

"And say what? And say *what*? That you're going to heist millions from a government facility? Good. That will take care of everything."

"No, you idiot."

Donne shook his head and started to walk away. Back toward the train station. Back to figure out what he was going to do next with his life.

"All I need to do is leave an anonymous tip with the NYPD."

Donne froze.

"Or maybe Elliot can do it, though I think he'd rather get his own revenge. But if you run?"

Donne turned back around to see Kenneth standing there, hands spread as if to say, "What do you got?"

"Think about it, Jackson. I leave one anonymous tip that I know who killed Bryan Hackett, or that Mosby. Any of your targets. Cops are good at their jobs. I say your name and I'm sure someone will recognize it. I'll put you on their radar again. Which has to be the last thing you want."

Donne exhaled. A bus leaned on its horn, piercing his eardrums. A group of drunks stumbled out of the bar on the corner laughing and shouting. Monday night drinking—a young person's game.

"You don't want to run again, not from the police."

"Like I won't have to run after executing your plan. From people more powerful than the police."

Kenneth shook his head. "Think about it. Right now, what do

you have? A credit card that's barely holding on before they shut it down? After we finish the job, you'll have millions. A lot easier to hide when you have money. New name. New life. Last time you told me you tried Vermont because of the beer. What's next? Colorado? They have some good stuff I hear. But you walk away right now? With nothing? My tip will be fucking specific. They *will* find you."

"I already put myself in jail. I can do it again."

Kenneth nodded. "You can. Sure. But last time you had me, right? Do you remember the six months before I came along? Watching your back every day? Do you think your arm healed as best it could? Does your brain work as well after those concussions? If they knew what happened to you in prison, those guys suing the NFL would have a field day on the penitentiary system."

A chill ran through Donne's stomach. New York prison would be worse. He didn't know anyone, and he wasn't about to play crazy to get protection. It wasn't in him. Prison wasn't fun, it was penance. And now that he was free again, he realized that maybe he'd repaid his sins.

Before he added more to the list, anyway.

Donne took a deep breath and then said, "What do you need from me?"

"To help. Follow the plan, stay out of my way."

"I want to know why Elliot wants me dead."

Kenneth nodded. "We have thirty-six hours before go time. We might be able to get some answers before then."

"Leave Matt out of this. I don't want him to become like me."

"You're not going to say a word to him. Nothing. This will make him whole. This will be my legacy. He'll finally be my son."

"Jesus. How did I not realize you were this crazy in prison?"

"Everyone in prison is crazy. Right on down to Fred Aguilera, our warden friend. No one ever notices." Kenneth went toward the front door. "Let's go upstairs. You can meet the whole family at once. And then we get to work."

Donne hesitated. He could run. He could stay ahead of the cops long enough to get back on his feet. Maybe Colorado would be nice.

But Matt Herrick was upstairs, holding on to life. Donne had thrown his away. He couldn't let that happen again.

And if Donne left, he would leave Herrick all alone.

It was time to pay Kenneth back for all the prison help. But maybe not the way Kenneth wanted.

He followed Kenneth into the apartment building.

CHAPTER 56

ERRICK LOOKED AROUND his apartment. The only thing missing was his basketball team. If they had been there, every important person in his life would be cramming their way in. As it was, with Donne, Kenneth, Sarah and Tammy here, it felt crowded.

Sarah was getting Tammy into bed, and Herrick could hear whispering. He wondered what Sarah was saying. Or was it Tammy talking? He hoped she would sleep. She needed it. They had to get her to a real doctor soon.

The other two, Donne and Kenneth, stood on opposite sides of the room. Donne was staring out the window while Kenneth was rooting through the kitchen. He had mentioned something about chips, but Herrick didn't keep those at home. He went bare bones, buying enough groceries for the week and keeping the crappy snacks away. Somehow, he thought he was sending a message to his team, even though they'd never been in his apartment. Sarah kept trying to get him to buy kale chips, but that was not happening.

"So," Kenneth said, slamming a cabinet shut. "Since there's nothing to eat, let's talk."

Herrick sat down on the couch. Donne still didn't face them. A ripple went down Herrick's back.

"Okay," Herrick said. "Talk."

"Well, Mr. Military, we need you."

"So you've said."

Donne turned from the window. His face was unreadable.

"You know the routines. You know how to act like you've been there before. You were military. You have to predict how they're going to respond. We need a strategy. We have the weapons. We need a plan."

Herrick bit his lip.

"Manuel already robbed the National Guard base. He and Haskins are military. You don't need me."

Kenneth blinked. "I don't need. I want. God damn it. The plan was my idea. And you're my son. My family. This is my plan! Not Elliot's."

Donne opened his mouth and Kenneth shot him a look. Again the ripple went down Herrick's back.

"Dad, walk away."

Kenneth slammed his fist down on the coffee table. The noise of the strike was so loud it made Sarah poke her head out of the bedroom.

"We are doing this!" Kenneth's voice burned fire from his mouth. "You are my son and you will listen to me."

Herrick shook his head. "Just two men with horrendous egos. One pissed because he didn't get his face on TV ten years ago, and another pissed because he lost ten years of playing the game."

Kenneth's nose crinkled and his nostrils flared.

"Kenneth," Donne said. His voice was even.

Kenneth's head snapped up in Donne's direction and his face relaxed. Herrick hadn't seen his dad react like that in a long time. If ever.

"Sorry," Kenneth said. "It's the stress."

Donne shot Kenneth another look, and this one was easy to read. Something along the lines of, "Tell him." Now Herrick's stomach cramped.

Sarah came out of the bedroom, looked around the living room and shook her head.

"Your mom's asleep," she said.

"You can't be here," Kenneth said.

"She lives here," Herrick said.

"Jesus Christ."

And they waited, silently, as if some momentous occasion was about to occur. Like waiting to see if the superstar would hit the shot at the buzzer. But nothing happened.

"Sarah," Herrick finally said.

"It's a school night," she said. "I'm not going anywhere."

"What time do you start work in the morning, dear?" Kenneth's voice was like strawberry syrup.

"I'll be out of here by seven."

Kenneth sat on the easy chair and reclined it. "We'll talk tomorrow, then."

Donne sat on the floor and put his head in his hands. Herrick shook.

Sarah came and sat next to him on the couch and put her head on his shoulder. He remembered this from a year and a half ago, the first time she did it—just hours after her apartment exploded. The last place he expected to be was here, potentially throwing his life away.

Herrick closed his eyes. Soon the tremors stopped, and he was asleep too.

CHAPTER 57

DONNE MOVED FROM the carpet to the wall and sat in the darkness. The slow breathing of the Herrick's sleep cycle kept rhythm in the room. Donne tried to rest, but sleep was not going to come.

After talking to Kenneth on the street, Donne realized there was only one way to make sure this was over with only minor collateral damage. He watched the clock. Three a.m. would be the witching hour. There would be other steps, but tonight was step one.

The clock ticked away the minutes, and then the hours. More and more, Donne was convinced this was the way to go. Too often in his career he reacted instead of being proactive. Someone had to die — usually someone close to him — before he made moves he needed to. If he had acted sooner, Katie would be alive. Mario would be alive. Even Bill Martin would still be alive. And already this time around, Jesus was dead. He was always a step too late.

Donne always chose to wait. And things then went to hell.

No more.

Three o'clock in the morning. He checked the time on the burner phone and then the cable box display to confirm. The time didn't matter, more that it needed to be late enough that no one was on the streets in Hoboken. On a Monday — no, now it was early Tuesday morning — the streets would be clear for sure. Even the hipsters didn't stay out too late on a random April Monday.

Donne stood up and edged over to Kenneth's seat on the couch. He watched his chest rise and fall for a moment before touching his shoulder. Kenneth jerked awake, eyes wide. He was about to say something, but Donne had a finger over his own lips. *Be quiet.*

Kenneth nodded.

Donne shook his head toward the door—*Let's take a walk.*

Kenneth nodded again and then inched himself out of the chair. He slipped on his shoes and then followed Donne into the hallway.

Once there, Kenneth said, "What's up?"

Donne shook his head. "Not here. Let's get outside."

They took the elevator down to the lobby. Donne led the way onto the street, which was now completely empty.

"Okay," Kenneth said. "What's up?"

This was the moment Donne had to sell Kenneth. To keep things from getting any worse, he had to get Kenneth to go along with his plan. He only needed ten minutes.

"Before I got to the apartment, you know, before you flashed a gun at me, I was coming to tell you something important. I wanted to show you something. It could help us. It's over near the train station. I saw it on my walk back here."

Kenneth said, "No. Tell me first."

"You know," Donne said, "the best leaders take advice from all corners. Take a look at this thing. I can't really describe it well. Kind of a car, but I think it can help."

Kenneth exhaled. "You woke me up at three in the morning for this?"

Donne shrugged. "I think we're going to have to steal it."

A glint appeared in Kenneth's eye. "Show me."

They walked down Washington to first and hung a left. Donne kept Kenneth a step behind, moving at a quick pace.

"Relax," Kenneth said. "Don't be nervous. You'll draw attention."

Donne pointed toward a narrow alleyway. "It's just up here."

Kenneth harrumphed, but before he could protest, Donne turned right up the corridor. A rat scuttled out of the way behind a small dumpster. On the other end, Donne could see the street. It was clear. Now or never.

"There's noth—"

Donne whirled around and caught Kenneth with a straight right. He felt the cartilage of Kenneth's nose crunch under his knuckles. Kenneth's head snapped back and an arc of blood followed it. He took a step backward and brought his hands up to his face. His jacket opened and Donne caught the glint of gun metal.

Do it fast, he thought.

Donne maneuvered inward and caught him with two body blows. The air went out of Kenneth with a whoosh. Donne connected his elbow to Kenneth's jaw and Kenneth went down to one knee. He wasn't screaming, instead making a small whining noise. Donne grabbed him by the back of his head and slammed it down into the asphalt ground with a sickening thud.

Kenneth managed, "I protected you."

Donne kicked him in the ribs. Hard.

"No," Kenneth hissed.

Donne didn't respond. He just brought the heel of his shoe down on Kenneth's head. An instant later, Kenneth was motionless and silent except for a soft gurgle. Donne waited until the gurgle stopped.

He rolled Kenneth on his back and dragged him into a sitting position against the dumpster. His face was hamburger and Donne bit his lip to keep from vomiting. He felt a trickle of blood run down his chin.

Reaching into Kenneth's jacket pocket, he found an envelope. It was yellow and thick. Donne opened it and flipped through. Ben Franklins. Just like the thick pack he had when they got out of prison. Maybe a hundred of them. Maybe more.

Kenneth certainly wasn't broke. Donne pocketed the envelope. A nest egg.

Then, he pulled the burner phone out. His second burner. The one he hadn't used yet but figured he'd need after the heist. He flipped it open, accessed the camera and snapped a picture. He opened the picture in a text and wrote, *Now I'm in charge*, and sent it to the other phone he'd been using. When that phone beeped, he checked to make sure the picture was clear.

It was.

He sent picture messages to two different phone numbers.

Donne destroyed the phone he used to take the photo and made his way back to Herrick's apartment. As he walked, he took his pulse. It ran at a pace equal to a short jog. The adrenaline that had been coursing through his system had already faded. He didn't even want a beer. He hadn't wanted one in almost three days.

He wondered what had changed in him. Was it prison? Maybe. Running for your life every minute of the day did things to a person.

But he'd seen so much violence in his life, so many people close to him had died, that prison didn't affect him.

Not as much as everything else. It was like all the murders he'd seen, and even the ones he'd committed, had reached inside him and changed his DNA.

Whatever.

This was who he was now.

And this was how he'd accomplish his goals and keep good people from dying.

His next goal was to break the news to Matt Herrick. Step two.

CHAPTER 58

DONNE SLIPPED BACK into the apartment building. He'd used the bathroom in the train station to wash the blood off his hands and shoes. At that time of night, only a few homeless watched him come and go.

Herrick snapped awake on the couch. That old military instinct that kept you alive when you most needed it to still swirled inside. For a second the air went from Donne. Did Herrick see Kenneth and Donne sneak out together?

"Is everything okay?" Herrick asked. "Where's my dad?"

He looked around the room and shifted his weight on the couch. Sarah turned her head and snuggled deeper into the cushions. Herrick got up and walked over to Donne.

"Tell me," he said.

Donne shook his head. "Not here. Out in the hall. Your mom has to sleep."

Herrick followed him into the hallway and closed the door behind them with a quiet *click*. Donne opened and closed his hands. He blinked a few times. He had to get this right.

"You okay? You're shaking."

"It's not good, Matt."

"Tell me." Herrick looked down the hall toward the elevator. "Where is my dad?"

Donne pulled out the good burner phone and flipped it open. He pulled up the picture of a bloody Kenneth Herrick and took a deep breath.

"This is really bad," he said. "At around one in the morning, your dad snuck out to see Elliot Cole. After two hours, I got really nervous and went to see if I could find him. I couldn't but I got a text from Cole a few minutes ago. It's bad, Matt."

Donne passed the phone to Herrick, who looked at the screen. He immediately recoiled as if he'd been punched.

"Jesus Christ," Herrick said.

"I'm sorry."

"Jesus Christ!"

Herrick dropped the phone and it bounced across the paisley carpet. Donne leaned over and picked it up. He gave Herrick a minute to catch his breath. Herrick didn't seem like he was going to puke, and once again Donne noticed that military background.

This guy had seen some shit.

"That's my…" Herrick sputtered. "That's my…"

Donne nodded. "Yeah. And it was Cole who sent me this text. Cole did that."

Herrick rubbed his face and then shook his head like he was getting water out of his hair. "I barely knew him. Not since I was eighteen."

"I know, kid." Kid? Donne was only a few years older than Herrick.

Herrick blinked it out, and then looked at Donne. "Are you okay?"

The words caught Donne off guard. "What do you mean?"

"He got you through prison. He got you *out* of prison. You knew him better than I did. To me, he was an asshole who left me out to dry. But to you…" Herrick trailed off.

Donne took a deep breath. "Your part of this is over now. I'm going to get Cole, and then I'll be finished also."

"What are you talking about?"

"Cole is still going to go after the reserve. You know that. Think about it, he had the same pieces as we did. The muscle in Manuel, the military guy in Haskins."

Herrick pinched the bridge of his nose. "I have a guy I can call. He works in corrections. Mack. He'll help."

"No," Donne said. "I want this one."

"Don't be stupid, Jackson."

Donne's stomach muscles knotted. Adrenaline surged through him, which was odd since it barely did when he was with Kenneth.

"No! Cole is mine. He got us out of that hellhole, but your dad kept me alive. Cole is mine."

"You can walk away, Jackson. Start anew. This doesn't have to be your life anymore. It shouldn't even be mine. I can go back to coaching. And menial work like peeping on future divorcees. You can start your life over. Let Mack take care of this now. Let's give him everything we have, and then walk away."

Donne shook his head. Electricity ran up his arms. This was not step two. Step two was Herrick breaking down into a puddle of emotion, telling Donne to do what needed to be done and walking away. He wasn't following the script.

"Fine," Donne said. "Call your man."

"I have to tell Mom. I have to tell Sarah. I'm supposed to meet with the military police tomorrow to talk about the robbery at the National Guard base."

"Fuck."

"What are you going to do?"

Donne shook his head. He needed to clear it. He needed to calm down. Maybe going through law enforcement was the smartest move.

"I need to get out of here."

"Stay until the sun comes up. Jackson, you're not handling this well."

Always so damn impulsive. Even when he planned things out, he was impulsive. But Kenneth was crazy too. He was going to ruin them, all in the name of putting his family together. Getting his son in the family business. He should just tell Herrick that. Tell him everything.

His dad was a bad man, and deserved to die. It was the only way. But the words wouldn't come.

"No," Donne said. "Call your guy. I have to go away. Get a clean start."

"Will I hear from you?"

When this is all over, he thought.

"Maybe," he said. "I don't know."

Donne turned to leave.

He heard Herrick mumble something about his father, and

thought about turning back.

Instead, he kept walking to the elevator. He pressed the button to call it. Behind him, the door to Herrick's apartment closed. The elevator dinged and the doors opened. Donne went down to the street. It was close to five a.m. There were delivery trucks out dropping off bread to some of the restaurants.

Donne kept walking. He didn't know where he was going to go, but he knew he couldn't be in Hoboken when they found Kenneth Herrick.

CHAPTER 59

ELLIOT COLE CLOSED out the picture message on his phone. He put the phone down and choked back the bile. Manuel's face didn't look *that* bad. He took a breath, pushed himself out of bed and woke Haskins and his partner.

"We need sleep, Boss," Haskins said.

Cole ushered them into the living room and then went to put on coffee. He needed to get the sick taste out of his mouth, and he knew he wouldn't be sleeping for quite some time.

When he came back in, Neil was resting his head on Manuel's shoulder. Cole put the coffee down and sat across from them.

"Kenneth Herrick is dead. Someone caved in his face." Cole didn't show them the picture message. "I'm glad you're both here."

Haskins said, "You didn't think it was us, did you?"

Cole cracked his neck and then took a sip of coffee. The bitterness washed away the bile.

"We are going to have to go bare bones on this one now."

Manuel leaned forward, Cole edged away from him.

"What do you mean?"

"No more Kenneth means no Matt and no Donne. Those were Kenneth's guys, and I don't want them near us. In fact, this can't go any further."

Manuel stood up. The black eye had finally started to clear.

"What do you mean?"

Cole licked his lips. "I mean tomorrow, you go over there and you take them all out. Matt, the girl..."

Manuel breathed in through his nose and clenched his hands into fists. Haskins patted him on the leg.

"What about Tammy?"

Cole waited a beat, then said, "Her too."

Manuel kicked the table over. The coffee cup flew and brown liquid splattered all over the wall. The ceramic mug shattered, pieces clattering down against the hardwood floors.

"She is your *wife*."

"And I can't trust her. She ran from us, Manuel." Cole stared at the puddle spreading on the ground, some of it soaking into the throw rug. "She knows too much. She's angry and Matt has her ear. You don't know what she'll do. In less than thirty-six hours, we are going to be four of the richest men alive."

Manuel tilted his head. "You convinced Adrik?"

"It didn't take much."

Haskins stood up and put his arm around Manuel.

"I won't kill her, Elliot. She's been too good to me through the years. When I was having those flashbacks to my high school days...the rituals. She talked me through it. We were trying to help her. She can't—"

Haskins put a finger to his lips and turned to Cole. "I'll do it. I was basically doing it anyway, with the chemo. When the sun comes up, I will take care of them."

Manuel turned toward Haskins, but didn't say anything. Haskins left the room.

Cole put his face in his hands. This was all falling apart, but he only needed to hold it together for a few more hours. Adrik would be here when the sun came up.

"How can we pull this gig with only four of us?" Manuel asked.

Cole shook his head. "We have a god damn rocket launcher. How can we fail?"

"There was supposed to be seven of us. Against the Army."

Cole grinned. "Just think, when this is all over, everyone will know us. Will know our faces."

Manuel shook his head. "You're losing your mind, Elliot. I want to enjoy the damn money."

Cole nodded. "You will. I promise. Just one more day."

CHAPTER 60

S ARAH WAS AWAKE when Herrick came back inside. She wiped
her eyes and watched him go into the kitchen. He started to
make coffee. It was early enough to be awake, and there wasn't
any way he would get to sleep now.

"What is it?" she said.

Herrick remembered he didn't have a good poker face. Still, he
didn't answer her. He couldn't bring himself to utter the words.
Not yet. He scooped grounds into the filter.

Sarah got up off the couch, stretched and walked over to him.

"Matt," she said. "What's wrong?"

Herrick went over to the sink and filled the pot with cold
water. After pouring the water into the basin, he pressed the on
button a little too hard.

"Where's Jackson?" she asked. "Where…where's your dad?"

Herrick turned and pulled her into a hug. Sarah returned it,
pressing her nails into his back, as if to scratch an itch.

"Dad's gone," he said finally, the image Donne showed him
rolling through his brain again. He pushed it away, just like he'd
pushed away the face of the boy with the bomb for years.

"Where did he go?" Sarah whispered. "With Jackson? Did
they…did they move on?"

Herrick looked toward his bedroom to make sure Tammy

was still asleep. He wasn't ready to do this to her yet. She'd been through enough. But maybe she didn't care about his father anymore. Maybe what Cole did was what she wanted as well. It didn't matter at the moment. She had to sleep.

"He's dead," Herrick said. "Elliot Cole or one of his cronies killed him in an alleyway and sent the picture to Donne."

A shudder went through Sarah as he held her.

"What are you going to do?" Sarah asked. "Be smart." Then she whispered it again. "Please, be smart."

Herrick stepped out of the embrace. The coffee maker gurgled behind them.

"I'm going to call Mack and tell him everything. He'll take care of it. I should have done that three days ago."

"I can't call in sick today," Sarah said. "Are you going to be all right?"

Herrick nodded. "I'm okay. I just—I didn't like seeing his picture. Not that way."

"My God," Sarah said.

"Yeah, I know."

Herrick ran a hand through his hair. "The other thing I need to do today is get my mother to a doctor. I want her checked by a real doctor and some real progress noted. I want to make sure she's actually cancer free."

"That Cole did that to her," Sarah said. "It's not just physical scars you have to worry about. I'll take her after work."

Herrick said, "My whole family is pretty fucked up."

"I love you anyway."

"You, too."

Sarah touched his shoulder and then walked over to the bathroom. A few seconds later, Herrick heard the shower running. The coffee stopped brewing. He poured himself a bowl of Cheerios, and then poured the coffee. His went into a mug with cream and sugar. Sarah's into a travel cup, just cream.

Herrick closed his eyes and smelled the bitter coffee, and was transported back to his childhood. His parents never used a coffee maker, and instead worked with a percolator—the kind with the plastic round top that you could watch bubble. His dad would sit and read the paper, mostly the police blotter. And in the winter, he'd pass Herrick the sports section, so he could read about the Knicks or the Nets.

Jason Kidd was the player Herrick loved to follow. The way the point guard shared the ball was both a sign of leadership and unselfishness—something Herrick felt were connected, but as a kid couldn't figure out how. Kenneth used to point it out to him, how giving up the rock would lead to an easy bucket, while other teams preferred isolation plays and often drove right into the teeth of the defense.

That must have been why he and Cole planned together. Why they played to their strengths. Tammy was the smooth talker. Cole was the strategist, and Kenneth was the muscle. Uncle Adrik was the GM, essentially. Kenneth was the brave one, barreling into situations and getting the job done.

Cole always hung back.

He never hit someone. Not that Herrick could remember. He'd run the getaway car or stand guard outside. He didn't get his hands dirty.

The shower turned off in the bathroom and Herrick drank some more coffee.

The bedroom light went on. Herrick could see it glowing from the crack in the door. He got up and went over to the door. He knocked.

Tammy said, "Come in."

Herrick took a deep breath before opening the door. His mom stood in the corner, near the dresser Sarah kept her clothes in, and stared at a picture. It was of Sarah and Herrick on their trip to the shore. Sarah was holding a Giants pennant, something she'd won on one of the wheel games. Herrick held her cotton candy.

"You two look good together," Tammy said.

"We are good together." Herrick scratched his wrist. "Mom—"

"I heard you talking in there. Heard what happened to your dad."

Herrick took a step forward. He wanted to hug her. He wanted to comfort her like she had when he was three and had an ear infection.

She held up a hand.

"Elliot Cole didn't do that to your father. It's not like him."

"Maybe one of his goons."

"Maybe. But what's the point? They were working together."

"That's what I have to figure out."

Tammy shook her head. "Don't bring the cops into this. He's

your dad."

Herrick nodded. "I'm trying to be smart about this."

"Smart is good. Smart and tough is better."

"I have to go talk to cops about something else today. I'll try to heed your advice. Sarah will take you to the doctor later. Why don't you get some more sleep?"

Tammy yawned. "I think I will."

"How are you feeling?"

Tammy smiled. "I'll be a lot better when Elliot is dead."

CHAPTER 61

THE SUN ROSE over Manhattan, and Donne stared at it from a bench on the Hoboken side of the Hudson River. For the first time in his life, he had no idea where to go. He was literally homeless. The first train left in twenty minutes, but he didn't want to be cooped up in a train station waiting. Better to do it in the open, where he could see what was coming, or, better yet, run.

His fists ached, and the muscles in his shoulders joined the party. His eyes felt heavy and he wanted to sleep. There wasn't time for that, however. Herrick was going to call this corrections officer and make things really tough for Donne.

Didn't Herrick get it?

Donne was trying to take it all on and lift the world off Herrick's shoulders. Any step Herrick took next could ruin his life, or worse, kill him. That was how deep Kenneth had dragged them. Less than a week ago, Donne was in prison, now he was a murderer.

Looking toward the train station, Donne pondered his next move. He could try to find Cole and head everything off at the pass, but that seemed unlikely. Dealing with Cole wasn't like dealing with Kenneth. Kenneth was someone Donne could handle.

But Cole was different. He had an entourage and he was mad. He was a man down, but Herrick's description of Haskins was worrisome. Taking out Cole before he moved on the Federal

Reserve was key, but that deserved a plan.

Or Donne could run.

He could get on a train and head off into nowhere. Herrick would talk to Mack, and Donne would be back on some watch list somewhere. Spend the rest of his days on the run.

Donne exhaled.

And then a cop came and sat down next to him. A uniformed cop, younger than Donne and a grin on his face. Donne's stomach knotted up.

"Good morning," the cop said. His badge read Culp.

"Morning," Donne said.

"You been out here all night?"

Donne shrugged. "It was warm enough. I like watching the city lights."

"That's all you looked at overnight?"

Donne turned to the cop, trying to keep his breathing even. "What do you mean?"

The cop looked straight ahead toward the river. A barge tooted its horn, saying good morning to New York City. A few joggers passed.

"There was a murder last night. An old man was beaten to a pulp in an alley a couple of blocks from here. Poor guy. They didn't even take his wallet ."

Donne closed his eyes for a moment. Couldn't even make it look like a robbery.

"Did you see or hear anything?" the cop asked.

"No. It was quiet last night."

"Murder like that, the guy usually screams."

"I did fall asleep for a couple of hours."

"On this bench?"

"More comfortable than the train station."

The cop shook his head. "Are you new to this whole homeless thing? Haven't learned the routine yet?"

Donne considered his options. Telling a cop he was just out of prison would set off all kinds of alarm bells. Saying he was an experienced homeless person just sounded ridiculous. And he hadn't had a drink in days, so he didn't sound like a boozer who missed the last train.

"I was in finance," Donne said. "Bottom dropped out of the stock market and I liquidated everything."

He had no idea if that was a legitimate reason, but it sounded good.

The cop agreed. "Fuck, man. That sucks. No family to speak of?"

Donne shook his head. "My sister is out in California. Parents are dead."

The cop shook his head. "Maybe take a walk for a while. I'm supposed to chase guys like you out of here. But with the body and all, it's been a busy morning."

Donne nodded. "Thanks. Good luck with the case."

"My name is Alvin Culp. You hear anything about this old guy, come back here and let me know. I work the midnight to eight shift."

"Looking for a big break to get off nights?"

The cop tilted his hat back on his head. "You know it."

"Thanks, Officer."

"Good luck, sir. Maybe find a shower too. Tough to go on job interviews after wearing the same set of clothes a couple of days in a row."

Donne and the cop stood up. The cop gave him a nod and Donne started walking. He headed in the direction of the train station. At least he could hop on the train for a stop or two. It would put some distance between Kenneth Herrick's body and himself. The first train would take him to Lyndhurst.

The sun was almost fully up now, and the chill in the air was lifting. It seemed like it was going to be a warm and sunny day, perfect for being aimless. He hustled to the station and got on the first train leaving the station.

Felt like he was in the middle of some song written in the 1960s.

Donne made his way to the back of the train, as far from the conductor as possible. He didn't want to cause a scene when asked for a ticket. The next stop was ten minutes away, and the cars were starting to crowd with people heading to their jobs. Might have been smarter to sneak into Manhattan, but he was sick of that town.

In three days, he'd made too many memories.

And that was when he realized the best strategy. It wasn't to go on the offensive, but to go and talk. Create a peace treaty. He needed to make his way back to Long Valley and talk to Elliot Cole and whoever else he had on the job.

Get Cole to run before he moved on the Reserve.

Or maybe join up with Cole.

Anything to keep Herrick safe. His life was too good. It was the exact reverse of Donne.

What Donne could have had if only he'd listened to Jeanne and stayed on the straight and narrow. Donne always made the wrong decisions. The dumb choices.

And it ruined more lives that just his.

Maybe today was the day to make some smarter choices.

Even if that included murder.

CHAPTER 62

TAMMY OPENED HER eyes and immediately knew something was wrong.

Now, in the dark, she wondered how long she had actually slept. The clock said it was nearing nine, so she'd gotten about two hours. But as she blinked her eyes into focus, something felt very wrong. It was quiet in the apartment. Maybe Matt and his lady friend were gone already?

No.

That wasn't it. The TV was humming, the introduction to the evening news played. And there was the tinkling of metal against something. Maybe they were getting the pots and pans out to cook.

No again.

Tammy's interior alarms were ringing loud. She hadn't heard them this loud since the Orchard Bank Affair, when the cops had burst in on the three of them mid job. She blinked the memory away and inched out of bed, landing on her tip toes. The room spun a bit. She got up too fast, so she put a hand on the bed stand to get her balance.

Then she creeped across the room, inch by inch. When she got to the door, the light outlining the hinges, she pulled it open just a hair and peeked out.

And saw that her instincts were right.

Matt stood close to the kitchen, hands up in the air like he was being held up. Sarah was over by the couch, knee on the cushion, looking toward the front door. And the front door had been kicked in. That, she suddenly remembered, was how she'd been awakened. She heard the crunch of the door. Originally, she thought it was from a dream. The metal tinkling she had heard was the chain lock bouncing off the door itself.

And standing in the doorway was a young man holding a pistol. He had a military haircut and wore a cammo jacket. The gun was something she'd seen cops and military police hold. But the familiarity came from his eyes, something she'd seen before. A glint, a look and even the color.

Haskins.

The one who stuck that damn IV in her arm every single day. Slowly killing her.

Tammy pushed the door wide open and everyone turned her way.

Matt said, "Mom!"

Haskins said, "There you are."

The gun whirled in Tammy's direction, and her stomach muscles tightened. If this was how things ended, there were worse ways to go. At least she gave her son a few more minutes to live.

But Matt lurched forward and grabbed Haskins' wrist. The gun clattered to the ground, sliding toward her on the hardwood floor. Sarah screamed and dropped flat on the ground. Tammy darted into the living room as fast as her tired legs would take her.

Matt and Haskins tumbled onto the floor together and Tammy heard the sound of fist on flesh. But that wasn't where her attention was focused.

Instead, she worried about the gun that was only a few feet from her. Her legs gave out and she fell to her knees. She crawled the last bit of distance and reached out for the weapon. Sarah screamed again, but Tammy ignored her.

She hefted the gun. It was heavier than she remembered. Looking toward the fight, she saw that Matt had Haskins on his back and was raining blows down on him. Haskins was bloody.

But he wasn't dead.

"Move," Tammy said, leveling the weapon.

Matt stopped swinging and looked at his mom. His eyes went wide.

"You can't—" he said, but the rest of the words were cut off by the right cross Haskins hit him with.

Matt flailed backward to the ground, and Haskins got to his feet. Exactly like Tammy had hoped. He took a step toward Matt, clearly not worrying about the gun or the doddering old woman.

Tammy squeezed hard and the trigger resisted at first. She squeezed harder, the air escaping from her lungs as she did. The soft wheeze of air was cut off by the loud retort of the gun going off. She squeezed two more times, and Haskins toppled over. All three bullets had embedded themselves in Haskins back.

Tammy dropped the gun.

Sarah ran to her and wrapped her in a hug. Her lungs were having trouble getting air to them, but she slumped into Sarah's arms. The girl was whispering something, but all Tammy heard was white noise. Her vision was clear, though, so that was good.

"Mom, Jesus Christ," Matt said. "Jesus."

"Is he dead?" she managed.

Herrick ran over to him and checked his pulse. Haskins opened and closed his mouth. Herrick put his ear to the mouth and it happened again. Then all movement stopped.

"Yeah, Mom. You killed a guy."

"Not my first rodeo," she said.

Sarah helped Tammy get to the couch. The air was starting to come more easily now. Her blood was on fire and she was more awake than she had been in weeks. Months even. Every color on the wall looked brighter. She could feel every bit of the couch's material. The world was alive.

Because Tammy had killed somebody.

She looked over at Matt, trying to fight the smile off her face. He was on the phone, essentially shouting. Maybe the gun shot had damaged his hearing too. How long before the cops got here? Ten minutes? Hoboken was small, Maybe it would be faster.

"Yeah," Matt said. "Yeah. Get over here. Fast. No. I meant to call you this morning, but now I have a real emergency on my hands."

Tammy sank into the couch and her muscles relaxed. A faint pain settled in her stomach, like someone gently prodding her with a needle.

"All right, Mack. See you soon. Thanks."

"Calling in a favor?" Tammy said.

"You have to rest," Sarah said.

Tammy laughed. "I feel better than I have in weeks."

Sarah shot Matt a look. He shrugged.

"Who did you call?" Sarah asked.

"Mack. He'll help. Somehow."

"The cops will get here first."

"Probably. We'll be okay."

"He was going to kill us," Sarah said.

"Yeah." Herrick looked at the ceiling. "His last words were 'tomorrow.'"

Their conversation continued, but Tammy didn't care. She focused on the TV, some old sitcom from the 80s she'd changed the channel to. The old Tammy was back, even if it was only for five minutes.

She laughed at one of the stupid guys on the screen.

CHAPTER 63

DONNE SAT BEHIND the wheel of a 1998 Honda Accord. The used car dealer on Riverside Ave in Lyndhurst nodded his approval. Probably more at the promise of fifteen hundred dollars in cash rather than loving the car Donne was about to buy. It didn't matter.

He'd changed his mind. A full tank of gas would take him a few more stops, and then he would get the hell out of Dodge. Kenneth's money would probably keep him going for a week or two.

"This car will take good care of you. Hondas are built to last," the dealer said.

Donne didn't answer, instead passing a fist full of cash through the window to the dealer.

"Are you in a hurry, sir? We have some paperwork we should fill out."

He got out of the car and followed the dealer into the office. There were pictures of him shaking hands with different customers in front of different cars, big grin on his face. There was also a frame of a dollar on the wall. His desk was a mess, paperwork, the newspaper and an outdated Mac computer resting precariously on the edge.

Donne took a seat and stared across the desk. The dealer— Donne didn't need to remember his name—shuffled through the papers on his desk. Maybe it was a stroke of luck for Donne. This guy was so disorganized that even if Donne passed his ID along, the guy would lose the photocopy. And by the time the police made their way to the car dealership, he'd be long gone.

"Let me see here," the dealer said. "Ah, here it is."

He passed Donne a contract to sign, which Donne barely scanned over. As he reached for a pen, the dealer stopped him.

"Did you forget to grab a napkin after breakfast, sir?" The dealer pointed at Donne's hand. He grinned, like they were buddies busting balls during a Happy Hour.

Donne looked at it and saw the dried blood. Jesus Christ. He thought he got the rest using the hose near an old warehouse.

"Yeah. Stupid Taylor Ham and egg. Let me go wash it off."

"Salt, pepper, ketchup?" The dealer laughed. "Get that stuff on the contract and it messes everything up."

Donne washed his hands in the bathroom and looked at his face in the mirror. It seemed like each day the lines on his face got deeper, and the circles under his eyes got darker. Maybe it was time to go back to the beard, and cover half his face up again.

Running was possible. Donne knew it. He'd done it once before. Jeanne had done it twice and, as far as he knew, had never been caught. She was somewhere warm raising her kid. Maybe he could find her.

After this was over.

He left the bathroom, and the dealer grinned.

"Much better," Donne said.

Donne took the pen and scribbled his name as illegibly as possible. Didn't want to make things too easy.

"The thing about Hondas," the dealer said, "is they're reliable. No matter how long you have them, as long you change the oil, they will survive. I've heard people put two hundred thousand miles on them. They just keep trucking. Get you out of a lot of jams. You'll never be stranded. Even in the snow."

Donne nodded. He knew that, it was why he wanted one. "And this one has barely a hundred thousand on it."

"Yeah, the previous owner hated giving it up. But time moves on, and we offer good deals."

The dealer took Donne's ID without looking at it. He photocopied it. When the piece of paper shot out of the copier, Donne's stomach knotted up. He inhaled and waited for the dealer to look at it. But he didn't.

It was amazing this guy was still in business. His attention to detail was awful. But good for Donne.

"We all finished here?" Donne stuck out his hand.

The dealer took Donne's hand. "Enjoy the car."

"I intend to give it a good run."

"You can count on it."

Ten minutes later, Donne was on the road, weaving through excess traffic. He found the Parkway and headed south.

When it was time to run, that was the direction he was headed.

This time, go south for the weather. No need to drink anymore, and there was nothing wrong with a good tan. Kenneth Herrick once told him he liked the winter. It was cold and felt pure. He felt clean in the winter. Donne didn't agree. He wanted the sun to burn the guilt off him.

The dealer was right. The car was handling well. He pressed the gas and got off the Turnpike exit that would take him to his old stomping grounds of New Brunswick. He was leaving this world behind.

He thought about the dealer one more time. The car was reliable. Saves you, even in the snow. Just like Donne tried to do for Herrick. Save him.

But Herrick had to show up this morning, didn't he? Couldn't leave well enough alone. And now, he was back in the shit. Herrick needed to give this gig up, it only caused a world of hurt. It may have toughened his skin to the point of unfeeling. And Herrick didn't need that.

Herrick needed someone to rely on one more time. Donne was a beat up Honda Accord, wasn't he?

Because the job wasn't over. Cole had gotten away with it, and six people had died. With Herrick there, the spotlight would be on him again. He saw the gun pressed to Herrick's head. He couldn't miss that scene.

And now Donne was just going to run away?

He shook his head and looked for the next exit. He couldn't run yet. It wasn't time. He still had to finish things.

Herrick wasn't a hero. Herrick needed a hero.

Jackson Donne.

CHAPTER 64

ONNE SQUEALED INTO New Brunswick and found a parking spot
easier than he probably ever had. He held the steering wheel
tightly with both hands and stared out the windshield. College
kids carrying book bags and staring at phone screens passed him.
He took a breath and closed his eyes.

Usually, he'd go to Jesus for this. But Jesus was dead. And
Donne didn't have the kind of contacts to take the next step deeper
into Sanchez's world. At this point, that was probably a good
thing. But he still didn't have guns. He had a pistol, but not the
firepower he'd need to help out Herrick.

Donne opened his eyes. Herrick. The radio had been playing
his news report for the last forty-five minutes. The dumbass who
didn't use a gun. Who got him into this situation just by passing
him a note. If Donne hadn't hooked up with Kenneth, none of this
would be happening to him. He'd still be sitting in prison, whiling
the hours away.

Or dead.

But he wouldn't be about to walk into the one place he'd
promised himself he wouldn't go.

The Olde Towne Tavern.

Well, it wasn't called that anymore. It was called Artie's Sports
Palace, rebuilt from the ground up after a nutjob had destroyed it

with a Molotov Cocktail before Donne went away. But, if the drug world didn't get you the shit you wanted, you could always try a bar.

Because the regulars in a bar could get you whatever you wanted.

Donne shook his head. *Here we go.*

He got out of the car, crossed the road and pushed the door to the bar open. The music didn't scratch silent like in old movies. In fact, no one even looked up from their drinks. Donne ambled past two college kids playing darts and found and empty seat at the edge of the bar. The Yankees were just getting started on the flatscreen TV overhead. Getaway day.

Appropriate.

The bartender, a woman who was probably a fifth year senior, walked up to him. She wore a halter top with the name of the bar written in script on it. Her bellybutton ring glittered under the light. Artie had really switched things up here.

Again.

"What can I get you?"

"A club soda, and Artie."

"Excuse me?"

"I need to talk to Artie."

The bartender nodded, passed him a club soda and moved on. She filled two more beers, the usual tap fare: Yuengling and Bud Light. Then she disappeared into the kitchen. Donne smelled the fryer and his stomach grumbled. He didn't know the last time he eaten. Thirty seconds later, Artie, now fully gray, came out from the kitchen.

"You son of a bitch," he said.

Donne spread his hands.

"You mother fucker."

"Let me have it," Donne said.

"Get out of my bar."

"I need help."

Artie slammed his palm on the bar. Some of Donne's club soda sloshed onto the wood. The patrons looked their way and then turned their focus back to their drinks or their dart game.

Lowering his voice to a whisper, Artie said, "I'm not helping you. I don't want you here. Every time you come in here, something explodes. Someone dies."

Donne nodded. "Because I don't finish the job the right way."

"You're supposed to be—" And then, as if a light went off in Artie's head, "Why the hell aren't you in jail?"

Donne gave him the quick rundown. Money. Kenneth Herrick. New York City. He tried to keep as much blood out of the story as possible.

But when you were about to ask a man for guns, you had to connect the dots with some gore.

"Who can you connect me with?" Donne asked. "Jesus sent me to you."

"I don't want anything to do with this."

"Listen, Artie, remember how we met?"

"You came here and got shitfaced on a nightly occurrence, I believe."

"Before that. Me, Bill Martin and Alex Robinson tracked a dealer here. He would come in here every night. I came in and asked you about him. I know shady people come in here all time."

Artie shook his head. "I rebranded. Not anymore. In fact, you can get the fuck out."

Donne pushed back from the bar. "If that's what you want."

"It is."

"Then all I want to do is say goodbye, Artie."

Artie rubbed his face in his hands. "Goodbye."

"Forever. Without your help, I'm probably going to die. I know you don't care. You probably want me dead. I get it. I bring hell everywhere I go. But I'm learning how to change that."

The New York Yankee pitcher struck out the batter and the inning was over. A commercial about a used car dealership popped on the screen.

Artie sighed. "What do you need?"

"I need to buy some guns. Good ones."

"You're in the wrong place."

"Am I?"

"Can't Jesus help you out with this?"

A chill went through Donne's nerves. "No."

Artie shook his head one more time, as if he was trying to rattle something loose. He stared at Donne for a long time. Enough for one commercial to end and the next—an exterminator—to begin. Finally, he said, "Come with me."

Donne followed Artie through the kitchen to a rundown office.

It was the same office Artie always had, where he kept the books. It was the one thing that hadn't changed about this place. The one area that was still the Olde Towne Tavern.

Artie reached into his desk and came out with a business card. He gave it to Donne.

"You able to pay?"

Donne said, "I have the money."

"Call that number. An old Vietnam buddy. One I hoped to forget. Of course, you'd remind me."

Donne didn't respond. He didn't need to.

"Now get the fuck out of my bar."

Donne started to say thank you, but changed his mind.

"Never come back," Artie said.

Donne left, hoping to comply.

CHAPTER 65

ERRICK STARED AT the front door of his apartment. It wouldn't
close right anymore, not after it had been kicked in. And, he
realized, he'd spent too much time this past week reacting and
not acting. Donne, his dad, Uncle Adrik, Cole and even his mother.
Each had been a chess piece that had put him on the defensive,
instead of being aggressive.

He would have much rather been coaching his team instead of
dealing with another life and death situation. But now, as the cops
worked around him, he wanted it to be different. The target was
on Cole's back now. Because Haskins had gone too far. And that
must have been because of Cole.

Tomorrow was the day.

For the moment, though, Herrick still waited, as much as that
burned his skin. He needed Mack here. He needed an ally to talk
his mom out of this mess. The detectives had taken Tammy back
into the bedroom to question her. Herrick asked if she could bring
Sarah, just to keep her cool, and the cops acquiesced. But Tammy
just grinned the whole way into the bedroom.

A smile Herrick hadn't seen since he brought a home straight
A report card in fifth grade. She was proud of herself.

Still Herrick waited. Where was Mack? It had been over an
hour. Herrick's gut twisted and churned old coffee.

Low voices came from the bedroom, and Herrick strained his ears to try to hear the conversation. The words didn't come. In the apartment hallway, a medical examiner talked to one of the cops who stood guard. Herrick got up and went into the kitchen, hoping he could get himself another cup of coffee. Of course, everything was evidence, so he was cut off at the pass.

When he came back into the living room, Mack stood there. Herrick's stomach settled and he took a calming breath.

"What the hell?" Mack strode over to him.

"A guy. His name is Neil Haskins, he came here to kill us. My mom—she shot him."

Mack ran his hand through his hair. "Jesus, Matt."

"I know, I know. I thought we were out of this."

"Out of what? I haven't talked to you since the mall."

Herrick filled him in as fast as he could, trying to leave no detail out. Donne, his dad—his dead dad. Elliot Cole and Uncle Adrik. All he left out was what the heist was. He told Mack he didn't know. As he spilled his guts, Sarah helped Tammy back into the living room, and the medical examiner finished his investigation. Two EMTs came and started to tend to Haskins' body. When he wrapped things up, Mack stared at him without anything to say.

"I need help, Mack. My mom can't go to jail."

"You should have called me." Mack tilted his head and wagged a finger. It reminded Herrick of a move Harrison Ford would make, even though they looked nothing alike. "You should have called me a week ago."

"You're right. But it was my dad. And my mother."

Mack shook his head. "Let me talk to the lead detective. I'll see what I can do. But—holy shit, Matt."

Herrick turned and walked over to Sarah and his mother.

"How is she?" he asked Sarah.

"I'm fine. This is the best I've felt in months. I told the cop that."

Sarah nodded. "She did great in there."

"Are you okay?" Herrick asked Sarah.

"When this is over, we need to talk," she said.

Herrick ignored the icepick in his side. "Mom. You could be looking at a prison sentence."

"They're not going to put me away."

Mack sauntered to them. "She's right."

Herrick shook his head. He thought he might fall over.

The cops were marking stuff up and finishing up. They'd been around nearly three hours, and day had turned into night. One of the detectives—he'd given Herrick his name, but Herrick had forgotten it in all the commotion—beckoned him. Herrick obeyed.

"Your friend talked to me, and you're a very lucky man. I'm not finished with this investigation yet, but I'm not going to bring your mother in. Not today anyway."

Herrick nodded.

"She's a very strong woman. You're all very lucky. He had another gun strapped to his leg. She saved you. Stay in town and I'll be in touch. Also, don't do anything stupid."

Herrick shook his hand and agreed, all the while planning on doing something incredibly stupid.

He took out his phone and texted Donne, *Tomorrow*.

Minutes later, Donne wrote back, *I know. It'll be early. Very early. Let's let the cops handle it.*

Hell no.

Knew you'd say that. It's why I didn't tell them. They wouldn't believe me anyway. And I don't want you anywhere near there.

No answer.

Herrick was going to do something stupid. Stop Donne from stopping Cole.

And then let the police handle it.

CHAPTER 66

||||||||||||||||||||||||||||||||||||||||||||||||||||||||||||||||||||||||||||||||||||||||||||||||||||||||||||||||||||||||||||||||||||||

MANUEL WAS WEEPING.

Cole and Adrik sat across from him, waiting for him to get control. It didn't appear that was happening anytime soon. They just needed him to calm down and get him back on point.

"I'm very sorry," Adrik said. "My police friends told me. They heard it on the scanner."

Another long sob.

"Get a hold of yourself," Cole said. "We have to get rest and be ready."

Manuel wiped his eyes, and for an instant, Cole thought he got through. But Manuel, giant among men, pulled his knees up to his chest in some sort of fetal position.

"Call it off," he said through the tears.

Cole shook his head.

Adrik said, "The time for mourning is when you are rolling in money."

"He was a good man," Manuel said. "He loved me."

Adrik said, "He was cra—"

Cole reached over and put a hand on Adrik's arm before he could say anymore.

Adrik nodded. "Now is not the time."

He went back to cleaning the automatic weapon in front of

him. "I've never done something like this before. I was always behind the scenes, giving you money and reaping the rewards. Was not as exciting."

"Shut up, Adrik," Cole said.

Manuel rolled onto his side and wiped his eyes. The couch shuddered underneath his girth.

"Just days ago," Cole said, "you grabbed Matt Herrick by the collar and threw him on his ass. You manhandled him no problem."

The words hung in the air as Manuel started to regain his composure. Cole got up and poured him a shot of whiskey. They never drank the night before a job, but Manuel needed to take the edge off.

"I did," Manuel finally said. He knocked the drink back. "I'm going to do it again. Right now."

He stood and Cole stood with him, his old knees aching in the process. "Tomorrow there will be three of us with a rocket launcher and machine guns. They will not be expecting us."

"How do you know Herrick didn't…?"

"Even if he did tell the cops, they blew him off. You know that. There's no evidence. Nothing."

"Tomorrow, we blow that shit up and we are rich." He put an arm around Manuel's shoulders. "You get through tomorrow and you have the rest of your life to kill Matt Herrick. No one will know who you are. They will only know me."

Manuel blinked. "I can barely focus right now. Can barely think."

Adrik looked up from the gun and caught Cole's eye. Cole shook him off. Adrik went back to the weapon.

"You know how to aim and fire," Adrik said.

"It's not that simple." Manuel wiped away a tear.

Cole shook his head. "Tomorrow will be a spectacle, a joke. Piece of cake."

"We went from seven to three."

"It will make our victory even better. I'll be even more famous."

"That's all you care about."

Cole flashed to the picture of Tammy. He loved that shot, her eyes so wide and blue. He'd kept a blurry copy in his wallet for years. Every time he looked at it, though, he knew one thing was missing. Himself.

"It doesn't matter. I'm going to care about you getting your revenge."

"You'll be in Cuba."

"I can still wire money. I still have my contacts."

Adrik said, "So do I."

Manuel took a deep breath. "Tomorrow, we will be rich."

"You have to focus."

Manuel nodded. Tears still streamed from his eyes. "I need more whiskey."

Cole passed him the bottle.

CHAPTER 67

DONNE SAT IN the bleachers again, high up, looking out over the Federal Reserve building. It wasn't yet six in the morning and the traffic on Route 17 was light. He counted a car passing just about every thirty seconds. In New Jersey, that was flat out an empty road.

Next to Donne was a rifle — the hunting kind. Artie's man called it a sniper rifle. It wasn't. It was something he hadn't handled in years, not since an afternoon in Jockey Hollow, putting bullets into the air and hoping to scare people into running away. Now he was going to have to be a pinpoint marksman, and he'd never done that.

Donne figured they had maybe twenty minutes to get the job done, if the caravan was on time. Kenneth once said the men at the reserve wanted to get the shipment out of there fast. After they shit the bed handing billions of dollars to Iraq, the people in charge kept their schedule quiet.

But if they took longer than twenty minutes, the witnesses would start coming out of the woodwork. Donne considered six a.m. the start of rush hour, but right now only early morning joggers were just starting to make their way to the track. Twenty more minutes and employees trying to get the jump on the day would fill up the road. In ten minutes, an armored car and two military vehicles would pull out of the reserve and head north, trying to make their way to Teterboro Airport.

Tight window.

Go time in seven minutes. Donne walked the bleachers over to the right corner, looking out at both the highway and the Federal Reserve building. The sun peeked out behind the buildings of New York in the east.

Time was running short.

Donne's stomach burned acid. He hefted the gun, checked the chamber and weight and then leveled it out toward the road. He took a look through the sight and saw movement on the reserve campus. Two men in green were talking to each other and pointing at the road. For an instant, Donne expected them to look in his direction, and his muscles seized. But they didn't, instead heading back toward a large garage door.

Bill Martin had held a gun like this once, and used it to end a senator's life. That bullet was the one that sent Donne into this spiral—into hiding, into jail and now homeless and hoping a few thousand stolen dollars would be a nest egg. Sweat formed at the back of his neck. Too many memories returning because of just one type of gun.

Two shots. All he would need were two shots, and then he'd run. Grab the money and be gone. But now that the time was near, his plan felt faulty. Could he really grab a handful of cash and get the cops here in time? He had no doubt that Manuel, Haskins, Adrik and Cole would engage the military dudes in a firefight. He had no doubt they'd planned for the contingency and would be able to get the back door of the car opened.

But he didn't know if he would be able to sneak in and out without, well, dying.

No other choices though.

It was the only way to keep Herrick home and out of this, and get himself started. The only way to stay alive.

Behind him, the metal clunked, as if someone set foot on the bleachers. Donne felt the weight shift, and he whirled, aiming the gun below him.

Matt Herrick stood there, arms in the air, and his mouth hanging open.

"Jackson," he said. "What the hell are you doing?"

"Go home," Donne said, lowering the gun.

"No." Herrick kept his hands up.

His phone buzzed signaling an alarm he'd set, and Donne took a look at it. *Four minutes. Get in position.* He could handle this.

"I'm doing it for you, Herrick. I don't want you to become like me. Your dad tried to drag you down, but you're a good person. You don't deserve this."

Herrick lost his balance on the bleacher for a moment, and had to put his left foot on the step below to balance himself. A car revved by, heading north. Donne glanced toward the reserve building, but didn't see any change. He only had scant minutes to talk Herrick away from here and get on with his job.

"For me? You're standing here like some crazed militia man waiting to rob an armored car." Herrick stepped back up. "I'm trying to save *you*."

Donne shook his head. "I've been here before. Go home, Matt. Help your mom. Mourn your dad. This is a bad place for you. It's going to be national news. You know that."

"And that's good for you?"

He turned his back to Herrick. *I need the money. I need to go back to jail. Maybe I need to die.*

He leveled the gun and realized how much he reminded himself of Bill Martin, stuck on the roof, aiming a rifle at the senator. And Herrick was his old self, a younger Donne, trying to fix things.

"I need to put things right," Donne said.

Herrick said, "Who killed my dad?"

"Cole did it. I told you."

Herrick didn't say anything.

"Maybe he sent Haskins. I don't know."

"Walk away and it's all over," Herrick said. "Haskins is dead now. The cops can catch them later. There are cameras everywhere. They can't escape this."

"For you, it's over. I got you into this. I'm ending it. Leave, Matt."

"I'm sorry my dad got you involved in everything. I'm sorry I gave you his name. But you don't have to fix everything."

"The only solution is a clean slate," Donne said.

Donne leveled the gun again. Through the sight, he watched the garage door open and the security gate rise. A black Jeep pulled out first, followed by the armored car, and then another Jeep. Just as Cole had said. Maybe Haskins had gotten him the information. It didn't matter.

"We have to stop Cole, but without anyone dying," Herrick said.

"That's the mistake people make," Donne said.

Herrick didn't answer.

The Jeep made the first left onto Route 17, traveling away from Donne. The armored car started its route. Donne looked through the sight again and gave the armored car a lead.

"Put the gun down, Jackson!"

Donne ignored the words, and Herrick watched his finger squeeze the trigger.

Before Donne could complete the act, something exploded.

CHAPTER 68

THE SHOCKWAVE TORE through them, and Donne's gun clattered down the bleachers. Herrick kept his balance and watched the rifle spin past him. It didn't go off. Donne fell to his knees.

After regaining his equilibrium, Herrick bounded the last three steps of the bleachers. As he peered over the edge next to Donne, he saw the armored car careening into the guardrail. A loud crunch reached their ears, along with the squeal of brakes. The armored car went up on two wheels, and for a moment it looked like it would right itself. But the top weight of the armored car took it over on the side. A fireball funneled toward the sky from a crater in the road.

Donne blew air out of his mouth. Herrick glanced at him. He grimaced.

"Are you okay?"

"You're going to win this time," Donne said. "I can't fight a war."

Herrick looked back at the brewing warzone. The soldiers from the Jeeps ran toward the wreckage, guns out. It was compelling to watch, as they ran a move Herrick had learned during his boot camp training. He'd never seen the movement from this high before. In fact, he'd only been involved in it. Two soldiers watched the road, slowly stepping backward, one guarding their six. Two others kept their eyes north and south. And two more rushed the armored car. They were talking, the words lost in the wind and hitting Herrick's ears as a garbled mess.

And then it happened, from the far side of Route 17, near a used car dealership, something arced through the air. Herrick saw it immediately and tried to scream and warn the soldiers. The words didn't reach their mark. Donne turned his head toward Herrick, reacting to the sound. A rocket soared through the air with a whistle, hit the armored car and blew it up, flipping the car on its side. The concussive blast sent two of the soldiers to the ground. Another fireball.

There was the rocket launcher Manuel had stolen.

"Shit," Donne said. "Shit, shit, shit."

He whirled and started down the bleachers. Herrick took a few more seconds to watch the scene unfold before him. From where the rocket had come, two men appeared with assault rifles. Behind the barrier, another man was putting the launcher down. He then hopped the barrier as well. They were all wearing Kevlar and helmets, keeping Herrick from identifying them from this distance.

But he could guess.

It was in that second that Herrick realized how truly unprotected he and Donne were. He turned to warn Donne, but found himself alone. Donne had disappeared. The gunfire started. Instinct sent Herrick to the ground, his face pressed against the cold steel of the bleacher seat. More shouting from the street. Herrick's heart pounded.

In his mind's eye, he saw the boy on the base again. Strapped in explosives. About to press the button. The memory of Herrick leveling his gun. The boy always returned at the worst time.

He blinked, snapping himself out of it. Air caught in his throat. The gunfire continued. Sirens emerged in the air, and somewhere helicopter blades *whupped*. Maybe a news chopper. Maybe the police. Herrick had no idea how much time had passed. And then there was another explosion, softer this time, like a magician's trick.

Pulling himself up, Herrick looked out over the scene again. He pulled his phone and opened the video app and started recording. There were two more bodies on the street — soldiers. Two of the men in armor were laying down cover fire as one of them made his way to the armored vehicle. The smoke was coming from the back doors, which had been blown open. The last two remaining soldiers were torn. Stop the guys laying down cover fire or move toward the man who had blown the doors. One stood up and his head immediately exploded in a puff of red dust. The last soldier was screaming. He fired several times and caught the big guy in the helmet and chest. He fell backward, body motionless. The military had powerful bullets.

Was the big guy Manuel? Had to be.

Herrick looked toward the Federal Reserve building. There was a commotion there as well. Men running. Probably arming themselves. Herrick supposed Cole and crew knew they had a finite amount of time, but could handle between six and ten soldiers guarding the truck.

The balls on them.

And then, Donne appeared.

"No," Herrick whispered.

The last soldier was down, a bullet must have caught him while Herrick had his eye on Donne. The two remaining Kevlar guys were hustling toward the vehicle now.

Donne reached into the back of the armored car, and that was when Herrick turned off his phone and took to the stairs. He was down to the bottom in Maybe four seconds. He didn't stand a chance with just an ASP, but he was going to run full-blown into the middle of a gunfight anyway.

Real smart, Matt.

But his legs wouldn't stop. He ran through the concourse of the stadium and out to the sidewalk. The sirens were louder now, as was the *whup* of the helicopter blades. Herrick ran toward Route 17, and the closer he got, the more chaos reigned. Broken glass, the smell of bullets in the air. He was in the sandbox again, but this time it was in the middle of New Jersey.

When Herrick finally got to the road, everything was quiet. The Kevlar guys were gone. Donne too. Herrick ran first to the back of the armored car and found it empty. Nothing he could do there. He looked south and saw an ambulance, lights whirling, siren screaming, racing toward him. There were shouts to get his hands in the air behind him. The scrambling troops at the reserve had gotten their asses in gear.

Herrick didn't stop, though. He didn't listen to the orders. He was moving from soldier to soldier, trying to find one breathing.

No luck. All he saw was spurting blood, bone fragment and smoke. There was nothing he could do. No one to save. Not even Manuel, whose empty eyes stared at him from the pavement.

He bit his lip to hold in a scream.

He turned toward the approaching troops and shot his hands up in the air. He screamed at them that he was a witness. That he wanted to help. They told him to get down on the ground. They repeated it.

Herrick had no choice.

He hit the ground, and the barrel of a gun was pressed hard into his neck.

If they had only listened to him instead of telling him to shut up, they would know he wasn't involved. And they would hear the names he kept shouting.

No deal.

CHAPTER 69

||||||||||||||||||||||||||||||||||||||||||||||||||||||||||||||||||||||||||||||||||||||||||||||||||||||||||||||||||||||||||||||||||||||||||||||||||||||||||||||||||||||

"So, YOUR LIFE the past two and a half years has been Jackson Donne gets you in shit and you try to unfuck it?"

The military cop crossed his arms and stared down his nose like Herrick was an underperforming power forward. No wonder his players hated that look. It was effective.

"Well," Herrick said, "Donne spent some of that time in prison. So I went out and got myself a girlfriend and a Playstation. Killed time until the next screw up."

He was lying about the Playstation.

"Son, you'd best figure out your next sentence before you say it." The guy was old, with gray clipped hair and a bushy gray moustache. His nametag said Montana. His voice had the effect of years in the Army, a bit southern, but mostly worn away like an eroded stone. "Otherwise, and maybe even still, you're in a world of hurt."

Herrick scrunched his nose like he smelled something awful. Maybe he shouldn't have mentioned Donne's name. But these guys had videotape, Herrick was sure of it. Montana would have shown him that eventually. And Herrick just wanted to get the hell out of here.

"Donne isn't the one you have to worry about. He wanted to stop the whole thing."

Montana nodded. "Yeah? Well, he didn't save any of my men. You want to be the ones to call their relatives?"

Herrick let that one go.

"Do I need a lawyer?"

"Are you guilty of anything?"

Herrick didn't answer. And Montana waited.

One thing that cops hated was silence. If you didn't answer their question right away, they filled the air with more words and sounds. More questions. The strategy was to get the witness or suspect so uncomfortable they talked just to shut the cops up. Montana was different. He kept as quiet as possible. Herrick liked the strategy.

But he hated the silence.

"Wrong place wrong time," he finally said.

"So you're a witness." Montana ran a hand through his hair. "You're not under arrest. But help us out here. Who are they?"

"The dead guy is Manuel Parada. There are two other guys who planned this whole thing. Elliot Cole and Adrik Vavilov. They both got away. They flipped the truck, they wanted the money."

"And you just happened to be there."

Herrick shrugged. "That's what I said."

"You were in the sandbox, right? I looked you up. You're not hard to find. I talked to Major Christenson. You do a good job with those kids at the school."

"You want any recruiting scoops?"

Montana shot him the same look. Guess that was a no.

"I see what you're doing. I've been there," Montana said. "It's respectable. You're trying to make up for something you did across the ocean by coaching those kids. I appreciate that you're trying to help. That's a commendable thing, son. Maybe you should stick to it. Become a full-time teacher. Because all this? You're going to get yourself killed. And by letting Donne go, by not calling us—you got a lot of good men killed. You balanced the scales. Save your brothers in Afghanistan and let my men die."

Herrick adjusted his position in the chair. He'd had the same conversations with Sarah over the past year. That Montana could read him so quickly made Herrick's fingers tingle. And it felt like a knife dug through his lower intestine as Montana talked more.

"Now you're just busting my balls," Herrick said. "I gave you three names. And the more time you waste with me, the harder it will be to catch them."

Montana shook his head. "If those are the right names, we'll get them."

"Bullshit. Elliot Cole is probably on a plane to Cuba already." Herrick blinked. "He told us he wanted to go to Cuba."

The words had tumbled from his mouth, and he knew he was giving too much away. Why did he want to protect these people? Probably because of what Montana uttered next.

"You knew about this? In advance? Why didn't you tell us? The cops. Anyone. Maybe you do need a lawyer."

Before Herrick could answer, a private ran up to Montana and handed him a computer printout. Montana snatched it from the private, dismissed him and then read over the paper. He dropped his arm to his side and turned his gaze back to Herrick.

"So, when were you going to tell me about your father?"

Herrick tilted his head.

"You've been in here what? Two hours? We've already got a ton of information on you, son."

Time to fake ignorance and annoyance. Anything to keep them from asking about his phone. It was too chaotic in the Reserve right now. Herrick didn't think they were thinking straight.

"Stop calling me—"

Montana held up a hand. "We know you shot a suicide bomber in Iraq. A kid. Commendable. But we also know your dad was in prison, with Jackson Donne, until about a week ago. Now your dad is found in a Hoboken alley—not far from your apartment—beaten to death. He was a bloody fucking pulp. I mean, thank God for fingerprints. And that was only a day ago. Jesus, Matt."

"People say that to me a lot these days. Listen, I don't know what to tell you. I know Cole was involved, I saw him on the street shooting up your soldiers. My dad came to visit me and talk to me after he got out of prison, and then he died. That was it."

Montana shook his head. "You also visited the National Guard station in New Brunswick a few days ago."

Herrick closed his eyes. He exhaled. Fine. They got everything on him.

"Cole and my dad were going to rob the reserve. They wanted my help. I think my dad was trying to get the family back together in his own sick way. I wanted nothing to do with it."

Montana slammed his hand down on the table. "Then *why*

didn't you tell us?"

Herrick exhaled again, trying to calm the rattling he felt in the back of his head. He had kept it together during a firefight. He was not about to have a breakdown now.

"Because it was my dad. Because it was my mom. Because it was Jackson Donne, who saved my life when I first met him. I was trying to stop them, but I didn't want them arrested again. They had their chance to live on the straight and narrow. This was the only way I could fix things. I thought my mom was sick. She was my number one concern."

Montana shook his head. "And instead, it blew up in your face."

Herrick didn't say anything.

"You really fucked up, Matt. Really fucked up."

"Maybe you did too. All of you. Couldn't put the pieces together. I talked to the National Guard and you talked to Christenson too. I talked to MPs when the rocket launchers were stolen. I was in contact, and you all couldn't be bothered to figure this out. I handed it to you on a silver platter."

"You should have called us and told us everything."

Herrick shook his head. "I didn't know everything. Until just now. Every time I turn around, someone is trying to kill me. I've talked to more cops than I can count."

Montana said, "Fine. I've got bigger things to worry about right now. You're a witness and we are going to be in touch. Get the fuck out of here."

CHAPTER 70

H ERRICK WAS BACK on the street.
  Minutes earlier, Montana had explained to him how important it was to find Donne or Cole, ASAP.

Herrick said, "Yeah. You wasted enough time."

"You hear anything, you call me. Do not keep it to yourself."

"I'll get right on that."

Montana didn't say any more, and Herrick left, trekking through security and onto the street near the stadium. His car was up on Hoboken Road about three quarters of a mile away. Before traveling there, he took one last glance at the carnage. The bodies had been removed, but cops and military police were examining the rest of the evidence. One guy in fatigues sat on the curb on the corner staring at his feet, hands between his legs.

Herrick had been there, that day in the sandbox. He remembered sitting on the fender of a Jeep and staring at the ground for a long time. He lost a friend that day too. And a lot of himself.

Before the tightness in his chest could start to constrain his heart, Herrick turned and headed toward Hoboken Road. He hoped to be back in Hoboken proper within two hours. With Route 17 closed in both directions and rush hour humming hard, that was wishful thinking.

IT TOOK MORE than three.

But Herrick was back in his apartment. His mother was sleeping again, and that was a good thing. It gave him time to think and process. Too much had gone on in the past twenty-four hours.

He wanted to get Tammy and Sarah to a hotel, but Sarah was able to persuade him otherwise, due to Tammy's health. She made sure the cops had collected as much evidence as they could and re-opened the apartment, so it wouldn't be contaminated. Detectives and the MPs would soon ask more questions. The media would probably pick up on it too. That was bad for his job as a basketball coach.

Working for a school, you never wanted to be the headline. Especially one that had someone's violent death in it.

Herrick sat down on the couch, rubbed his face and then got down to it. Time to do some real detective work. If Cole were on his way to Cuba by now, there'd be no catching him. But something about that line of thinking seemed off. Tammy was his reason for going to Cuba. Judging by what she had said when she got there, this wasn't about saving Tammy. It couldn't have been.

So where would Cole start?

He already had two safe houses. The one in Paterson that had been cleaned out, and the one in Long Valley, that was likely cleaned out as well. The key was to get as far away as possible with the money. Out of the public eye. That was the problem with the Lufthansa heist, wasn't it? Spent the money too quickly and with too much flash. At least, that was what *Goodfellas* said.

And then there was Donne. Where would he go?

Step one: buy a car. First stop, cash for a cheap vehicle that moved. Donne would get the hell out of Dodge. It was his M.O. Vermont. Jail. Wherever the violence wasn't.

Herrick got up and walked to his bedroom door. He tapped on it lightly, hoping to wake his mother as gently as possible.

"How are you feeling?" he asked as he poked his head through the door.

"Better, I think. Maybe this is running its course. Turn on the lights and come sit down."

Herrick did as he was told. The edge of the bed was still cold. Her feet didn't reach that far.

"They pulled it off, Mom. I couldn't stop them."

She adjusted her position on the bed to look at him. "Did you expect otherwise? You went after them with nothing but your mouth and your fists. Elliot Cole is not someone you can talk out of ideas."

"But Jackson Donne is."

"I don't think he's the man you once knew. I know your father wasn't. Prison changed him. Hardened him even more. Messed with his head." Tammy tapped her temple. "Makes you want to do crazy things. He wanted you to help him rob a federal building. I can barely stand for more than an hour. As he lifted weights and snapped necks in jail, I rotted. The Bonnie and Clyde days are over, but he couldn't figure that out."

Herrick nodded. "I guess you don't notice times changing when you're staring at prison bars for ten years."

"He thought you were a lot like him too—anything to get the job done. I bet he thought that because of what you did in Iraq. With the kid."

Herrick turned his head. "I had no choice. We would have all died."

Now, Tammy reached over and put her hand on his shoulder. "I know, Matt. I know. You're more like me. When we were young, you know what I wanted to do anytime we stole? I didn't want to be Bonnie. It was the 70s. I wanted to be Robin Hood. I wanted to go into the bad neighborhoods—like Newark after the riots. I wanted to use the money to help rebuild. Your dad and Cole were harbingers of the eighties. They wanted it for themselves."

Herrick exhaled, and listened.

"You did what you had to do to save people. You coach basketball for the same reason, I'm sure."

"It's not right what they did, Mom." Herrick rubbed his hands together. "Where would Cole go?"

"He told me Cuba."

Herrick shook his head. "That was a lie and you know it. He told that lie to keep you quiet. What would he want to do with all that money? What was he willing to destroy people's lives for?"

Tammy thought. They were quiet for a while. Herrick stared at the empty dresser top. He needed pictures of him with Sarah.

Finally, Tammy said, "He wants to be famous. He wants to be the next Dillinger. A superstar."

"There's no way he gets away with this without fleeing the country."

Tammy shook her head. "You're right. Who was that guy who robbed the plane and disappeared? Back in the day."

"D.B. Cooper."

"That's what Elliot loved. The last second escape. He's not gone yet. They didn't almost catch him. He needs that adrenaline."

And it all came flooding to Herrick at that moment. He grinned and said, "Thanks, Mom."

She gave him a kiss on the cheek. The first one since he was in high school. Herrick suppressed another grin.

CHAPTER 71

HERRICK TOOK THE PATH. It was quicker, despite all the police presence, than trying to drive into the city. The doors pinged open at 33rd and Herrick stepped onto the platform, pushed past the crowds and made his way up to the street.

Manhattan on a warm April afternoon.

A slight breeze, the sun on your face and not a hint of the garbage smell that wafted into the city in July. And since Herrick hardly knew the subway, he decided to hoof it seventeen blocks. *Think of it as exercise,* he reminded his body. He hadn't been to a shootaround since that night with Sarah. He needed it. Somehow, running for your life didn't actually feel like a workout.

Herrick brushed past tourists and businessmen on their cell phones as he made his way uptown. Twenty minutes later, Herrick found himself in front of Rockefeller Center, and the headquarters for NBC news. There wasn't a sign of Elliot Cole. That wasn't what Herrick was here for. Instead, it was to give Cole what he wanted.

An audience.

The lobby for NBC wasn't all that hard to get into. But the newsroom was. Herrick walked up to the receptionist. When she asked if she could help him, he let her have it.

"I want to talk to a reporter," he said. "I know who the culprits are in the Federal Reserve armored car heist."

The receptionist smiled. "You can call our tipline at 1-8 — "

"No. I want to speak to a reporter."

The receptionist's smile got wider. Like she'd been through this rodeo before.

"I'm afraid I can't do that, sir. If you have information, call our tipline and someone will be in touch."

Herrick pulled out his phone and held it up. He pressed play on the video he had taken, the bullets flying. The screaming. The smile went away.

"They can have this video — free. But I want to talk to them."

The receptionist picked up a phone behind the desk and said something. She took Herrick's ID, photocopied it, and seconds later a man dressed in an NBC security uniform escorted him back to the newsroom.

T HE MAKE-UP ON Herrick's cheeks felt weird. Sticky and powdery, more like a donut topping than something to make him look better on TV.

The news anchor, a woman with overly sprayed black hair named Kelly Battle, smiled in his direction.

"In two minutes, we are going to cut away from Produce Pete and then focus on you. Breaking news."

Herrick shot her a grin. "I thought Produce Pete was a weekend feature."

"He can't do this weekend. But he has to appear per his contract. You're a viewer?"

Herrick shrugged. "I'm a fan."

"I thought I was supposed to be making you comfortable. Not vice versa."

The studio was smaller than he'd expected. There was a news desk and a screen with the silhouette of Manhattan in the background. Facing the desk to the left was a green screen for the weather. To the right, another separate desk for sports. They put Herrick at the main desk to the left of the anchor.

"Ninety seconds." The voice came from behind the bright lights shining in Herrick's eyes.

He'd never been in a TV studio. All the appearances he'd done for the team had been when a beat reporter stuck a microphone in his face just as the team was running off the court. He was more comfortable there than here. Here he felt like he had to be prepared. Spur of the moment wasn't a thing when you were in a news studio. Spur of the moment was for the reporter on the street.

"I'm going to ask you some questions about this morning. Answer them as clearly as you can. Speak slowly, so the viewers can understand you. Got it?" Battle shuffled papers on her desk. The weather guy was playing on his phone.

"Piece of cake."

Battle nodded. "Before we start, we will show the footage from your phone. I'll do some voice over. Make sense?"

"Like I said, I watch."

Battle nodded. Someone started counting down from twenty.

"Here we go," she said.

The countdown stopped at three, and as if finishing it in her head, Battle nodded. Then said, "Pete, we will come back to you when we can. This is breaking news. The shocking phone footage you're about to watch was taken by Matt Herrick, a local high school basketball coach. If you have kids in the room, be warned, this footage is graphic. Herrick was on the scene this morning during the dramatic attack on an armored car moving money from the Federal Reserve to Teterboro Airport. The military has been scarce with details from the attack, refusing to say how much money was taken. They've also refused to identify the victims and the assailants involved in this attack."

The video played on monitors behind the camera. Herrick didn't want to watch, but couldn't look away.

Battle took another beat, then. "Welcome back to the four o'clock live news. I'm here with Mr. Herrick who is going to give us his eyewitness report on the attack. Matt?"

As if it was an instinct from years of watching the news, Herrick said, "Good to be here, Kelly."

"What can you tell us about the attack?"

"Well, as you can see from the video, three men appeared from behind the barrier near the car dealership and opened fire. They took out the armored car and the Jeeps escorting the vehicle."

Herrick's phone started to buzz in his pocket. He ignored it, trying to keep his eyes on the camera.

"And what were you doing in the area this morning?"

Herrick thought, *Keep Donne out of it. For now. This is about Cole.* His phone continued vibrating.

"I was out for a morning jog at the track nearby. I heard the gun shots and climbed the bleachers to get the footage you just showed."

"What else can you tell us? How many people were injured?"

"From my count, one of the assailants was killed, and there were six soldiers murdered. The attackers got away with all the money."

Battle tilted her head. "All of it?"

"The military appeared completely unprepared."

"And you would know, you are, after all, former military."

The words surprised Herrick, though they shouldn't have. He'd been in the newsroom for nearly two hours being vetted. Of course they'd find out about his time in Iraq.

"Yes, I am a veteran of the Afghanistan war."

"How would you have handled this situation differently, Mr. Herrick?"

Herrick went for it. "I don't think I can even begin to speculate on that, Kelly. But I can give you a scoop."

Battle said, "Please do."

"I know the name of the ringleader of this case. His name is Elliot Cole, and he also killed my father, Kenneth Herrick."

Battle didn't say anything. She had her finger pressed to her earpiece. A producer was talking to her.

"Uh, Mr. Herrick, I —"

Herrick spoke some more. "I'd love to hash this out with you, Cole. I'm sure you're watching, and even if you aren't, this is going to be big news and you'll hear about it anyway. I'm a loose end, aren't I? Just me sticking around here. There's a way to wrap this all up and get all the Bonnie and Clyde buzz you want. Just meet me at Lattieri Park, remember that place? By the basketball nets at nine p.m."

Herrick pulled the microphone out of his shirt and dropped it on the desk. He stood up before Battle could ask any more questions and stormed toward the door of the studio. A producer stepped in front of him, but he pushed the guy out of the way and kept moving. That was the secret to getting out of here without anyone stopping him. It sounded silly, but it was true.

Eyes forward, he just kept walking until it was time to leave the city. His phone vibrated like crazy.

At Lattieri Park. The place where he remembered making his first lay-up.

This wasn't going to be a lay-up, that was for sure.

CHAPTER 72

THE POLICE HAD already started to scout Lattieri Park. Donne was lying in the weeds a good football field away, using the rifle sight to get a look.

The perimeter the cops set up was probably fifty yards. They were just hoping Cole and Herrick would walk up to the park without seeing them. Guess what? If Donne could see them, then Elliot Cole wasn't going to miss them either.

Local cops were usually dumb. These were no different.

Clifton, New Jersey was a city Donne had been in before. Years earlier. It felt like a lifetime ago. Back when cops weren't predictable. The detective he worked with back then was a smart guy named Iapicca who did his damnedest to save Donne's sister. But Iapicca became yet another victim that plagued Donne. Another person he couldn't save.

Fuck that.

It wasn't going to happen anymore. If Donne had his way, Elliot Cole wouldn't be walking off in handcuffs. He'd be carted out in a body bag.

Matt Herrick was a bleeding heart. He hadn't learned how to get results on the street. He kept trying to keep people alive, only getting them arrested. But that blowback eventually came down on you and your friends. The only way to truly keep people safe was with a pre-emptive strike.

Donne didn't know what Herrick's plan was. You didn't go on NBC and expect everyone besides the target of your rant would ignore you.

Before he tried to foil the heist, getting the guns was easier than expected. Donne dropped Artie's name—something he never expected would work—and the man gave him fifteen minutes to meet. They ended up in a small New Brunswick side road near Robert Wood Johnson Hospital. Donne passed the cash along, and the short man wearing a ski mask loaded a machine gun, a "sniper" rifle and a hunting knife into his trunk. He had scars on his fingers, visible when he took the last of Kenneth's cash.

Suppressing the memory, Donne hoped the equipment paid off now. The money wasn't the problem. He got himself some more this morning.

He eyed the street, looking for approaching cars. Instead, there were only news vans and live news feed set-ups. Another brilliant move. When the gunfire broke out, the collateral damage meant a reporter could take a headshot.

What Donne was trying to avoid.

The clock ticked closer to 8:45. Herrick wasn't going to be late. He was too smart for that. Unless this was Herrick's plan all along: pick a location, and no show. Cole would then walk into the teeth of the police.

But Cole wasn't that stupid either. Couldn't be.

Donne exhaled again, trying to slow the hammering of his heart. He could hear the blood rushing through his ears. The sharp tips of the newly grown grass pressed into his forearms, pinching his skin.

At that moment, Donne figured it out. And he cursed himself for being such a fool.

Yes, he was the idiot. Herrick needed to get Cole's attention, and the news was a surefire way to do it. But Lattieri Park was a ploy. Some sort of subtle message. Herrick and Cole had known each other for a long time.

There was a hidden meaning that Donne and the cops had missed.

Donne closed his eyes. Herrick was going to walk in, unarmed, to a meeting with a guy who managed to murder six soldiers and steal billions of dollars.

There was no way he was going to walk out.

But where would he go? Donne replayed the previous days through his brain, searching for clues, something Herrick or Cole had said. All he needed was a tip, a hint.

He pulled out the burner phone and texted Herrick.

Where are you? I'm here to help.

Putting the phone down next to him, Donne scanned the scene again. Several cops were putting on flak jackets, much like Cole had worn this morning. Two others were pointing at something on a phone. Donne looked toward the basketball courts and saw they were empty. And the road was still silent.

No one approached.

The phone buzzed.

Stay out of this.

Donne read the message twice, debating about what to type back. He wrote: *Cops all over Lattieri Park. I know the park was a plant. Cole will kill you. You know you need back-up. I'm here to help.*

Donne put the phone down again. The "stay out of this" was a sign he was right. The meeting wouldn't be here. Instead, it would be at a place where Herrick was a sitting duck. Donne stood up, staying behind his car and out of the cops' sightline. He put the sniper rifle into the backseat and then got in the driver's seat.

He stared at the phone. Willed it to give him a location. Herrick needed to smarten up. This wasn't the middle of the desert anymore. He didn't have a battalion around the protect him. He was on his own.

Come on, Matt, he thought.

Donne scanned the area one more time. Nothing had changed except a few news vans had popped on their lights and cameras for a report.

Because that was secure.

His phone buzzed again. The location was one he was familiar with, only a few miles away. Memorial Park in Rutherford, right on the Passaic River. Only a few blocks from a fight he'd had with his adopted brother. The past was swirling around Donne and he did not appreciate it.

But what twisted his stomach even more was the follow-up message.

You don't have time to get here anyway. It's too late.

Donne started the car and slammed on the gas. It was probably a ten-minute drive. Eight if he blew stop signs and stop lights.

He prayed Herrick was wrong.

CHAPTER 73

HERRICK STARED AT the playground of his youth. The basketball hoops didn't have nets anymore, only rusted rims. The pavement was cracked and in need of new asphalt. The playground to his right was plastic and new. It looked as if it hadn't been played in at all.

But this broken down court was a connection to his childhood. His one connection to Elliot Cole. The only time they'd bonded together.

The one time he'd ever gone out with Elliot Cole was to Lattieri Park—except this wasn't Lattieri Park. This was where they ended up instead. Herrick couldn't remember where his parents had been that day—perhaps out planning a job, or hell, even pulling one off. All he remembered was he was in a very frustrated Elliot Cole's care. He kept saying he couldn't believe he had to spend the day babysitting.

Herrick decided they should go shoot baskets, and Cole wanted to drive around for a while. Cole knew of Lattieri Park, and got within ear shot of it, but made a wrong turn, and instead, they ended up at Memorial Park.

One wrong turn.

It seemed that Herrick had made the wrong decision when he took Alex Robinson's money to find Jackson Donne a year and a half ago.

Herrick got out of the car and walked over to the basketball court. He'd left his phone in the car after texting Donne his location—he ignored Sarah's texts. Her calls. His principal's texts. He only answered Donne. Someone needed to know where he was. No way Donne could get here that fast. Cole would either be here soon or expect a trap and not show up. But Herrick hoped that by saying Lattieri Park, it would tip only him off. *Just the two of us.*

The lapping of the Passaic River against a dock. The smell of dead fish was strong. When you're a kid, that sort of thing didn't matter. All that mattered was the rock and getting to the hole. You played through anything. Right now, though, Herrick couldn't control his thoughts. He couldn't settle himself and focus. All he could think about were dead fish.

The cars on Route 21, just across the river, melded with the sound of the water against the shore. For a park that was closed and an area of town that was quiet, there was a lot to mess with Herrick's senses. He took a breath.

And that was when the SUV rolled up. A Toyota RAV-4—gray with tinted windows. Not enough to carry a billion dollars, Herrick thought. The headlights flashed in his eyes and then went dark. Herrick steeled himself and waited.

He could make the free throw with no time left on the clock.

He could shoot a kid to save a battalion.

But this was causing his heart to rat-a-tat-tat and the sweat on his palms to reflect the street lights.

Elliot Cole stepped out of the driver's side and slammed the door shut. In his free hand, he held a pistol. Of course.

"You don't need that," Herrick said. "I'm not the type of guy to shoot you."

Cole grinned. The lines around his mouth had gotten deeper. Herrick wondered how much depth they gained after today.

"Maybe I'm the kind of guy to shoot you. You're my last relic of this job. What's that on your hip?"

Herrick tapped the ASP and shook his head. "What about Donne?"

"He got away with some cash. He's not going to talk." Cole shook his head and leveled the gun at Herrick. "I want your last thought to be this: your mother knows. Your girlfriend knows."

Herrick said, "The whole fucking world knows, Elliot. I said it on TV. It's probably on YouTube. I gave you your moment."

The gun barrel twitched, but Cole righted it. He nodded in agreement

"Give yourself up, Elliot. This is stupid. The only reason there isn't an army of police raining down on this park is because I lied to them."

Cole didn't say anything. Herrick was convinced a bullet would pierce his own brain in less than a second. But he kept talking.

"How far back do we go? To this park, right? Even further. I get it, you want to be the king. You're not a superstar. You're not John Dillinger. Can't keep running forever. Not in this day and age. It's a global world."

Cole shrugged. "Either way, I'm a legend now. Thanks for that."

"To get there you dragged people you've loved to their lowest possible points."

"Way of the world," Cole said.

The gun went off. A loud crack that echoed off the walls of the apartment buildings in the distance. Someone screamed. Herrick flinched, waiting for the pain. But Cole dropped the gun, his brain exploding in a cloud of red dust. He slumped to his knees, and then, wordlessly, went face down to the ground.

Herrick exhaled. Opened and closed his hands in fists. Tried to focus on breathing. There were spots of blood on him. Just like when the boy died.

Blood everywhere.

Herrick blinked and blinked. He wasn't sure how much time had passed, but a lone siren in the air snapped him out of it. He jogged to Cole and pressed his fingers to his throat. No pulse. Not surprising.

Sinking to the ground, Herrick wanted to let the panic overtake him. Wanted to huddle and rock for a while. This was all too familiar.

"Donne!" he screamed, and his throat burned. "Donne!"

No answer came.

The siren grew louder. The noise overwhelmed the lapping of the waves, cutting through the night air like a blade through flesh.

Herrick forced himself to his feet and ran to his car. He opened the door and got in. He called Sarah. The phone rang twice.

"I'm okay," he said after her greeting.

"I'm so mad at you." Usually when she said that there was a playful tone with it. Not tonight.

"Cole is dead." The words felt odd coming out of his mouth.

"What? How could you do something so stupid?"

"Tell my mom. He's gone."

"You killed him? I thought you didn't do that sort of thing."

He pictured her on the couch, legs tucked underneath her staring at a muted TV. He wondered if she was gnawing on her nails.

"No," Herrick said. "You know that's not me."

"Who did?"

Herrick knew Sarah already understood the answer. He didn't say the name.

"I love you."

"Come home," she said. "We need to talk."

"I will," he said. "It's over."

"Come home," she said again. There was an edge to her voice.

Herrick took a deep breath and disconnected the conversation.

CHAPTER 74

ONNE STOOD OUTSIDE the palatial estate. Somewhere a cricket chirped, and the wind buzzed through the leaves of the trees. He opened and closed his hands and eyed the house for security concerns. He didn't notice any, but when you were stalking a millionaire, not seeing them didn't mean they weren't there.

He crept up the hill of the front lawn, constantly stopping and scanning his surroundings. Nothing out of the ordinary. If Donne tripped some sort of security system, it'd be more likely that some sort of private security force showed up instead of the police.

It happened that way when you were a multi-million-dollar thief. Cops wouldn't do the dirty work. You hired people to do it for you. Nasty people. But Donne had dealt with their type before.

Adrik's house was tall and brick, like an oven. He wondered how much the air conditioning bill ran in the summer. Donne sprinted across the grass and pressed himself up against the wall of the house adjacent to the garage. No lights went on. No alarms were tripped.

In the distance, Donne could smell the faint waft of a skunk. A dog barked. Donne edged his way around the side of the house to the backyard. He wished he'd inspected the interior better the last time he was here. He had an idea where the kitchen was, that was the way Cole had appeared. And he assumed the bedrooms were upstairs.

But he didn't have a ladder to climb upstairs and break in that way. So through the kitchen window he went. He used the knife he'd purchased off the guy Artie knew to pop the lock on the window and slide it open. Still no alarm.

Adrik had balls.

Unless he wasn't here. Maybe he did run. After ending up with a ton of cash, the smart thing to do would be to disappear. But this guy was experienced. Hiding in plain sight was the smart move. It didn't reek of panic. Even with Herrick giving the police, military and anyone watching the evening news his name, Adrik's face wasn't on the video. He could talk his way out.

He could always disappear in a week.

Donne climbed through the window and landed softly on the tile floor next to the kitchen table. He pulled the window shut and moved through the dark house. The hard wood floor didn't creak as he stepped, and Donne was feeling lucky.

He turned at the stairs and ascended them. The stairs squeaked, and Donne had to stop on each one to listen for the sound of someone waking up. Instead, he heard snoring.

Adrik *was* home.

When he reached the second floor, Donne began peeking into rooms. The bathroom, an office, the two empty guest rooms and finally the master bedroom. He pushed the door open and inched into the room. Once he was standing over the bed, he stared at the two bodies asleep in it. The bed was a king size and the two bodies weren't entwined. The woman on the right was naked.

A night of celebrating after a big score?

Didn't matter.

Donne pulled the knife from his belt.

And Adrik woke up, reaching for the light on the nightstand. He clicked it on and the woman he was with rolled over and screamed.

"Son of a bitch," Adrik said.

"You cocky bastard."

Adrik didn't answer. He pushed himself out of bed and stood, nude, in front of Donne.

"I knew I should have killed you," Adrik said.

Donne grinned. "He's gone too."

"Shit."

The woman screamed again as Donne approached Adrik. He ignored her and brought the knife up hard. Adrik feinted right and went left, so Donne only caught his arm, sending a spray of blood across the mattress. The woman was reaching for her phone.

Donne didn't care.

Adrik backed up into his dresser, sending picture frames flying. Glass shattered against the floor. The woman was yelling at 911. Donne needed to get this over with quick.

He hit Adrik in the face with a quick jab. Adrik covered his face, and blood dripped through his fingers. Donne stepped in, left foot first, and followed through with his right hand, embedding the knife in Adrik's gut. Adrik gurgled and sank to the floor. Donne pulled hard, releasing the knife. He jammed it down in Adrik's back. An arc of blood flew through the room.

The woman screamed again. She dropped the phone.

Adrik's chest neither rose nor fell.

Good.

Maybe now Herrick could live the life he deserved and not be held prisoner of the past.

He looked at the woman and said, "I'll be gone before the cops get here."

Tears streaked her face. Her breath came in huge gasps.

"This is for the best," Donne said.

With that, he retraced his steps back downstairs and let himself out the front door. The smell of the skunk was stronger now. The dog didn't bark anymore. Donne held onto the knife and ran down the block to where he parked the shitty Honda.

Once inside, he drove in circles for a while, waiting for the adrenaline to calm down. Waited for the guilt to kick in, but it never did. Instead, a twitch started in his eyelid. He tried to blink it away but it didn't stop.

Miles later, he pulled over on a Parkway overpass shoulder. This time he tossed the knife into the Passaic. His grandfather used to troll rivers for bodies during the Great Depression. Donne wondered how many knives and guns he came across.

Things like that didn't matter. The past shouldn't matter. The future was where he aimed himself now.

Donne kept driving. He'd head south soon enough, but first he had one more stop to make. He exited onto Route 3. Traffic was light and the sky was clear. The New York skyline grew bigger and bigger in his vision the closer he got to Hoboken.

He needed to see Herrick one last time. Explain to him that things were okay now.

Donne hit the gas even harder.

CHAPTER 75

ERRICK STOOD AT the corner of the parking deck only minutes after the phone call. He wasn't letting Donne into his apartment anymore. And, if not for Mack, Herrick wouldn't have even picked up the phone when Donne called. But Mack gave him the nod.

"Meet with him," Mack said. "And if you give me a signal, we can take him down."

Herrick had called Mack before Cole's body was cold. Donne was losing it, he needed help, and the only person he could think of was Mack. He didn't want the real cops involved, not yet. He needed to hear Donne say the words about his dad.

Good man or bad man, Kenneth was still his dad. He didn't need to be beaten to death.

Donne had done too much, but maybe Mack could slow Donne down. Herrick didn't want the cops on Donne's back if he hadn't done what Herrick thought he might have. He needed answers first, and Herrick thought he could trust Mack long enough to get them.

Now, Herrick walked down the driveway into the empty deck. It was late, the bars were closed and the morning commuters hadn't filtered in. He saw Mack on the other end of the deck, crouched behind an abandoned car. If Donne freaked or ran, Herrick would give Mack a signal, or, hell, even shout for him. Something about Donne's demeanor made Herrick think of a rabid dog.

One person wouldn't be able to take him down.

"Donne," Herrick called out. The words reverberated off the concrete walls. "I know you're here."

"I am."

The voice came from Herrick's left, and he turned in that direction. Donne stood there, half covered in shadow. Behind him were only empty parking spots. Herrick wondered how he got in so silently. Wraith-like.

Donne's face seemed like it'd been worn down by the wind. Leathery and sharp.

"You're safe now, Matt."

"You're scaring me, Jackson. What did you do? What happened?" Herrick let the words spill from his mouth like the last drops in a bourbon.

"I'm going to go away for a while, but you can find me when you need me."

Herrick tilted his head. "I don't understand."

"You're not going to leave this investigative work. But you won't do what it takes. You're going to keep getting yourself in trouble."

Herrick didn't say anything.

"I know you. You love those kids. The ones who play their hearts out for you. I don't know what you think, if you're saving them or whatever, but you won't give that up either."

"No. I won't."

Donne nodded. "So, if that's the case, there's no way you'll go to the ends necessary to get cases finished. Believe me, I've been there. I tried to save people, and make sure the bad guys got punished by the system. But sometimes you have to do things. Bad things."

Herrick took a deep breath. "What happened to my dad, Jackson?"

"He's gone. Cole killed him."

Herrick shook his head. "Cole denied it when were in the park."

Donne took a deep breath. "You're safe now. And you'll need me again, I promise."

A tremor went through Herrick's body. He opened his mouth

to call for Mack, but the words didn't come. Herrick was safe now, whatever that meant. Donne thought he was a savior.

What did my father do to you in prison?

Donne's insides were leather too now, worn down by the grind of life. The life he'd chosen.

"When you need me, find me. It won't be hard," Donne said. "I'll help you. You're a good man. You don't need any blood on your hands."

"What did you do, Jackson?"

Donne turned and headed back toward the street. "Tell your cop friend the money is in Adrik's basement. Maybe he can get there before anyone else finds it."

"What did you do?"

"You'd better hold on to Sarah too. She's good for you." Donne wiped his chin. "When you need me, call me. And you *will* need me."

"Tell me, Jackson!"

"You're going to need me, because you can't stand up for yourself. You won't do what has to be done. I understand. Say hi to your mom for me."

Donne disappeared, leaving Herrick with too many unanswered questions. Seconds later, a beat up Honda Accord sped up Washington Street out of Hoboken. It blew two reds.

Mack ran up to Herrick.

"What did he say?"

Herrick told him where to find the money. Mack shook his head. They had the airport staked out for Adrik. He'd bought multiple plane tickets in his name. No one was at the house all day. He must have waited them out.

"What about Donne?"

Herrick didn't answer. Instead, he said, "I'm going home."

He felt hollow inside. He walked away from Mack and headed back to his apartment.

The streets were so quiet, but you could hear the rats on the basement doors of the shops, making them creak. The wind whistled through the corridors, the building creating a wind tunnel. Herrick ignored them and kept walking. He wasn't going to call Donne. He dealt with his career his own way.

As Herrick thought about his father and Donne's words, a knot formed in his gut. Sarah met him at the door. She took one look at his face and wrapped her arms around him.

"Are you okay?"

Herrick nodded. "Will you still be here in the morning?"

"Of course."

"What about next week? A month from now? I love you."

"Come to bed," Sarah said.

He nodded. The questions could be answered later on. It was time to sleep.

EPILOGUE

THE SCORE

1989

THE ALARM RANG, *its wail piercing Tammy's ears like never before. The gun felt heavy in her arm, and the gurgle in her stomach wasn't a good sign.*

Three more minutes.

The tellers behind the glass filled the bags with money while everyone else sat in the corner watching her. Kenneth had killed the manager. There wasn't a choice. He'd made a move for the gun, and they couldn't stand for that. They weren't peaceful bank robbers if people wouldn't let them be.

Kenneth was shouting instructions, but Tammy couldn't focus on them over the rumbling in her gut. The smell of gun smoke was irritating her. She'd never smelled that on a gig before. Usually that shit just dissipated.

Today was different, wasn't it?

The tellers handed over the two duffel bags to Kenneth. They were heavy, and he struggled to sling them over his shoulders. The movements snapped Tammy back into action, and she started shooting out the cameras. The ski masks would protect their identities, but she went and got the tape anyway.

As they were about to leave, Kenneth whispered to her, "It's amazing how we've gotten away with this stuff."

"Here's to another hundred years, Babe," she said. Her stomach cramped even more. "We have to go."

They hustled out into the street, searching for Elliot's car. The police sirens were howling in the air, but still far enough off that they'd be long gone.

If Elliot was there. But Tammy didn't see the car. Kenneth let a curse go.

"Where the hell is he?"

"He'll be here," she said.

"Better be soon."

The sirens got louder.

But not as loud as the squeal of brakes as the Toyota rounded the corner. Elliot leaned on the horn as the car screeched to a halt in front of them. Cole rolled the windows down, and flashed a big grin.

"Get in," he shouted.

Kenneth pulled his ski mask off. "Where the hell were you?"

"A dramatic entrance. Cool right?"

"You're an asshole. Stick to the plan. You made it."

Kenneth threw the two duffel bags into the trunk and ran around the passenger seat. He got in. Tammy pulled her mask off, opened the door and turned her head to vomit in the street. The sirens grew louder as her body rid itself of its contents.

"Are you okay?" Kenneth started to get back out of the car.

Tammy held up a hand, spit the last bit and said, "I'm fine. I have news."

Kenneth tilted his head.

"Let's get out of here first."

She got in the backseat and fastened her belt. The car jerked out of park and headed toward the nearest highway. Tammy didn't know Union all that well, so the streets were foreign to her.

Kenneth turned and looked between the seats. "Are you okay?"

Tammy grinned. "I am. I have news, like I said."

Kenneth nodded to her.

"We're having a baby!"

He went pale, and then he turned to Elliot.

"Pull over," he shouted.

"What?"

"Pull the fuck over."

Elliot did. Kenneth got out of the car and pulled the back door open.

He hopped in next to Tammy.

"Go!"

They peeled back out again as Kenneth wrapped her in his arms. "I can't believe this."

"I took the test this morning."

"Why didn't you…?"

"I didn't want to distract you. Not today."

He leaned in and kissed her, and she hoped he didn't taste the vomit. She pulled him close using the collar of his shirt. Elliot said something in the front of the car, but they didn't hear him.

"I love you."

"You too."

"We're going to be parents. This is…this is…"

"I know, Ken. I know."

Now the scenery familiarized around Tammy. Elliot pulled onto the Parkway South. They were heading toward the shore. Toward her happy place. The summer was here, and living was easy.

"I hope he'll be a lefty," Kenneth said. "We can teach him how to throw a slider."

"What makes you think it's going to be a him?"

"We'll teach her how to throw a slider."

They laughed. Tammy caught Elliot eyeing them in the mirror. They were going to be a family now. And he was out.

"Maybe we can teach him the family business," Kenneth said. "Or her."

Tammy sucked in air through her nose. "Don't joke."

"I'm…"

"You're joking. That's how we are going to handle what you just said. No more talk about that."

"You can't smoke anymore."

"Nine months without won't kill me."

Kenneth buried his face in her hair. She held him tight, jamming her nails into his back. The two duffel bags rustled next to them as Elliot switched lanes. That would be a good nest egg. Maybe they could go straight now. Clean up their act. The fugitive game was fun when you were in your twenties without a care in the world. But in nine months, life was going to get a lot tougher.

Tammy's ear felt wet. She wiped at it. Kenneth pulled away from her.

"Are you crying?" she asked.

"I'm so happy. We're going to raise him right. I promise."

Tammy nodded, even though Kenneth couldn't see her.

"We have a great support system. Elliot. Adrik. He'll be okay."

Tammy took a deep breath. She looked out at the expanse of road in front of them. No traffic. No sign of the cops. A clean slate. A fresh start.

"He'll be more than okay," she said. "He'll be better than us."

ACKNOWLEDGEMENTS

This book is dedicated to my good friend and fantastic writer, Duane Swierczynski. I consider Duane a great mentor, and he's never been shy about his advice for Jackson Donne. In fact, his first suggestion was to kill Donne off in the very first novel, *When One Man Dies*. Of course, I didn't listen to that one—good thing. But Duane has always been a great listener, and never too shy to help a writer out. Thanks, man.

Inspiration comes from everywhere, and *Blind to Sin* is no different. Two of my favorite writers are the late Robert B. Parker and Richard Stark pseudonym of Donald Westlake. There is so much of the both of them in this book that I'd be remiss if I didn't point the influence out. If you haven't read either of them, please put this down and buy their books.

Big thanks to Jason Pinter and Polis Books. Jason has always believed in my writing and I hope he knows it doesn't go unnoticed. I am also grateful for my new agent Dara Hyde, whose enthusiasm and patience is contagious.

My mother, Carol White, and mother-in-law, Eleanore Richard, provided extra sets of eyes on this manuscript. The book is better for it. Thanks a ton.

I am nothing without Erin and Ben. My wife and son have believed in me, supported me, and loved me. I love them both so much.

To everyone else who's taken a chance on any of my books—including this one—thank you all! It means so much to me. I hope you've enjoyed the ride.

ABOUT THE AUTHOR

Dave White is the Derringer Award–winning author of six novels: *When One Man Dies, The Evil That Men Do, Not Even Past, An Empty Hell,* and *Blind to Sin* in his Jackson Donne series, and the acclaimed thriller *Witness to Death.* His short story "Closure," won the Derringer Award for Best Short Mystery Story. *Publishers Weekly* gave the first two novels in his Jackson Donne series starred reviews, calling *When One Man Dies* an "engrossing, evocative debut novel" and writing that *The Evil That Men Do* "fulfills the promise of his debut." He has received praise from crime fiction luminaries such as bestselling, Edgar Award–winning Laura Lippman and the legendary James Crumley. *Witness to Death,* was an ebook bestseller upon release and named one of the Best Books of the Year by the *Milwaukee Journal-Sentinel.* He lives in Nutley, NJ. Follow him at @Dave_White.